# To the Sea Again

# TO THE SEA AGAIN

*Classic Sailing Stories*

## EDITED BY
## TOM MCCARTHY

LYONS PRESS
Guilford, Connecticut
*An imprint of Globe Pequot Press*

To buy books in quantity for corporate use
or incentives, call **(800) 962-0973**
or e-mail **premiums@GlobePequot.com**.

Lyons Press is an imprint of Globe Pequot Press.

Project editor: Staci Zacharski
Layout artist: Sue Murray

Library of Congress Cataloging-in-Publication Data is available on file.

ISBN 978-0-7627-9648-9
Printed in the United States of America

10 9 8 7 6 5 4 3 2 1

*To Valerie, Maggie, and Britta—*
*classics in their own right.*

# Contents

Acknowledgments . . . . . . . . . . . . . . . . . . . . . ix

Introduction . . . . . . . . . . . . . . . . . . . . . xi

The Sea, with a Ship—Afterwards an Island. . . . . . . . 1
by William Shakespeare

The Capture: A True Account . . . . . . . . . . . . . 7
by Aaron Smith

Dirty Weather . . . . . . . . . . . . . . . . . . . . .23
by Joseph Conrad

An Introduction to Informality . . . . . . . . . . . . .45
by Erskine Childers

Yammerschooner. . . . . . . . . . . . . . . . . . . .71
by Joshua Slocum

Young Ironsides . . . . . . . . . . . . . . . . . . . .83
by James Fenimore Cooper

Rounding Cape Horn . . . . . . . . . . . . . . . . . .91
by Herman Melville

Loss of a Man—Superstition . . . . . . . . . . . . . 111
by Richard Henry Dana

Mal de Mer . . . . . . . . . . . . . . . . . . 119
by Jerome K. Jerome

MS. Found in a Bottle . . . . . . . . . . . . . . . 127
by Edgar Allan Poe

The Unfortunate Voyage . . . . . . . . . . . . . 145
by Master John Hawkins

The Siege of the Round-House . . . . . . . . . . . 159
by Robert Louis Stevenson

Owen Chase's Narrative . . . . . . . . . . . . . . 169
by Owen Chase

The White Whale . . . . . . . . . . . . . . . . 183
by Herman Melville

Escape from the Ice . . . . . . . . . . . . . . . 225
by Ernest Shackleton

Sources . . . . . . . . . . . . . . . . . . . . 279

# Acknowledgments

To ALL THOSE WHO SUGGESTED STORIES, MANY THANKS, especially: John Vigor, Twain Braden, Tom Kiley and Barb Hills, Jay McCullough, Scott Kirkman, and Jim Babb, who introduced me to Jerome K. Jerome, lo those many years ago.

# Introduction

What is it about the sea that lends itself to so many indelibly classic stories?

The sea itself is easy pickings for writers looking for backdrop rich in metaphor or symbolism. It's dark, or brooding, or deep. It's serene, mysterious, unforgiving. It's angry, seductive, cruel. The possibilities are nearly endless. The sea is a wonderful stage on which to unroll a dramatic narrative or introduce a heroic character. And writers of both the truly memorable works and the wretchedly clichéd clunkers have availed themselves of the sea as a setting. Richness of backdrop aside, any sea story worthy of being called classic must offer much more than the fact that it has endured. The fifteen stories included here do so, I hope.

A brief mention of the process of putting together this collection is necessary. The most difficult aspect of this most enjoyable task was eliminating stories I had selected as "sure things." Such is the volume of wonderful writing available that I could have easily filled another book of similar size with those stories I reluctantly dropped. It is the nature of anthologies to spark debate over the selections, and indeed, any discussion about the contents herein might well focus on what isn't here rather than what is. In the end, my selections were governed by a decidedly personal criterion—I was moved by the story and enriched and informed by its content.

In selecting these stories I tried for balance, to offer a collection rich in both drama and history, perhaps both. And while each of these fifteen stories is above everything else enduring—Richard Hakluyt, for example, wrote more than four hundred years ago—each I hope also offers something unique. You'll find here a good mixture of fact and fiction, of unvarnished true accounts and of polished, robust fiction oftentimes based on true accounts. The former selections are poignant in their chilling reality, and the latter in their depth and richness of character, and their dramatic pacing.

Fact or fiction, sea stories are, plain and simple, wonderful springboards for vicarious adventure. Few people would want to test their mettle in an ice-encrusted boat with Ernest Shackleton, sail the Straits of Magellan with Joshua Slocum, or watch with Owen Chase as an angry whale sends his ship to the bottom thousands of miles from the nearest land. But it's quite another thing to read these true accounts while settled into a favorite chair. Shackleton and Chase persevered in the face of travails that would have given even Job pause. Their stoic accounts are stronger and more dramatic for their total lack of affectation, their frankness, and their lack of ego. Their gripping stories are custommade for the imaginative reader who seeks adventure in a more controlled environment, safe and warm, and well fed. *Civilized* readers with their armchairs anchored firmly to the living room floor.

As I mentioned earlier, these stories have endured, have been read and studied and enjoyed by generations. Chronologically, Hakluyt's presentation of Master John Hawkins's voyage to the Americas in 1567 is earliest. Hawkins's first-hand account is a clear window through which readers can view the vicissitudes of that era's colonial explorers, though his casual treatment—cold indifference actually—of the natives of the Caribbean is repugnant. Hakluyt was a contemporary of William Shakespeare. He died in 1616, about six months after the Bard.

This collection opens with a short piece from Shakespeare, "The Sea with a Ship," which is the opening scene from *The Tempest*, Shakespeare's tale of hurt, loss, and betrayal. It's a wonderful opening scene—a stormtossed ship hurled into its final moments, whiles its crew curses fate, and each other.

"The Capture," by Aaron Smith is a true account of the author's abduction by Cuban pirates while en route from Jamaica to England in 1822. Smith subsequently gained his freedom, but his bad karma continued when he was later arrested as a pirate in Havana, returned to England in chains, and put on trial for his life.

Another first-hand account of the travails of life at sea is Owen Chase's chilling retelling of watching his whaler, the *Essex* out of Nantucket, being rammed by a white whale and sunk. Chase was only one of eight crew to survive an ordeal that included spending ninetythree days adrift in a whaleboat after the ship was sunk. Chase's 1821 narrative inspired Melville to write *Moby Dick*, a portion of which appears here. Of Chase's story Melville wrote, "The reading of this wondrous story upon the landless sea, and very close to the latitude of the shipwreck has a surprising effect on me." Melville, the icon, appears here also with "Rounding Cape Horn," from his 1850 work, *White-Jacket*. Melville's contemporary Richard Henry Dana presents an interesting glimpse into the highly superstitious life of a sailor in "Loss of a Man—Superstition," from *Two Years Before the Mast*.

No collection of sea stories, classic or not, would be complete without Joseph Conrad. "Dirty Weather," from *Typhoon*, contains the requisite storm, but Conrad's portrayal of Captain MacWhirr is masterful and rich and unforgettable. Like Robert Louis Stevenson, Conrad was seen by contemporaries primarily as a writer of boys' sea stories. "The Seige of the Roundhouse" is taken from Stevenson's *Kidnapped*.

It is impossible to read Erskine Childers's 1903 novel *The Riddle of the Sands* and not want to chuck it all, find a small boat, and go gunkholing for months on end. "An Introduction to Informality," in which the stiff, vain, excessively formal Curutthers meets up with his unglamorous acquaintance Arthur Davies, is taken from *The Riddle*, a book *The Irish Times* called "one of the most famous of all thrillers and one of the best of all sea stories." It was the only work of fiction Childers produced. Turning his attention to the vast difficulties of Irish politics and independence, Childers was executed by the British in 1922.

Joshua Slocum, who at one point commanded some of the finest tall ships of his era, became in 1898 the first man to sail around the world singlehandedly, in his small sloop *Spray*—a 46,000mile trip he began three years earlier at age 51. "Yammerschooner" is taken from his incomparable *Sailing Alone Around the World*.

What can one say about legendary Sir Ernest Shackleton? Leader of perhaps the greatest, or at least the most remarkable survival feats ever, Shackleton was an unflappable character whose story would be deemed unbelievable if it had been presented as fiction. "Escape from the Ice" is taken from his account, *South*.

"MS Found in a Bottle," included here in its entirety, brings us brooding Edgar Allan Poe at his best. Poe not surprisingly has a darker take on a sea journey. After Poe won a $50 prize for this story, he began a career as a magazine writer.

*Three Men in a Boat*, from which "Mal de Mer" is excerpted, is considered British writer Jerome K. Jerome's great comic masterpiece. Though humor rarely travels or ages well, *Three Men in a Boat* is, more than one hundred years after Jerome wrote it, still funny.

It might strike some as unusual to see a piece by James Fenimore Cooper—an author better known for the landlocked Natty Bumpo and *The Last of the Mohicans*, in a collection of sea stories. But Cooper was a longtime aficionado of the American Navy. His account of the early days of the USS *Constitution* appears in "Young Ironsides."

I hope readers find this collection broad, balanced, and interesting. These stories, having stood the test of time, are classics indeed. But more than anything else, they're good reading.

Tom McCarthy
July 2003

# The Sea, with a Ship—
# Afterwards an Island

## *William Shakespeare*

[On a ship at sea; a tempestuous noise of thunder and lightning heard]

[Enter a SHIPMASTER and a BOATSWAIN severally]

MASTER: Boatswain!
BOATSWAIN: Here, master: what cheer?

MASTER: Good! Speak to the mariners: fall to't yarely, or we run ourselves aground: bestir, bestir.
[Exit]

[Enter MARINERS]

BOATSWAIN: Heigh, my hearts! cheerly, cheerly, my hearts! yare, yare! Take in the topsail. Tend to th' master's whistle.—
Blow till thou burst thy wind, if room enough.

1

[Enter ALONSO, SEBASTIAN, ANTONIO, FERDI-
NAND, GONZALO, and OTHERS]

ALONSO: Good boatswain, have care. Where's the master?
Play the men.
BOATSWAIN: I pray now, keep below.
ANTONIO: Where is the master, bosun?
BOATSWAIN: Do you not hear him? You mar our labour:
keep your cabins: you do assist the storm.
GONZALO: Nay, good, be patient.
BOATSWAIN: When the sea is. Hence! What cares these
roarers for the name of king? To cabin! silence! Trouble us not.
GONZALO: Good, yet remember whom thou hast aboard.
BOATSWAIN: None that I more love than myself. You are
counsellor: if you can command these elements to silence, and
work the peace of the present, we will not hand a rope more.
Use your authority: if you cannot, give thanks you have lived so
long, and make yourself ready in your cabin for the mischance
of the hour, if it so hap.—Cheerly, good hearts!—Out of our
way, I say.

[Exit]

GONZALO: I have great comfort from this fellow.
Methinks he hath no drowning mark upon him: his complexion is perfect gallows. Stand fast, good Fate, to his hanging! Make the rope of his destiny our cable, for our own

doth little advantage! If he be not born to be hang'd, our case is miserable.

[Exeunt]

[Re-enter BOATSWAIN]

BOATSWAIN: Down with the topmast! yare! lower, lower! Bring her to try wi' th' maincourse. [A cry within] A plague upon this howling! They are louder than the weather or our office.

[Re-enter SEBASTIAN, ANTONIO, and GONZALO]

Yet again! What do you here? Shall we give o'er, and drown? Have you a mind to sink?
SEBASTIAN: A pox o' your throat, you bawling, blasphemous, incharitable dog!
BOATSWAIN: Work you, then.
ANTONIO: Hang, cur, hang! You whoreson, insolent noisemaker, we are less afraid to be drowned than thou art.
GONZALO: I'll warrant him for drowning, though the ship were no stronger than a nutshell, and as leaky as an unstanched wench.
BOATSWAIN: Lay her ahold, a-hold! set her two courses: off to sea again: lay her off.

[Enter MARINERS, wet]

MARINERS: All lost! To prayers, to prayers! All lost!

[Exeunt]

BOATSWAIN: What, must our mouths be cold?
GONZALO: The King and Prince at prayers! let us assist them, for our case is as theirs.
SEBASTIAN: I am out of patience.
ANTONIO: We are merely cheated of our lives by drunkards.—
This wide-chapp'd rascal—would thou might'st lie drowning
The washing of ten tides!
GONZALO: He'll be hang'd yet,
Though every drop of water swear against it,
And gape at wid'st to glut him.
[A confused noise within:—'Mercy on us!'—
'We split, we split!'—'Farewell, my wife and children!'—
'Farewell, brother!'—'We split, we split, we split!'—]
ANTONIO: Let's all sink wi' the King.

[Exit]

SEBASTIAN: Let's take leave of him.

[Exit]

GONZALO: Now would I give a thousand furlongs of sea for an acre of barren ground; long heath, brown furze, any thing. The wills above be done! but I would fain die dry death.

[Exit]

# The Capture: A True Account

## *Aaron Smith*

AT TWO O'CLOCK, P.M., WHILE WALKING THE DECK IN CONVER-sation with Captain Cowper, I discovered a schooner standing out towards us from the land; she bore a very suspicious appearance, and I immediately went up aloft with my telescope to examine her more closely. I was instantly convinced that she was a pirate, and mentioned it to Captain Cowper, who coincided with me, and we deemed it proper to call Mr. Lumsden from below & inform him. When he came on deck we pointed out the schooner and stated our suspicions, recommending him to alter his course and avoid her. We were at this moment about six leagues from Cape Roman, which bore S.E. by E. Never did ignorance, with its concomitant obstinacy, betray itself more strongly than on this occasion; he rejected our advice and refused to alter his course, and was infatuated enough to suppose, that, because he bore the English flag, no one would dare to molest him. To this obstinacy and infatuation I must attribute all my subsequent misfortunes—the unparalleled cruelties which I have suffered—the persecutions and prosecutions which I have undergone—the mean and wanton insults which have been heaped upon me—and the villany and dishonesty to which I have been exposed from the author of them all; who, not satisfied with having occasioned my sufferings, would have basely taken advantage of them to defraud my friends of what little of my property had escaped the general plunder. In about half an hour after this conversation, we began to discover that the deck of the schooner was full of men, and that she was beginning to hoist out her boats. This circumstance greatly alarmed Mr. Lumsden, and he ordered the course to be altered two points, but it was then too late, for the stranger was within gunshot. In a short time she was within hail, and, in English, ordered us to lower our stern boat and send the captain on board of her. Mr. Lumsden either did not understand the order, or pretended not to do so, and the corsair, for such she now proved to be, fired a volley of musketry. This increased his terror, which he expressed in hurried exclamations of Aye, aye! Oh, Lord God! and then gave orders to lay the main yard aback. A boat from the pirate now boarded the *Zephyr*, containing nine or ten men, of a most ferocious aspect, armed with muskets, knives, and cutlasses, who immediately took charge of the brig, and ordered Captain Cowper, Mr. Lumsden, the ship's carpenter, and myself, to go on board the pirate, hastening our departure by repeated blows with the flat part of their cutlasses over our backs, and threatening to shoot us. The rapidity of our movements did not give us much time for consideration; and, while we were rowing towards the corsair, Mr. Lumsden remarked that he had been very careless in leaving the books, which contained the account of all the money on board, on the cabin table. The captain of the pirate ordered us on deck immediately on our arrival. He was a man of most uncouth and savage appearance, about five feet six inches in height, stout in proportion, with an aquiline nose, high cheek bones, a large mouth, and very large full eyes. His complexion was sallow, and his hair black, and he appeared to be about two and thirty years of age. In his appearance he very much resembled an Indian, and I was afterwards informed that his father was a Spaniard and his mother a Yucatan Squaw. He first addressed Mr. Lumsden, & inquired in broken English what the vessels were that he saw ahead. On being informed that they were French merchantmen, he gave orders for all hands to go in chase. The *Zephyr* was observed in the mean time to make sail and stand in the direction of Cape Roman.

The captain now addressed himself to Mr. Lumsden on the subject of his cargo, which he was informed consisted of sugars, rum, coffee, arrow root, dye woods, & co. He then severally inquired who and what we were; and then whether we had spoken any vessel on our passage. On being informed of the schooner from New Brunswick, he asked if we thought she had specie on board. We told him that those vessels in general sold their cargoes for cash and he seemed very anxious to learn whether she was ahead or astern of us, and whether she was armed. Mr. Lumsden now entreated the captain to make a signal to the *Zephyr* not to stand nearer to the land, as he was apprehensive of her going on shore, and was told that he need not be under any alarm, as there was a very experienced pilot on board of her. He was, however, dissatisfied with this reply, and repeated his entreaty, when the other, in a menacing tone, enjoined silence, and went forward. In a short time he returned and questioned Mr. Lumsden as to what money he had on board, and when told that there was none, he replied, 'Do not imagine that I am a fool, Sir; I know that all vessels going to Europe have specie on board; & if you will give up what you have, you shall proceed on your voyage without further molestation.' Mr. Lumsden repeated his answer, and the pirate declared that if the money was not produced, he would detain the *Zephyr*, throw her cargo overboard, and, if any was found concealed, he would burn her with every soul belonging to her. He then asked whether there were any candles, wine, or porter, on board; and Mr. Lumsden foolishly replied, not any that he could spare, without appearing to consider that we were in his power, and that he could if he pleased possess himself of any thing he might wish without consulting his convenience.

The night was at this time fast approaching, and the breeze had begun to die away. The captain appeared to despair of coming up with his chase, which we could not clearly perceive to be a ship and a brig, and asked Captain Cowper and myself whether he should be able to overtake them before dark. We replied in the negative, and he then gave orders to shorten sail and stand towards the *Zephyr*. The pirates then began to prepare for supper, and were very liberal in serving out spirits to our boat's crew, and also offered us a share, or wine if we preferred it, but we declined both.

The captain now turned to me and said, that, as he was in a bad state of health and none of his ship's company understood navigation, he should detain me for the purpose of navigating the schooner. I tried as much as possible to conceal my emotions at this intimation, and endeavoured to work upon his feelings by telling him that I was married and had three children—that they, together with my wife and aged parents, were anxiously expecting me at home; and represented, in as pathetic language as I could, the misery & distraction which it would cause them, beseeching him to spare my wife and children, and not bring down the grey hairs of my unfortunate parents with sorrow to the grave. But I appealed to a monster, devoid of all feeling, inured to crime, and hardened in iniquity. Mr. Lumsden in the mean time interfered, and hoped that he would not deprive him of my services: but he savagely told him, 'If I do not keep him, I shall keep you.' This threat evidently alarmed and agitated him, and he seemed to regret the part he had taken.

A few minutes, however, displayed the unfeeling & selfish character of this man in the strongest light. 'Mr. Smith,' said he, turning to me, 'for God's sake do not importune the captain, or he will certainly take me: you are a single man, but I have a large family dependent upon me, who will become orphans and be utterly destitute. The moment I am liberated, I shall proceed to the Havannah, and despatch a man of war in search of the corsair, and at the same time publish to the world the manner in which you have been forcibly detained. Nay, I will represent the whole affair at Lloyd's; and, should the pirate be captured hereafter, and you found on board, no harm shall befall you. Whatever property you have shall be safely delivered to your family, and mine will for ever bless you for the kind and generous act.' During this address he was much affected, and the tears streamed from his eyes. I sympathized in his feelings, and replied, that I hoped that neither of us would be detained; but if the lot must fall upon one, under these circumstances, and on these conditions, I could consent to become the victim. This declaration calmed his agitated spirits; but little did I think of the treachery and duplicity that had been masked beneath them, and which subsequent events have too clearly demonstrated.

Supper having been prepared, the captain and his officers, six or seven in number, sat down to it, and invited us to join them, which, for fear of giving offence and exciting their brutality, we did. Our supper consisted of garlic and onions chopped fine and mixed up with bread in a bowl, for which there was a general scramble, every one helping himself as he pleased, either with his fingers or any instrument with which he happened to be supplied.

During supper Mr. Lumsden begged to be allowed to go on board the *Zephyr* to the children, as he was fearful that they would be alarmed at our absence and the presence of strangers, in which request I joined; but he replied, that no one would injure them, and that, as soon as the two vessels came to an anchor, he would accompany us on board.

The corsair was at this time fast approaching the *Zephyr*, when the captain ordered a musket to be fired, and then tacked in shore; the signal was immediately answered, & the brig followed our movements. One of our boat's crew was then ordered to the lead, with directions to give notice the moment he found soundings, and the captain then inquired if we had any Americans on board as seamen. He expressed himself very warmly against them, and declared he would kill all belonging to that nation in revenge for the injuries that he had sustained at their hands, one of his vessels having been lately taken and destroyed by them; adding, at the same time, that if he discovered that we had concealed the fact from him, he would punish us equally. To the Americans he said that he should never give quarter; but as all nations were hostile to Spain, he would attack all.

The man at the lead, during this conversation, gave notice of soundings in fourteen fathoms, and the captain ordered the boat down, and told Mr. Lumsden he would accompany him on board his vessel. The men we had brought were ordered into the boat, but Captain Cowper, the carpenter, and myself, were not allowed to go into her. The boat then proceeded towards the *Zephyr*, with Mr. Lumsden and the captain of the corsair, and shortly after returned with some of the men whom the pirate had put on board; who brought with them Captain Cowper's watch, the ship's spyglass, and my telescope, together with some of my clothes, and a goat. The goat had no sooner reached the deck, than one of these inhuman wretches cut its throat, and proceeded to flay it while it was yet alive, telling us at the same time, that we should all be served in the same manner if no money was found on board. The corsair had then got into four fathoms' water and came to an anchor, as also did the *Zephyr*, about fifty yards from her, and the pirates that were on board began hailing their companions, & congratulating one another at their success.

The watch on board the corsair was now set, and Captain Cowper, the carpenter, and myself, were ordered to sleep on the Companion. Thither we repaired; but to sleep was impossible. The carpenter then took an opportunity of informing us that there was specie on board, and expressed his apprehension, that, if discovered, the cruel threat would be put into execution. Captain Cowper and myself, however, were ignorant of the circumstance, and felt rather inclined to believe that the carpenter was mistaken, but he assured us that such was the case, and that Mr. Lumsden had consulted him a day or two before about a place for its concealment. The expression which had dropped from him in the boat then occurred to us; but we still felt inclined to believe that it was some private money of his own. The whole night was passed in giving way to various conjectures, and hope and fear and the dread of assassination completely drove sleep away. Each reflected on what might be his future fate, and imparted his hopes or his apprehensions to his fellow-sufferers.

At daylight we perceived the pirates on board beating the *Zephyr*'s crew with their cutlasses, & began to tremble for our own safety. After this we perceived the sailors at work hoisting out her boats, and hauling a rope cable from the afterhatchway and coiling it on deck, as if preparing to take out the brig's cargo. The crew of the corsair meanwhile began to take their coffee, and the officers invited us to partake of some, which we willingly did, & found it very refreshing after a night spent in sleepless apprehension.

At seven o'clock the captain hailed his crew from the *Zephyr*, where he had passed the night, and ordered the boat to be sent, in which he returned in a short time, with some curiosities belonging to myself. On his arrival, he approached me, and, brandishing a cutlass over my head, told me to go on board the *Zephyr*, & bring every thing necessary for the purposes of navigation, as it was his determination to keep me. To this mandate I made no reply; so, brandishing his cutlass again, he asked me, with an oath, if I heard him. I replied that I did, when, with a ferocious air, he said, 'Mind and obey me then, or I will take off your skin.' At this threat I went into the boat, and pulled towards the *Zephyr*, and on my arrival found Mr. Lumsden at the gangway. I told him the nature of my visit, at which he expressed his sorrow, but advised me not to oppose the pirate, lest it might produce bad usage, as he seemed bent upon detaining me. He then informed me that they had taken possession of every thing, and that he himself had narrowly escaped assassination on account of his watch.

On entering my cabin, I found my chest broken to pieces, & contents taken away, with two diamond rings and some articles of value. From a seaman, I received my gold watch, sextant, and some other valuable things, which I had previously given to him to conceal; and with these I returned to my own stateroom, and proceeded to pack up what few clothes had been left by the plunderers. My books, parrot, and various other articles, I gave in charge to Mr. Lumsden, who engaged to deliver them safely into the hands of my friends, should he reach England.

The corsair had, during the interim, weighed anchor and hauled alongside of the *Zephyr*; and, having made fast, the crew had commenced moving all the trunks on board of her. Among these was the desk of Captain Cowper, containing all his papers and vouchers, which he begged me to claim as mine and recover for him, for which purpose he gave me the key. Well aware of the serious loss he would sustain, I undertook the dangerous task; and, passing into the corsair, informed the captain that my desk had been taken, and begged, as it only contained papers, which were of importance to my family, that it might be restored. He ordered me to open it, and, having examined the interior, he granted my request; and I had the pleasure of obliging Captain Cowper, who, in return, promised to represent my case to the underwriters at Lloyd's.

The pirates next commenced taking out the *Zephyr*'s cargo, at which Mr. Lumsden & myself were compelled to assist; but the former was soon after removed on board the schooner, in consequence of the crying of the children, who, the captain said, had been instigated by him to do so. There he was employed in striking the cargo into the hatchways. The pirates in the mean time became intoxicated, and gave way to the most violent excesses. All subordination was at an end, and quality seemed to be the order of the day. Mr. Lumsden was now called on board the *Zephyr*, and questioned as to the cargo down the main hatchway, when he read & explained the manifesto. Orders were immediately given to four sailors and myself to prepare for hoisting the cargo up, and to clear away the dye wood that was in our way. Mr. Lumsden directed us to throw it overboard, which we commenced doing, and threw some over; but this was prevented by the captain, who said that he only wanted to throw the ship's cargo overboard, in order to say that it was taken from him, and defraud the underwriters. We continued our occupation until we had hoisted up two scroons of indigo, a quantity of arrow root, and as much coffee as they thought sufficient. The seamen were then ordered to send down the foretop gallant mast and yard, both of which were taken on board the pirate, with whatever spars they thought would be of utility. Even the playful innocence of the children could not protect them from the barbarity of these ruffians; their earrings were taken out of their ears, and they were left without a bed to lie upon or a blanket to cover them.

They next commenced taking out the ship's stores, with all the live stock and some water; and Mr. Lumsden and Captain Cowper were then ordered on the quarter deck, and told that if they did not either produce the money or tell where it was concealed, the *Zephyr* should be burned and they with her. On this occasion the same answer was given as before, and the inhuman wretch instantly prepared to put his threat into execution, by sending the children on board the schooner, and ordering those two gentlemen to be taken below decks and to be locked to the pumps. The mandate was no sooner issued than it was obeyed by his fiendlike myrmidons, who even commenced piling combustibles round them. The apparent certainty of their fate extorted a confession from Lumsden, who was released and taken on deck, where he went to the round house and produced a small box of doubloons, which the pirate exhibited with an air of exultation to the crew. He then insisted that there was more; and, notwithstanding that the other made the most solemn asseverations to the contrary, and that even what he had given was not his own, he was again lashed to the pumps. The question was then applied to Captain Cowper, and fire was ordered to be put to the combustibles piled round him. Seeing his fate inevitable, he offered to surrender all he had, and, being released, he gave them about nine doubloons, declaring that what he had produced was all he had, and had been entrusted to his care for a poor woman, who, for aught he knew, might at this moment be in a state of starvation. 'Do not speak to me of poor people,' exclaimed the fiend, "I am poor, and your countrymen and the Americans have made me so; I know there is more money, and will either have it, or burn you and the vessel.' The unfortunate man was then once more ordered below and fire directed to be applied. In vain did they protest that he had got all; he persisted in his cruelty. The flames now began to approach their persons, and their cries were heart-rending, while they implored him to turn them adrift in a boat, at the mercy of the waves, rather than torture them thus, and keep the *Zephyr*; when, if there was money, he would surely find it.

Finding that no further confession was extorted, he began to believe the truth of these protestations, & ordered his men to throw water below and quench the flames. The unfortunate sufferers were then released and taken into the round house, and the seamen, children, and myself, allowed to go on board the brig. There we were left for a while at liberty, while the pirates caroused and exulted over their booty.

When they had finished their meal, the captain told them that it was now time to return to their own vessel, and ordered me to accompany them. I hesitated at first to obey; but he was not to be thwarted, and, drawing his knife, threatened with an oath to cut my head off if I did not move instanter. I thought it best to pretend ignorance of his order, and said that I had not heard him at first, and hoped, as I had some accounts to settle with Mr. Lumsden, that he would give me time to do so before he took me away. He complied, with some difficulty. I then requested Mr. Lumsden to sign a written bill of lading for the two tierces of coffee belonging to me on board, consigned to Mr. Watson, ship-chandler, in London, and also a promissory note for eighteen pounds ten shillings, payable to the same person, on account of monies due to me.

Having made these arrangements, I returned on board the schooner, and the captain asked me if I had my watch. I answered in the affirmative; he took it from me and looked at it, and, admiring it, gave very strong hints that he should like to have it. I took no notice of the hint, and said that it was a gift from my aged mother, whom I never expected to see again, and should like to send it to her by Mr. Lumsden; but I was afraid that his people would take it away from that person, if I gave it into his hands. 'Your people have a very bad opinion of us,' he replied; 'but I will convince you that we are not so bad as we are represented to be; come along with me, and your watch shall go safely home.' Saying this, he took me on board the *Zephyr*, with the watch in his hand, and gave it to Mr. Lumsden, and desired his people not to take it from him on any account. I then asked to remain awhile, & bid farewell to the children and crew; which he, with some difficulty, allowed me to do. In this interval, the owner's son, who was on board learning navigation, said that his quadrant and all his clothes had been taken away, and begged me to recover them for him, if possible. I promised him I would do my best, and represented to the pirate that he was the son of poor parents, and could ill afford the loss, and begged that they might be restored. He sulkily replied, that I was presuming too much, but this must be my last request; and the lad might have his things, with the exception of checked shirts, which must be left for his crew. Having performed this good office, the captain became impatient for my return, and I was obliged to take a hasty but affecting leave of my former messmates, to become one of a desperate banditti. The inhuman wretch thought even this affecting ceremony too long, and drove me on board at the point of his knife.

When I had reached the deck of the corsair, he asked me if I had got every instrument necessary to the purposes of navigation; and if not, to go and get them, for he would have no excuses by and by, and if I made any he would kill me. I answered, that I had got all that was necessary, and he then gave orders to cast loose from the *Zephyr*, and told Mr. Lumsden he might proceed on his voyage, but on no account to steer for the Havannah; for, if he overtook him on that course, he would destroy him and his vessel together. He promised that he would not touch there, and the vessels were accordingly cast loose, in a short time afterwards. Mr. Lumsden, Captain Cowper, & the children, stood on the gangway and bade me adieu, and my heart sunk within me as the two vessels parted.

The horrors of my situation now rushed upon my mind; I looked upon myself as a wretch, upon whom the world was closed for ever: exposed to the brutality of a ferocious and remorseless horde of miscreants—doomed to destruction and death, and, perhaps, to worse, to disgrace and ignominy; to become the partaker of their enormities, and be compelled, I knew not how soon, to embrue my hands in the blood of a fellow-creature, and, perhaps, a fellow-countryman. The distraction, grief, and painful apprehensions of my parents, and of one to whom I was under the tenderest of all engagements, filled my mind with terror. I could no longer bear to look upon the scene my fancy presented to me, and I would have sought a refuge from my own miserable thoughts, in self-destruction; but my movements were watched, and I was secured, and a guard set over me. The captain then addressed me, and told me that if I made a second attempt I should be lashed to a gun, and there left to die through hunger; and, for the sake of security, ordered me below; but, at my earnest entreaty, I was allowed to remain on deck till it was dark.

# Dirty Weather

## *Joseph Conrad*

OBSERVING THE STEADY FALL OF THE BAROMETER, CAPTAIN MacWhirr thought, "There's some dirty weather knocking about." This is precisely what he thought. He had had an experience of moderately dirty weather—the term dirty as applied to the weather implying only moderate discomfort to the seaman. Had he been informed by an indisputable authority that the end of the world was to be finally accomplished by a catastrophic disturbance of the atmosphere, he would have assimilated the information under the simple idea of dirty weather, and no other, because he had no experience of cataclysms, and belief does not necessarily imply comprehension. The wisdom of his county had pronounced by means of an Act of Parliament that before he could be considered as fit to take charge of a ship he should be able to answer certain simple questions on the subject of circular storms such as hurricanes, cyclones, typhoons; and apparently he had answered them, since he was now in command of the *Nan-Shan* in the China seas during the season of typhoons. But if he had answered he remembered nothing of it. He was, however, conscious of being made uncomfortable by the clammy heat. He came out on the bridge, and found no relief to this oppression. The air seemed thick. He gasped like a fish, and began to believe himself greatly out of sorts.

The *Nan-Shan* was ploughing a vanishing furrow upon the circle of the sea that had the surface and the shimmer of an undulating piece of gray silk. The sun, pale and without rays, poured down leaden heat in a strangely indecisive light, and the Chinamen were lying prostrate about the decks. Their bloodless, pinched, yellow faces were like the faces of bilious invalids. Captain MacWhirr noticed two of them especially, stretched out on their backs below the bridge. As soon as they had closed their eyes they seemed dead. Three others, however, were quarrelling barbarously away forward; and one big fellow, half naked, with herculean shoulders, was hanging limply over a winch; another, sitting on the deck, his knees up and his head drooping sideways in a girlish attitude, was plaiting his pigtail with infinite languor depicted in his whole person and in the very movement of his fingers. The smoke struggled with difficulty out of the funnel, and instead of streaming away spread itself out like an infernal sort of cloud, smelling of sulphur and raining soot all over the decks.

"What the devil are you doing there, Mr. Jukes?" asked Captain MacWhirr. This unusual form of address, though mumbled rather than spoken, caused the body of Mr. Jukes to start as though it had been prodded under the fifth rib. He had had a low bench brought on the bridge, and sitting on it, with a length of rope curled about his feet and a piece of canvas stretched over his knees, was pushing a sailneedle vigorously. He looked up, and his surprise gave to his eyes an expression of innocence and candour.

"I am only roping some of that new set of bags we made last trip for whipping up coals," he remonstrated, gently. "We shall want them for the next coaling, sir."

"What became of the others?"

"Why, worn out of course, sir."

Captain MacWhirr, after glaring down irresolutely at his chief mate, disclosed the gloomy and cynical conviction that more than half of them had been lost overboard, "if only the truth was known," and retired to the other end of the bridge. Jukes, exasperated by this unprovoked attack, broke the needle at the second stitch, and dropping his work got up and cursed the heat in a violent undertone.

The propeller thumped, the three Chinamen forward had given up squabbling very suddenly, and the one who had been plaiting his tail clasped his legs and stared dejectedly over his knees. The lurid sunshine cast faint and sickly shadows. The swell ran higher and swifter every moment, and the ship lurched heavily in the smooth, deep hollows of the sea.

"I wonder where that beastly swell comes from," said Jukes aloud, recovering himself after a stagger.

"Northeast," grunted the literal MacWhirr, from his side of the bridge. "There's some dirty weather knocking about. Go and look at the glass."

When Jukes came out of the chart-room, the cast of his countenance had changed to thoughtfulness and concern. He caught hold of the bridge-rail and stared ahead.

The temperature in the engineroom had gone up to a hundred and seventeen degrees. Irritated voices were ascending through the skylight and through the fiddle of the stokehold in a harsh and resonant uproar, mingled with angry clangs and scrapes of metal, as if men with limbs of iron and throats of bronze had been quarrelling down there. The second engineer was falling foul of the stokers for letting the steam go down. He was a man with arms like a blacksmith, and generally feared; but that afternoon the stokers were answering him back recklessly, and slammed the furnace doors with the fury of despair. Then the noise ceased suddenly, and the second engineer appeared, emerging out of the stokehold streaked with grime and soaking wet like a chimneysweep coming out of a well. As soon as his head was clear of the fiddle he began to scold Jukes for not trimming properly the stokehold ventilators; and in answer Jukes made with his hands deprecatory soothing signs meaning:

"No wind—can't be helped—you can see for yourself."

But the other wouldn't hear reason. His teeth flashed angrily in his dirty face. He didn't mind, he said, the trouble of punching their blanked heads down there, blank his soul, but did the condemned sailors think you could keep steam up in the Godforsaken boilers simply by knocking the blanked stokers about? No, by George! You had to get some draught, too—may he be everlastingly blanked for a swabheaded deckhand if you didn't! And the chief, too, rampaging before the steamgauge and carrying on like a lunatic up and down the engineroom ever since noon. What did Jukes think he was stuck up there for, if he couldn't get one of his decayed, goodfornothing deckcripples to turn the ventilators to the wind?

The relations of the "engineroom" and the "deck" of the *Nan-Shan* were, as is known, of a brotherly nature; therefore Jukes leaned over and begged the other in a restrained tone not to make a disgusting ass of himself; the skipper was on the other side of the bridge. But the second declared mutinously that he didn't care a rap who was on the other side of the bridge, and Jukes, passing in a flash from lofty disapproval into a state of exaltation, invited him in unflattering terms to come up and twist the beastly things to please himself, and catch such wind as a donkey of his sort could find. The second rushed up to the fray. He flung himself at the port ventilator as though he meant to tear it out bodily and toss it overboard. All he did was to move the cowl round a few inches, with an enormous expenditure of force, and seemed spent in the effort. He leaned against the back of the wheelhouse, and Jukes walked up to him.

"Oh, Heavens!" ejaculated the engineer in a feeble voice. He lifted his eyes to the sky, and then let his glassy stare descend to meet the horizon that, tilting up to an angle of forty degrees, seemed to hang on a slant for a while and settled down slowly.

"Heavens! Phew! What's up, anyhow?"

Jukes, straddling his long legs like a pair of compasses, put on an air of superiority. "We're going to catch it this time," he said. "The barometer is tumbling down like anything, Harry. And you trying to kick up that silly row. . . ."

The word "barometer" seemed to revive the second engineer's mad animosity. Collecting afresh all his energies, he directed Jukes in a low and brutal tone to shove the unmentionable instrument down his gory throat. Who cared for his crimson barometer? It was the steam—the steam—that was going down; and what between the firemen going faint and the chief going silly, it was worse than a dog's life for him; he didn't care a tinker's curse how soon the whole show was blown out of the water. He seemed on the point of having a cry, but after regaining his breath he muttered darkly, "I'll faint them," and dashed off. He stopped upon the fiddle long enough to shake his fist at the unnatural daylight, and dropped into the dark hole with a whoop.

When Jukes turned, his eyes fell upon the rounded back and the big red ears of Captain MacWhirr, who had come across. He did not look at his chief officer, but said at once,

"That's a very violent man, that second engineer."

"Jolly good second, anyhow," grunted Jukes. "They can't keep up steam," he added, rapidly, and made a grab at the rail against the coming lurch. Captain MacWhirr, unprepared, took a run and brought himself up with a jerk by an awning stanchion.

"A profane man," he said, obstinately. "If this goes on, I'll have to get rid of him the first chance."

"It's the heat," said Jukes. "The weather's awful. It would make a saint swear. Even up here I feel exactly as if I had my head tied up in a woollen blanket."

Captain MacWhirr looked up.

"D'ye mean to say, Mr. Jukes, you ever had your head tied up in a blanket? What was that for?"

"It's a manner of speaking, sir," said Jukes, stolidly.

"Some of you fellows do go on! What's that about saints swearing? I wish you wouldn't talk so wild. What sort of saint would that be that would swear? No more saint than yourself, I expect. And what's a blanket got to do with it—or the weather either. . . . The heat does not make me swear—does it? It's filthy bad temper. That's what it is. And what's the good of your talking like this?"

Thus Captain MacWhirr expostulated against the use of images in speech, and at the end electrified Jukes by a contemptuous snort, followed by words of passion and resentment: "Damme! I'll fire him out of the ship if he don't look out."

And Jukes, incorrigible, thought: "Goodness me! Somebody's put a new inside to my old man. Here's temper, if you like. Of course it's the weather; what else? It would make an angel quarrelsome—let alone a saint."

All the Chinamen on deck appeared at their last gasp. At its setting the sun had a diminished diameter and an expiring brown, rayless glow, as if millions of centuries elapsing since the morning had brought it near its end. A dense bank of cloud became visible to the northward; it had a sinister dark olive tint, and lay low and motionless upon the sea, resembling a solid obstacle in the path of the ship. She went floundering towards it like an exhausted creature driven to its death. The coppery twilight retired slowly, and the darkness brought out overhead a swarm of unsteady, big stars, that, as if blown upon, flickered exceedingly and seemed to hang very near the earth. At eight o'clock Jukes went into the chartroom to write up the ship's log.

He copied neatly out of the rough-book the number of miles, the course of the ship, and in the column for "wind" scrawled the word "calm" from top to bottom of the eight hours since noon. He was exasperated by the continuous, monotonous rolling of the ship. The heavy inkstand would slide away in a manner that suggested perverse intelligence in dodging the pen. Having written in the large space under the head of "Remarks," "Heat very oppressive," he stuck the end of the penholder in his teeth, pipe fashion, and mopped his face carefully.

"Ship rolling heavily in a high cross swell," he began again, and commented to himself, "Heavily is no word for it." Then he wrote:

"Sunset threatening, with a low bank of clouds to N. and E. Sky clear overhead."

Sprawling over the table with arrested pen, he glanced out of the door, and in that frame of his vision he saw all the stars flying upwards between the teakwood jambs on a black sky. The whole lot took flight together and disappeared, leaving only a blackness flecked with white flashes, for the sea was as black as the sky and speckled with foam afar. The stars that had flown to the roll came back on the return swing of the ship, rushing downwards in their glittering multitude, not of fiery points, but enlarged to tiny discs brilliant with a clear wet sheen.

Jukes watched the flying big stars for a moment, and then wrote: "8 p.m. Swell increasing. Ship labouring and taking water on her decks. Battened down the coolies for the night. Barometer still falling." He paused, and thought to himself, "Perhaps nothing whatever'll come of it." And then he closed resolutely his entries: "Every appearance of a typhoon coming on."

On going out he had to stand aside, and Captain Mac-Whirr strode over the doorstep without saying a word or making a sign.

"Shut the door, Mr. Jukes, will you?" he cried from within. Jukes turned back to do so, muttering ironically: "Afraid to catch cold, I suppose." It was his watch below, but he yearned for communion with his kind; and he remarked cheerily to the second mate: "Doesn't look so bad, after all—does it?"

The second mate was marching to and fro on the bridge, tripping down with small steps one moment, and the next climbing with difficulty the shifting slope of the deck. At the sound of Jukes' voice he stood still, facing forward, but made no reply.

"Hallo! That's a heavy one," said Jukes, swaying to meet the long roll till his lowered hand touched the planks.

This time the second mate made in his throat a noise of an unfriendly nature.

He was an oldish, shabby little fellow, with bad teeth and no hair on his face. He had been shipped in a hurry in Shanghai, that trip when the second officer brought from home had delayed the ship three hours in port by contriving (in some manner Captain MacWhirr could never understand) to fall overboard into an empty coallighter lying alongside, and had to be sent ashore to the hospital with concussion of the brain and a broken limb or two.

Jukes was not discouraged by the unsympathetic sound. "The Chinamen must be having a lovely time of it down there," he said. "It's lucky for them the old girl has the easiest roll of any ship I've ever been in. There now! This one wasn't so bad."

"You wait," snarled the second mate.

With his sharp nose, red at the tip, and his thin pinched lips, he always looked as though he were raging inwardly; and he was concise in his speech to the point of rudeness. All his time off duty he spent in his cabin with the door shut, keeping so still in there that he was supposed to fall asleep as soon as he had disappeared; but the man who came in to wake him for his watch on deck would invariably find him with his eyes wide open, flat on his back in the bunk, and glaring irritably from a soiled pillow. He never wrote any letters, did not seem to hope for news from anywhere; and though he had been heard once to mention West Hartlepool, it was with extreme bitterness, and only in connection with the extortionate charges of a boarding-house. He was one of those men who are picked up at need in the ports of the world. They are competent enough, appear hopelessly hard up, show no evidence of any sort of vice, and carry about them all the signs of manifest failure. They come aboard on an emergency, care for no ship afloat, live in their own atmosphere of casual connection amongst their shipmates who know nothing of them, and make up their minds to leave at inconvenient times. They clear out with no words of lea-vetaking in some God-forsaken port other men would fear to be stranded in, and go ashore in company of a shabby sea-chest, corded like a treasure-box, and with an air of shaking the ship's dust off their feet.

"You wait," he repeated, balanced in great swings with his back to Jukes, motionless and implacable.

"Do you mean to say we are going to catch it hot?" asked Jukes with boyish interest.

"Say? . . . I say nothing. You don't catch me," snapped the little second mate, with a mixture of pride, scorn, and cunning, as if Jukes' question had been a trap cleverly detected. "Oh, no! None of you here shall make a fool of me if I know it," he mumbled to himself.

Jukes reflected rapidly that this second mate was a mean little beast, and in his heart he wished poor Jack Allen had never smashed himself up in the coal-lighter. The far-off blackness ahead of the ship was like another night seen through the starry night of the earth—the starless night of the immensities beyond the created universe, revealed in its appalling stillness through a low fissure in the glittering sphere of which the earth is the kernel.

"Whatever there might be about," said Jukes, "we are steaming straight into it."

"You've said it," caught up the second mate, always with his back to Jukes. "You've said it, mind—not I."

"Oh, go to Jericho!" said Jukes, frankly; and the other emitted a triumphant little chuckle.

"You've said it," he repeated.

"And what of that?"

"I've known some real good men get into trouble with their skippers for saying a dam' sight less," answered the second mate feverishly. "Oh, no! You don't catch me."

"You seem deucedly anxious not to give yourself away," said Jukes, completely soured by such absurdity. "I wouldn't be afraid to say what I think."

"Aye, to me! That's no great trick. I am nobody, and well I know it."

The ship, after a pause of comparative steadiness, started upon a series of rolls, one worse than the other, and for a time Jukes, preserving his equilibrium, was too busy to open his mouth. As soon as the violent swinging had quieted down somewhat, he said: "This is a bit too much of a good thing. Whether anything is coming or not I think she ought to be put head on to that swell. The old man is just gone in to lie down. Hang me if I don't speak to him."

But when he opened the door of the chartroom he saw his captain reading a book. Captain MacWhirr was not lying down: he was standing up with one hand grasping the edge of the bookshelf and the other holding open before his face a thick volume. The lamp wriggled in the gimbals, the loosened books toppled from side to side on the shelf, the long barometer swung in jerky circles, the table altered its slant every moment. In the midst of all this stir and movement Captain MacWhirr, holding on, showed his eyes above the upper edge, and asked, "What's the matter?"

"Swell getting worse, sir."

"Noticed that in here," muttered Captain MacWhirr. "Anything wrong?"

Jukes, inwardly disconcerted by the seriousness of the eyes looking at him over the top of the book, produced an embarrassed grin.

"Rolling like old boots," he said, sheepishly.

"Aye! Very heavy—very heavy. What do you want?"

At this Jukes lost his footing and began to flounder. "I was thinking of our passengers," he said, in the manner of a man clutching at a straw.

"Passengers?" wondered the Captain, gravely. "What passengers?"

"Why, the Chinamen, sir," explained Jukes, very sick of this conversation.

"The Chinamen! Why don't you speak plainly? Couldn't tell what you meant. Never heard a lot of coolies spoken of as passengers before. Passengers, indeed! What's come to you?"

Captain MacWhirr, closing the book on his forefinger, lowered his arm and looked completely mystified. "Why are you thinking of the Chinamen, Mr. Jukes?" he inquired.

Jukes took a plunge, like a man driven to it. "She's rolling her decks full of water, sir. Thought you might put her head on perhaps—for a while. Till this goes down a bit—very soon, I dare say. Head to the eastward. I never knew a ship roll like this."

He held on in the doorway, and Captain MacWhirr, feeling his grip on the shelf inadequate, made up his mind to let go in a hurry, and fell heavily on the couch.

"Head to the eastward?" he said, struggling to sit up. "That's more than four points off her course."

"Yes, sir. Fifty degrees. . . . Would just bring her head far enough round to meet this. . . ."

Captain MacWhirr was now sitting up. He had not dropped the book, and he had not lost his place.

"To the eastward?" he repeated, with dawning astonishment. "To the . . . Where do you think we are bound to? You want me to haul a fullpowered steamship four points off her course to make the Chinamen comfortable! Now, I've heard more than enough of mad things done in the world—but this. . . . If I didn't know you, Jukes, I would think you were in liquor. Steer four points off. . . . And what afterwards? Steer four points over the other way, I suppose, to make the course good. What put it into your head that I would start to tack a steamer as if she were a sailingship?"

"Jolly good thing she isn't," threw in Jukes, with bitter readiness. "She would have rolled every blessed stick out of her this afternoon."

"Aye! And you just would have had to stand and see them go," said Captain MacWhirr, showing a certain animation. "It's a dead calm, isn't it?"

"It is, sir. But there's something out of the common coming, for sure."

"Maybe. I suppose you have a notion I should be getting out of the way of that dirt," said Captain MacWhirr, speaking with the utmost simplicity of manner and tone, and fixing the oilcloth on the floor with a heavy stare. Thus he noticed neither Jukes' discomfiture nor the mixture of vexation and astonished respect on his face.

"Now, here's this book," he continued with deliberation, slapping his thigh with the closed volume. "I've been reading the chapter on the storms there."

This was true. He had been reading the chapter on the storms. When he had entered the chartroom, it was with no intention of taking the book down. Some influence in the air—the same influence, probably, that caused the steward to bring without orders the Captain's sea-boots and oilskin coat up to the chart-room—had as it were guided his hand to the shelf; and without taking the time to sit down he had waded with a conscious effort into the terminology of the subject. He lost himself amongst advancing semi-circles, left- and right-hand quadrants, the curves of the tracks, the probable bearing of the centre, the shifts of wind and the readings of barometer. He tried to bring all these things into a definite relation to himself, and ended by becoming contemptuously angry with such a lot of words, and with so much advice, all headwork and supposition, without a glimmer of certitude.

"It's the damnedest thing, Jukes," he said. "If a fellow was to believe all that's in there, he would be running most of his time all over the sea trying to get behind the weather."

Again he slapped his leg with the book; and Jukes opened his mouth, but said nothing.

"Running to get behind the weather! Do you understand that, Mr. Jukes? It's the maddest thing!" ejaculated Captain MacWhirr, with pauses, gazing at the floor profoundly. "You would think an old woman had been writing this. It passes me. If that thing means anything useful, then it means that I should at once alter the course away, away to the devil somewhere, and come booming down on Fu-chau from the northward at the tail of this dirty weather that's supposed to be knocking about in our way. From the north! Do you understand, Mr. Jukes? Three hundred extra miles to the distance, and a pretty coal bill to show. I couldn't bring myself to do that if every word in there was gospel truth, Mr. Jukes. Don't you expect me. . . ."

And Jukes, silent, marvelled at this display of feeling and loquacity.

"But the truth is that you don't know if the fellow is right, anyhow. How can you tell what a gale is made of till you get it?

"He isn't aboard here, is he? Very well. Here he says that the centre of them things bears eight points off the wind; but we haven't got any wind, for all the barometer falling. Where's his centre now?"

"We will get the wind presently," mumbled Jukes.

"Let it come, then," said Captain MacWhirr, with dignified indignation. "It's only to let you see, Mr. Jukes, that you don't find everything in books. All these rules for dodging breezes and circumventing the winds of heaven, Mr. Jukes, seem to me the maddest thing, when you come to look at it sensibly."

He raised his eyes, saw Jukes gazing at him dubiously, and tried to illustrate his meaning.

"About as queer as your extraordinary notion of dodging the ship head to sea, for I don't know how long, to make the Chinamen comfortable; whereas all we've got to do is to take them to Fuchau, being timed to get there before noon on Friday. If the weather delays me—very well. There's your logbook to talk straight about the weather. But suppose I went swinging off my course and came in two days late, and they asked me: 'Where have you been all that time, Captain?' What could I say to that?

'Went around to dodge the bad weather,' I would say. 'It must've been dam' bad,' they would say. 'Don't know,' I would have to say; 'I've dodged clear of it.' See that, Jukes? I have been thinking it all out this afternoon."

He looked up again in his unseeing, unimaginative way. No one had ever heard him say so much at one time. Jukes, with his arms open in the doorway, was like a man invited to behold a miracle. Unbounded wonder was the intellectual meaning of his eye, while incredulity was seated in his whole countenance.

"A gale is a gale, Mr. Jukes," resumed the Captain, "and a fullpowered steamship has got to face it. There's just so much dirty weather knocking about the world, and the proper thing is to go through it with none of what old Captain Wilson of the Melita calls 'storm strategy.' The other day ashore I heard him hold forth about it to a lot of shipmasters who came in and sat at a table next to mine. It seemed to me the greatest nonsense.

"He was telling them how he outmanoeuvred, I think he said, a terrific gale, so that it never came nearer than fifty miles to him. A neat piece of headwork he called it. How he knew there was a terrific gale fifty miles off beats me altogether. It was like listening to a crazy man. I would have thought Captain Wilson was old enough to know better."

Captain MacWhirr ceased for a moment, then said, "It's your watch below, Mr. Jukes?"

Jukes came to himself with a start. "Yes, sir."

"Leave orders to call me at the slightest change," said the Captain. He reached up to put the book away, and tucked his legs upon the couch. "Shut the door so that it don't fly open, will you? I can't stand a door banging. They've put a lot of rubbishy locks into this ship, I must say."

Captain MacWhirr closed his eyes.

He did so to rest himself. He was tired, and he experienced that state of mental vacuity which comes at the end of an exhaustive discussion that has liberated some belief matured in the course of meditative years. He had indeed been making his confession of faith, had he only known it; and its effect was to make Jukes, on the other side of the door, stand scratching his head for a good while.

Captain MacWhirr opened his eyes.

He thought he must have been asleep. What was that loud noise? Wind? Why had he not been called? The lamp wriggled in its gimbals, the barometer swung in circles, the table altered its slant every moment; a pair of limp seaboots with collapsed tops went sliding past the couch. He put out his hand instantly, and captured one.

Jukes' face appeared in a crack of the door: only his face, very red, with staring eyes. The flame of the lamp leaped, a piece of paper flew up, a rush of air enveloped Captain MacWhirr.

Beginning to draw on the boot, he directed an expectant gaze at Jukes' swollen, excited features.

"Came on like this," shouted Jukes, "five minutes ago . . . all of a sudden."

The head disappeared with a bang, and a heavy splash and patter of drops swept past the closed door as if a pailful of melted lead had been flung against the house. A whistling could be heard now upon the deep vibrating noise outside. The stuffy chartroom seemed as full of draughts as a shed. Captain MacWhirr collared the other seaboot on its violent passage along the floor. He was not flustered, but he could not find at once the opening for inserting his foot. The shoes he had flung off were scurrying from end to end of the cabin, gambolling playfully over each other like puppies. As soon as he stood up he kicked at them viciously, but without effect.

He threw himself into the attitude of a lunging fencer, to reach after his oilskin coat; and afterwards he staggered all over the confined space while he jerked himself into it. Very grave, straddling his legs far apart, and stretching his neck, he started to tie deliberately the strings of his sou'wester under his chin, with thick fingers that trembled slightly. He went through all the movements of a woman putting on her bonnet before a glass, with a strained, listening attention, as though he had expected every moment to hear the shout of his name in the confused clamour that had suddenly beset his ship. Its increase filled his ears while he was getting ready to go out and confront whatever it might mean. It was tumultuous and very loud—made up of the rush of the wind, the crashes of the sea, with that prolonged deep vibration of the air, like the roll of an immense and remote drum beating the charge of the gale.

He stood for a moment in the light of the lamp, thick, clumsy, shapeless in his panoply of combat, vigilant and red-faced.

"There's a lot of weight in this," he muttered.

As soon as he attempted to open the door the wind caught it. Clinging to the handle, he was dragged out over the doorstep, and at once found himself engaged with the wind in a sort of personal scuffle whose object was the shutting of that door. At the last moment a tongue of air scurried in and licked out the flame of the lamp.

Ahead of the ship he perceived a great darkness lying upon a multitude of white flashes; on the starboard beam a few amazing stars drooped, dim and fitful, above an immense waste of broken seas, as if seen through a mad drift of smoke.

On the bridge a knot of men, indistinct and toiling, were making great efforts in the light of the wheelhouse windows that shone mistily on their heads and backs. Suddenly darkness closed upon one pane, then on another. The voices of the lost group reached him after the manner of men's voices in a gale, in shreds and fragments of forlorn shouting snatched past the ear. All at once Jukes appeared at his side, yelling, with his head down.

"Watch—put in—wheelhouse shutters—glass—afraid—blow in."

Jukes heard his commander upbraiding.

"This—come—anything—warning—call me."

He tried to explain, with the uproar pressing on his lips.

"Light—air—remained—bridge—sudden—northeast—could turn—thought—you—sure—hear."

They had gained the shelter of the weathercloth, and could converse with raised voices, as people quarrel.

"I got the hands along to cover up all the ventilators. Good job I had remained on deck. I didn't think you would be asleep, and so . . . What did you say, sir? What?"

"Nothing," cried Captain MacWhirr. "I said—all right."

"By all the powers! We've got it this time," observed Jukes in a howl.

"You haven't altered her course?" inquired Captain Mac-Whirr, straining his voice.

"No, sir. Certainly not. Wind came out right ahead. And here comes the head sea."

A plunge of the ship ended in a shock as if she had landed her forefoot upon something solid. After a moment of stillness a lofty flight of sprays drove hard with the wind upon their faces.

"Keep her at it as long as we can," shouted Captain MacWhirr.

Before Jukes had squeezed the salt water out of his eyes all the stars had disappeared.

# An Introduction to Informality

### *Erskine Childers*

FROM FLUSHING EASTWARD TO HAMBURG, THEN NORTH-ward to Flensburg, I cut short the next day's sultry story. Past dyke and windmill and still canals, on to blazing stubbles and roaring towns; at the last, after dusk, through a quiet level region where the train pottered from one lazy little station to another, and at ten o'clock I found myself, stiff and stuffy, on the platform at Flensburg, exchanging greetings with Davies.

"It's awfully good of you to come."

"Not at all; it's very good of you to ask me."

We were both of us ill at ease. Even in the dim gas-light he clashed on my notions of a yachtsman—no cool white ducks or neat blue serge; and where was the snowy crowned yachting cap, that precious charm that so easily converts a landsman into a dashing mariner? Conscious that this impressive uniform, in high perfection, was lying ready in my portmanteau, I felt oddly guilty. He wore an old Nor-folk jacket, muddy brown shoes, grey flannel trousers (or had they been white?), and an ordinary tweed cap. The hand he gave me was horny, and appeared to be stained with paint;

the other one, which carried a parcel, had a bandage on it which would have borne renewal. There was an instant of mutual inspection. I thought he gave me a shy, hurried scrutiny as though to test past conjectures, with something of anxiety in it, and perhaps (save the mark!) a tinge of admiration. The face was familiar, and yet not familiar; the pleasant blue eyes, open, clean-cut features, unintellectual forehead were the same; so were the brisk and impulsive movements; there was some change; but the moment of awkward hesitation was over and the light was bad; and, while strolling down the platform for my luggage, we chatted with constraint about trivial things.

"By the way," he suddenly said, laughing, "I'm afraid I'm not fit to be seen; but it's so late it doesn't matter. I've been painting hard all day, and just got it finished. I only hope we shall have some wind tomorrow—it's been hopelessly calm lately. I say, you've brought a good deal of stuff," he concluded, as my belongings began to collect.

Here was a reward for my submissive exertions in the far east!

"You gave me a good many commissions!"

"Oh, I didn't mean those things," he said, absently. "Thanks for bringing them, by the way. That's the stove, I suppose; cartridges, this one, by the weight. You got the riggingscrews all right, I hope? They're not really necessary, of course" (I nodded vacantly, and felt a little hurt); "but they're simpler than lanyards, and you can't get them here. It's that portmanteau," he said, slowly, measuring it with a doubtful eye. "Never mind! we'll try. You couldn't do with the Gladstone only, I suppose? You see, the dinghy—h'm, and there's the hatchway, too"—he was lost in thought.

"Anyhow, we'll try. I'm afraid there are no cabs; but it's quite near, and the porter'll help."

Sickening forebodings crept over me, while Davies shouldered my Gladstone and clutched at the parcels.

"Aren't your men here?" I asked, faintly.

"Men?" He looked confused. "Oh, perhaps I ought to have told you, I never have any paid hands; it's quite a small boat, you know—I hope you didn't expect luxury. I've managed her singlehanded for some time. A man would be no use, and a horrible nuisance." He revealed these appalling truths with a cheerful assurance, which did nothing to hide a naive apprehension of their effect on me. There was a check in our mobilization.

"It's rather late to go on board, isn't it?" I said, in a wooden voice. Someone was turning out the gaslights, and the porter yawned ostentatiously. "I think I'd rather sleep at an hotel tonight." A strained pause.

"Oh, of course you can do that, if you like," said Davies, in transparent distress of mind. "But it seems hardly worth while to cart this stuff all the way to an hotel (I believe they're all on the other side of the harbour), and back again to the boat tomorrow. She's quite comfortable, and you're sure to sleep well, as you're tired."

"We can leave the things here," I argued feebly, "and walk over with my bag."

"Oh, I shall have to go aboard anyhow," he rejoined; "I never sleep on shore."

He seemed to be clinging timidly, but desperately, to some diplomatic end. A stony despair was invading me and paralysing resistance. Better face the worst and be done with it.

"Come on," I said, grimly.

Heavily loaded, we stumbled over railway lines and rubble heaps, and came on the harbour. Davies led the way to a stairway, whose weedy steps disappeared below in gloom.

"If you'll get into the dinghy," he said, all briskness now, "I'll pass the things down."

I descended gingerly, holding as a guide a sodden painter which ended in a small boat, and conscious that I was collecting slime on cuffs and trousers.

"Hold up!" shouted Davies, cheerfully, as I sat down suddenly near the bottom, with one foot in the water.

I climbed wretchedly into the dinghy and awaited events.

"Now float her up close under the quay wall, and make fast to the ring down there," came down from above, followed by the slack of the sodden painter, which knocked my cap off as it fell. "All fast? Any knot'll do," I heard, as I grappled with this loathsome task, and then a big, dark object loomed overhead and was lowered into the dinghy. It was my portmanteau, and, placed athwart, exactly filled all the space amidships. "Does it fit?" was the anxious inquiry from aloft.

"Beautifully."

"Capital!"

Scratching at the greasy wall to keep the dinghy close to it, I received in succession our stores, and stowed the cargo as best I could, while the dinghy sank lower and lower in the water, and its precarious superstructure grew higher.

"Catch!" was the final direction from above, and a damp soft parcel hit me in the chest. "Be careful of that, it's meat. Now back to the stairs!"

I painfully acquiesced, and Davies appeared.

"It's a bit of a load, and she's rather deep; but I think we shall manage," he reflected. "You sit right aft, and I'll row."

I was too far gone for curiosity as to how this monstrous pyramid was to be rowed, or even for surmises as to its foundering by the way. I crawled to my appointed seat, and Davies extricated the buried sculls by a series of tugs, which shook the whole structure, and made us roll alarmingly. How he stowed himself into rowing posture I have not the least idea, but eventually we were moving sluggishly out into the open water, his head just visible in the bows. We had started from what appeared to be the head of a narrow loch, and were leaving behind us the lights of a big town. A long frontage of lamplit quays was on our left, with here and there the vague hull of a steamer alongside. We passed the last of the lights and came out into a broader stretch of water, when a light breeze was blowing and dark hills could be seen on either shore.

"I'm lying a little way down the fiord, you see," said Davies. "I hate to be too near a town, and I found a carpenter handy here—There she is! I wonder how you'll like her!"

I roused myself. We were entering a little cove encircled by trees, and approaching a light which flickered in the rigging of a small vessel, whose outline gradually defined itself.

"Keep her off," said Davies, as we drew alongside.

In a moment he had jumped on deck, tied the painter, and was round at my end.

"You hand them up," he ordered, "and I'll take them."

It was a laborious task, with the one relief that it was not far to hand them—a doubtful compensation, for other reasons distantly shaping themselves. When the stack was transferred to the deck I followed it, tripping over the flabby meat parcel, which was already showing ghastly signs of disintegration under the dew. Hazily there floated through my mind my last embarkation on a yacht; my faultless attire, the trim gig and obsequious sailors, the accommodation ladder flashing with varnish and brass in the August sun; the orderly, snowy decks and basket chairs under the awning aft. What a contrast with this sordid midnight scramble, over damp meat and littered packingcases! The bitterest touch of all was a growing sense of inferiority and ignorance which I had never before been allowed to feel in my experience of yachts.

Davies awoke from another reverie over my portmanteau to say, cheerily: "I'll just show you round down below first, and then we'll stow things away and get to bed."

He dived down a companion ladder, and I followed cautiously. A complex odour of paraffin, past cookery, tobacco, and tar saluted my nostrils.

"Mind your head," said Davies, striking a match and lighting a candle, while I groped into the cabin. "You'd better sit down; it's easier to look round."

There might well have been sarcasm in this piece of advice, for I must have cut a ridiculous figure, peering awkwardly and suspiciously round, with shoulders and head bent to avoid the ceiling, which seemed in the halflight to be even nearer the floor than it was.

"You see," were Davies's reassuring words, "there's plenty of room to sit upright" (which was strictly true; but I am not very tall, and he is short). "Some people make a point of headroom, but I never mind much about it. That's the centreboard case," he explained, as, in stretching my legs out, my knee came into contact with a sharp edge.

I had not seen this devilish obstruction, as it was hidden beneath the table, which indeed rested on it at one end. It appeared to be a long, low triangle, running lengthways with the boat and dividing the naturally limited space into two.

"You see, she's a flatbottomed boat, drawing very little water without the plate; that's why there's so little headroom. For deep water you lower the plate; so, in one way or another, you can go practically anywhere."

I was not nautical enough to draw any very definite conclusions from this, but what I did draw were not promising.

The latter sentences were spoken from the forecastle, whither Davies had crept through a low sliding door, like that of a rabbithutch, and was already busy with a kettle over a stove which I made out to be a battered and disreputable twin brother of the No. 3 Rippingille.

"It'll be boiling soon," he remarked, "and we'll have some grog."

My eyes were used to the light now, and I took in the rest of my surroundings, which may be very simply described. Two long cushion-covered seats flanked the cabin, bounded at the after end by cupboards, one of which was cut low to form a sort of miniature sideboard, with glasses hung in a rack above it. The deck overhead was very low at each side but rose shoulder high for a space in the middle, where a "coachhouse roof" with a skylight gave additional cabin space. Just outside the door was a fold-up washingstand. On either wall were long net-racks holding a medley of flags, charts, caps, cigarboxes, banks of yam, and such like. Across the forward bulkhead was a bookshelf crammed to overflowing with volumes of all sizes, many upside down and some coverless. Below this were a pipe-rack, an aneroid, and a clock with a hearty tick. All the woodwork was painted white, and to a less jaundiced eye than mine the interior might have had an enticing look of snugness. Some Kodak prints were nailed roughly on the after bulkhead, and just over the doorway was the photograph of a young girl.

"That's my sister," said Davies, who had emerged and saw me looking at it. "Now, let's get the stuff down." He ran up the ladder, and soon my portmanteau blackened the hatchway, and a great straining and squeezing began. "I was afraid it was too big," came down; "I'm sorry, but you'll have to unpack on deck—we may be able to squash it down when it's empty." Then the wearisome tail of packages began to form a fresh stack in the cramped space at my feet, and my back ached with stooping and moiling in unfamiliar places. Davies came down, and with unconcealed pride introduced me to the sleeping cabin (he called the other one "the saloon"). Another candle was lit and showed two short and narrow berths with blankets, but no sign of sheets; beneath these were drawers, one set of which Davies made me master of, evidently thinking them a princely allowance of space for my wardrobe.

"You can chuck your things down the skylight on to your berth as you unpack them," he remarked. "By the way, I doubt if there's room for all you've got. I suppose you couldn't manage—"

"No, I couldn't," I said shortly.

The absurdity of argument struck me; two men, doubled up like monkeys, cannot argue.

"If you'll go out I shall be able to get out too," I added. He seemed miserable at this ghost of an altercation, but I pushed past, mounted the ladder, and in the expiring moonlight unstrapped that accursed portmanteau and, brimming over with irritation, groped among its contents, sorting some into the skylight with the same feeling that nothing mattered much now, and it was best to be done with it; repacking the rest with guilty stealth ere Davies should discover their character, and strapping up the whole again. Then I sat down upon my white elephant and shivered, for the chill of autumn was in the air. It suddenly struck me that if it had been raining things might have been worse still. The notion made me look round. The little cove was still as glass; stars above and stars below; a few white cottages glimmering at one point on the shore; in the west the lights of Flensburg; to the east the fiord broadening into unknown gloom. From Davies toiling below there were muffled sounds of wrenching, pushing, and hammering, punctuated occasionally by a heavy splash as something shot up from the hatchway and fell into the water.

How it came about I do not know. Whether it was something pathetic in the look I had last seen on his face—a look which I associated for no reason whatever with his bandaged hand; whether it was one of those instants of clear vision in which our separate selves are seen divided, the baser from the better, and I saw my silly egotism in contrast with a simple generous nature; whether it was an impalpable air of mystery which pervaded the whole enterprise and refused to be dissipated by its most mortifying and vulgarizing incidents—a mystery dimly connected with my companion's obvious consciousness of having misled me into joining him; whether it was only the stars and the cool air rousing atrophied instincts of youth and spirits; probably, indeed, it was all these influences, cemented into strength by a ruthless sense of humour which whispered that I was in danger of making a mere commonplace fool of myself in spite of all my laboured calculations; but whatever it was, in a flash my mood changed. The crown of martyrdom disappeared, the wounded vanity healed; that precious fund of fictitious resignation drained away, but left no void. There was left a fashionable and dishevelled young man sitting in the dew and in the dark on a ridiculous portmanteau which dwarfed the yacht that was to carry it; a youth acutely sensible of ignorance in a strange and strenuous atmosphere; still feeling sore and victimized; but withal sanely ashamed and sanely resolved to enjoy himself. I anticipate; for though the change was radical its full growth was slow. But in any case it was here and now that it took its birth.

"Grog's ready!" came from below. Bunching myself for the descent I found to my astonishment that all trace of litter had miraculously vanished, and a cosy neatness reigned. Glasses and lemons were on the table, and a fragrant smell of punch had deadened previous odours. I showed little emotion at these amenities, but enough to give intense relief to Davies, who delightedly showed me his devices for storage, praising the "roominess" of his floating den. "There's your stove, you see," he ended; "I've chucked the old one overboard." It was a weakness of his, I should say here, to rejoice in throwing things overboard on the flimsiest pretexts. I afterwards suspected that the new stove had not been "really necessary" any more than the riggingscrews, but was an excuse for gratifying this curious taste.

We smoked and chatted for a little, and then came the problem of going to bed. After much bumping of knuckles and head, and many giddy writhings, I mastered it, and lay between the rough blankets. Davies, moving swiftly and deftly, was soon in his.

"It's quite comfortable, isn't it?" he said, as he blew out the light from where he lay, with an accuracy which must have been the fruit of long practice.

I felt prickly all over, and there was a damp patch on the pillow, which was soon explained by a heavy drop of moisture falling on my forehead.

"I suppose the deck's not leaking?" I said, as mildly as I could.

"I'm awfully sorry," said Davies, earnestly, tumbling out of his bunk. "It must be the heavy dew. I did a lot of caulking yesterday, but I suppose I missed that place. I'll run up and square it with an oilskin."

"What's wrong with your hand?" I asked, sleepily, on his return, for gratitude reminded me of that bandage.

"Nothing much; I strained it the other day," was the reply; and then the seemingly inconsequent remark: "I'm glad you brought that prismatic compass. It's not really necessary, of course; but" (muffled by blankets) "it may come in useful."

I dozed but fitfully, with a fretful sense of sore elbows and neck and many a draughty hiatus among the blankets. It was broad daylight before I had reached the stage of torpor in which such slumber merges. That was finally broken by the descent through the skylight of a torrent of water. I started up, bumped my head hard against the decks, and blinked leaden-eyed upwards.

"Sorry! I'm scrubbing decks. Come up and bathe. Slept well?" I heard a voice saying from aloft.

"Fairly well," I growled, stepping out into a pool of water on the oilcloth. Thence I stumbled up the ladder, dived overboard, and buried bad dreams, stiffness, frowsiness, and tormented nerves in the loveliest fiord of the lovely Baltic. A short and furious swim and I was back again, searching for a means of ascent up the smooth black side, which, low as it was, was slippery and unsympathetic. Davies, in a loose canvas shirt, with the sleeves tucked up, and flannels rolled up to the knee, hung over me with a rope's end, and chatted unconcernedly about the easiness of the job when you know how, adjuring me to mind the paint, and talking about an accommodation ladder he had once had, but had thrown overboard because it was so horribly in the way. When I arrived, my knees and elbows were picked out in black paint, to his consternation. Nevertheless, as I plied the towel, I knew that I had left in those limpid depths yet another crust of discontent and self-conceit.

As I dressed into flannels and blazer, I looked round the deck, and with an unskilled and doubtful eye took in all that the darkness had hitherto hidden. She seemed very small (in point of fact she was seven tons), something over thirty feet in length and nine in beam, a size very suitable to weekends in the Solent, for such as liked that sort of thing; but that she should have come from Dover to the Baltic suggested a world of physical endeavour of which I had never dreamed.

I passed to the aesthetic side. Smartness and beauty were essential to yachts, in my mind, but with the best resolves to be pleased I found little encouragement here. The hull seemed too low, and the mainmast too high; the cabin roof looked clumsy, and the skylights saddened the eye with dull iron and plebeian graining. What brass there was, on the tiller-head and elsewhere, was tarnished with sickly green. The decks had none of that creamy purity which Cowes expects, but were rough and grey, and showed tarry exhalations round the seams and rusty stains near the bows. The ropes and rigging were in mourning when contrasted with the delicate buff manilla so satisfying to the artistic eye as seen against the blue of a June sky at Southsea. Nor was the whole effect bettered by many signs of recent refitting. An impression of paint, varnish, and carpentry was in the air; a gaudy new burgee fluttered aloft; there seemed to be a new rope or two, especially round the diminutive mizzenmast, which itself looked altogether new. But all this only emphasized the general plainness, reminding one of a respectable woman of the workingclasses trying to dress above her station, and soon likely to give it up.

That the *ensemble* was businesslike and solid even my untrained eye could see. Many of the deck fittings seemed disproportionately substantial. The anchor-chain looked contemptuous of its charge; the binnacle with its compass was of a size and prominence almost comically impressive, and was, moreover, the only piece of brass which was burnished and showed traces of reverent care. Two huge coils of stout and dingy warp lay just abaft the mainmast, and summed up the weather-beaten aspect of the little ship. I should add here that in the distant past she had been a lifeboat, and had been clumsily converted into a yacht by the addition of a counter, deck, and the necessary spars. She was built, as all lifeboats are, diagonally, of two skins of teak, and thus had immense strength, though, in the matter of looks, all a hybrid's failings.

Hunger and "Tea's made!" from below brought me down to the cabin, where I found breakfast laid out on the table over the centreboard case, with Davies earnestly presiding, rather flushed as to the face, and sooty as to the fingers. There was a slight shortage of plate and crockery, but I praised the bacon and could do so truthfully, for its crisp and steaming shavings would have put to shame the efforts of my London cook. Indeed, I should have enjoyed the meal heartily were it not for the lowness of the sofa and table, causing a curvature of the body which made swallowing a more lengthy process than usual, and induced a periodical yearning to get up and stretch—a relief which spelt disaster to the skull. I noticed, too, that Davies spoke with a zest, sinister to me, of the delights of white bread and fresh milk, which he seemed to consider unusual luxuries, though suitable to an inaugural banquet in honour of a fastidious stranger. "One can't be always going on shore," he said, when I showed a discreet interest in these things. "I lived for ten days on a big rye loaf over in the Frisian Islands."

"And it died hard, I suppose?"

"Very hard, but" (gravely) "quite good. After that I taught myself to make rolls; had no baking powder at first, so used Eno's fruit salt, but they wouldn't rise much with that. As for milk, condensed is—I hope you don't mind it?"

I changed the subject, and asked about his plans.

"Let's get under way at once," he said, "and sail down the fiord." I tried for something more specific, but he was gone, and his voice drowned in the fo'c'sle by the clatter and swish of washing up. Thenceforward events moved with bewildering rapidity. Humbly desirous of being useful I joined him on deck, only to find that he scarcely noticed me, save as a new and unexpected obstacle in his round of activity. He was everywhere at once—heaving in chain, hooking on halyards, hauling ropes; while my part became that of the clown who does things after they are already done, for my knowledge of a yacht was of that floating and inaccurate kind which is useless in practice. Soon the anchor was up (a great rusty monster it was!), the sails set, and Davies was darting swiftly to and fro between the tiller and jib-sheets, while the *Dulcibella* bowed a lingering farewell to the shore and headed for the open fiord. Erratic puffs from the high land behind made her progress timorous at first, but soon the fairway was reached and a true breeze from Flensburg and the west took her in its friendly grip. Steadily she rustled down the calm blue highway whose soft beauty was the introduction to a passage in my life, short, but pregnant with moulding force, through stress and strain, for me and others.

Davies was gradually resuming his natural self, with abstracted intervals, in which he lashed the helm to finger a distant rope, with such speed that the movements seemed simultaneous. Once he vanished, only to reappear in an instant with a chart, which he studied, while steering, with a success that its reluctant folds seemed to render impossible. Waiting respectfully for his revival I had full time to look about. The fiord here was about a mile broad. From the shore we had left the hills rose steeply, but with no rugged grandeur; the outlines were soft; there were green spaces and rich woods on the lower slopes; a little white town was opening up in one place, and scattered farms dotted the prospect. The other shore, which I could just see, framed between the gunwale and the mainsail, as I sat leaning against the hatchway, and sadly missing a deckchair, was lower and lonelier, though prosperous and pleasing to the eye.

Spacious pastures led up by slow degrees to ordered clusters of wood, which hinted at the presence of some great manor house. Behind us, Flensburg was settling into haze. Ahead, the scene was shut in by the contours of hills, some clear, some dreamy and distant. Lastly, a single glimpse of water shining between the folds of hill far away hinted at spaces of distant sea of which this was but a secluded inlet. Everywhere was that peculiar charm engendered by the association of quiet pastoral country and a homely human atmosphere with a branch of the great ocean that bathes all the shores of our globe.

There was another charm in the scene, due to the way in which I was viewing it—not as a pampered passenger on a "fine steam yacht," or even on "a powerful modern schooner," as the yacht agents advertise, but from the deck of a scrubby little craft of doubtful build and distressing plainness, which yet had smelt her persistent way to this distant fiord through I knew not what of difficulty and danger, with no apparent motive in her single occupant, who talked as vaguely and unconcernedly about his adventurous cruise as though it were all a protracted afternoon on Southampton Water.

I glanced round at Davies. He had dropped the chart and was sitting, or rather half lying, on the deck with one bronzed arm over the tiller, gazing fixedly ahead, with just an occasional glance around and aloft. He still seemed absorbed in himself, and for a moment or two I studied his face with an attention I had never, since I had known him, given it. I had always thought it commonplace, as I had thought him commonplace, so far as I had thought at all about either.

It had always rather irritated me by an excess of candour and boyishness. These qualities it had kept, but the scales were falling from my eyes, and I saw others. I saw strength to obstinacy and courage to recklessness, in the firm lines of the chin; an older and deeper look in the eyes. Those odd transitions from bright mobility to detached earnestness, which had partly amused and chiefly annoyed me hitherto, seemed now to be lost in a sensitive reserve, not cold or egotistic, but strangely winning from its paradoxical frankness.

Sincerity was stamped on every lineament. A deep misgiving stirred me that, clever as I thought myself, nicely perceptive of the right and congenial men to know, I had made some big mistakes—how many, I wondered? A relief, scarcely less deep because it was unconfessed, stole in on me with the suspicion that, little as I deserved it, the patient fates were offering me a golden chance of repairing at least one. And yet, I mused, the patient fates have crooked methods, besides a certain mischievous humour, for it was Davies who had asked me out—though now he scarcely seemed to need me—almost tricked me into coming out, for he might have known I was not suited to such a life; yet trickery and Davies sounded an odd conjuncture.

Probably it was the growing discomfort of my attitude which produced this backsliding. My night's rest and the "ascent from the bath" had, in fact, done little to prepare me for contact with sharp edges and hard surfaces. But Davies had suddenly come to himself, and with an "I say, are you comfortable? Have something to sit on?" jerked the helm a little to windward, felt it like a pulse for a moment, with a rapid look to windward, and dived below, whence he returned with a couple of cushions, which he threw to me. I felt perversely resentful of these luxuries, and asked:

"Can't I be of any use?"

"Oh, don't you bother," he answered. "I expect you're tired. Aren't we having a splendid sail? That must be Ekken on the port bow," peering under the sail, "where the trees run in. I say, do you mind looking at the chart?" He tossed it over to me. I spread it out painfully, for it curled up like a watchspring at the least slackening of pressure. I was not familiar with charts, and this sudden trust reposed in me, after a good deal of neglect, made me nervous.

"You see Flensburg, don't you?" he said. "That's where we are," dabbing with a long reach at an indefinite space on the crowded sheet. "Now which side of that buoy off the point do we pass?"

I had scarcely taken in which was land and which was water, much less the significance of the buoy, when he resumed:

"Never mind; I'm pretty sure it's all deep water about here. I expect that marks the fairway for steamers."

In a minute or two we were passing the buoy in question, on the wrong side I am pretty certain, for weeds and sand came suddenly into view below us with uncomfortable distinctness. But all Davies said was: "There's never any sea here, and the plate's not down," a dark utterance which I pondered doubtfully. "The best of these Schleswigwaters," he went on, "is that a boat of this size can go almost anywhere. There's no navigation required. Why—" At this moment a faint scraping was felt, rather than heard, beneath us.

"Aren't we aground?" I asked, with great calmness.

"Oh, she'll blow over," he replied, wincing a little.

She "blew over," but the episode caused a little naive vexation in Davies. I relate it as a good instance of one of his minor peculiarities. He was utterly without that didactic pedantry which yachting has a fatal tendency to engender in men who profess it. He had tossed me the chart without a thought that I was an ignoramus, to whom it would be Greek, and who would provide him with an admirable subject to drill and lecture, just as his neglect of me throughout the morning had been merely habitual and unconscious independence. In the second place, master of his *métier* as I knew him afterwards to be, resourceful, skilful, and alert, he was liable to lapse into a certain amateurish vagueness, half irritating and half amusing. I think truly that both these peculiarities came from the same source, a hatred of any sort of affectation. To the same source I traced the fact that he and his yacht observed none of the superficial etiquette of yachts and yachtsmen, that she never, for instance, flew a national ensign, and he never wore a "yachting suit."

We rounded a low green point which I had scarcely noticed before.

"We must jibe," said Davies. "Just take the helm, will you?" and, without waiting for my cooperation, he began hauling in the mainsheet with great vigour. I had rude notions of steering, but jibing is a delicate operation. No yachtsman will be surprised to hear that the boom saw its opportunity and swung over with a mighty crash, with the mainsheet entangled round me and the tiller.

"Jibed all standing," was his sorrowful comment. "You're not used to her yet. She's very quick on the helm."

"Where am I to steer for?" I asked, wildly.

"Oh, don't trouble, I'll take her now," he replied.

I felt it was time to make my position clear. "I'm an utter duffer at sailing," I began. "You'll have a lot to teach me, or one of these days I shall be wrecking you. You see, there's always been a crew—"

"Crew!"—with sovereign contempt—"why, the whole fun of the thing is to do everything oneself."

"Well, I've felt in the way the whole morning."

"I'm awfully sorry!" His dismay and repentance were comical. "Why, it's just the other way; you may be all the use in the world." He became absent.

We were following the inward trend of a small bay towards a cleft in the low shore.

"That's Ekken Sound," said Davies; "let's look into it," and a minute or two later we were drifting through a dainty little strait, with a peep of open water at the end of it. Cottages bordered either side, some overhanging the very water, some connecting with it by a rickety wooden staircase or a miniature landing-stage. Creepers and roses rioted over the walls and tiny porches. For a space on one side, a rude quay, with small smacks floating off it, spoke of some minute commercial interests; a very small tea-garden, with neglected-looking bowers and leaf-strewn tables, hinted at some equally minute tripping interest. A pervading hue of mingled bronze and rose came partly from the weather-mellowed woodwork of the cottages and stages, and partly from the creepers and the trees behind, where autumn's subtle fingers were already at work. Down this exquisite sealane we glided till it ended in a broad mere, where our sails, which had been shivering and complaining, filled into contented silence.

"Ready about!" said Davies, callously. "We must get out of this again." And round we swung.

"Why not anchor and stop here?" I protested; for a view of tantalizing loveliness was unfolding itself.

"Oh, we've seen all there is to be seen, and we must take this breeze while we've got it." It was always torture to Davies to feel a good breeze running to waste while he was inactive at anchor or on shore.

The "shore" to him was an inferior element, merely serving as a useful annexe to the water—a source of necessary supplies.

"Let's have lunch," he pursued, as we resumed our way down the fiord. A vision of iced drinks, tempting salads, white napery, and an attentive steward mocked me with past recollections.

"You'll find a tongue," said the voice of doom, "in the starboard sofa-locker; beer under the floor in the bilge. I'll see her round that buoy, if you wouldn't mind beginning." I obeyed with a bad grace, but the close air and cramped posture must have benumbed my faculties, for I opened the portside locker, reached down, and grasped a sticky body, which turned out to be a pot of varnish.

Recoiling wretchedly, I tried the opposite one, combating the embarrassing heel of the boat and the obstructive edges of the centreboard case. A medley of damp tins of varied sizes showed in the gloom, exuding a mouldy odour. Faded legends on dissolving paper, like the remnants of old posters on a disused hoarding, spoke of soups, curries, beefs, potted meats, and other hidden delicacies. I picked out a tongue, reimprisoned the odour, and explored for beer.

It was true, I supposed, that bilge didn't hurt it, as I tugged at the plank on my hands and knees, but I should have myself preferred a more accessible and less humid wine-cellar than the cavities among slimy ballast from which I dug the bottles. I regarded my hard-won and illfavoured pledges of a meal with giddiness and discouragement.

"How are you getting on?" shouted Davies; "the tin-opener's hanging up on the bulkhead; the plates and knives are in the cupboard."

I doggedly pursued my functions. The plates and knives met me half-way, for, being on the weather side, and thus having a downward slant, its contents, when I slipped the latch, slid affectionately into my bosom, and overflowed with a clatter and jingle on to the floor.

"That often happens," I heard from above. "Never mind! There are no breakables. I'm coming down to help." And down he came, leaving the *Dulcibella* to her own devices.

"I think I'll go on deck," I said. "Why in the world couldn't you lunch comfortably at Ekken and save this infernal pandemonium of a picnic? Where's the yacht going to meanwhile? And how are we to lunch on that slanting table? I'm covered with varnish and mud, and ankle-deep in crockery. There goes the beer!"

"You shouldn't have stood it on the table with this list on," said Davies, with intense composure, "but it won't do any harm; it'll drain into the bilge" (ashes to ashes, dust to dust, I thought). "You go on deck now, and I'll finish getting ready." I regretted my explosion, though wrung from me under great provocation.

"Keep her straight on as she's going," said Davies, as I clambered up out of the chaos, brushing the dust off my trousers and varnishing the ladder with my hands. I unlashed the helm and kept her as she was going.

We had rounded a sharp bend in the fiord, and were sailing up a broad and straight reach which every moment disclosed new beauties, sights fair enough to be balm to the angriest spirit. A red-roofed hamlet was on our left, on the right an ivied ruin, close to the water, where some contemplative cattle stood kneedeep. The view ahead was a white strand which fringed both shores, and to it fell wooded slopes, interrupted here and there by low sandstone cliffs of warm red colouring, and now and again by a dingle with cracks of greensward.

I forgot petty squalors and enjoyed things—the coy tremble of the tiller and the backwash of air from the dingy mainsail, and, with a somewhat chastened rapture, the lunch which Davies brought up to me and solicitously watched me eat.

Later, as the wind sank to lazy airs, he became busy with a larger topsail and jib; but I was content to doze away the afternoon, drenching brain and body in the sweet and novel foreign atmosphere, and dreamily watching the fringe of glen cliff and cool white sand as they passed ever more slowly by.

# Yammerschooner

## *Joshua Slocum*

ON FEBRUARY 1 THE *SPRAY* ROUNDED CAPE VIRGINS AND entered the Strait of Magellan. The scene was again real and gloomy; the wind, northeast, and blowing a gale, sent feather-white spume along the coast; such a sea ran as would swamp an illappointed ship. As the sloop neared the entrance to the strait I observed that two great tide-races made ahead, one very close to the point of the land and one farther offshore. Between the two, in a sort of channel, through combers, went the *Spray* with close-reefed sails. But a rolling sea followed her a long way in, and a fierce current swept around the cape against her; but this she stemmed, and was soon chirruping under the lee of Cape Virgins and running every minute into smoother water. However, long trailing kelp from sunken rocks waved forebodingly under her keel, and the wreck of a great steamship smashed on the beach abreast gave a gloomy aspect to the scene.

I was not to be let off easy. The Virgins would collect tribute even from the *Spray* passing their promontory. Fitful rain-squalls from the northwest followed the northeast gale. I reefed the sloop's sails, and sitting in the cabin to rest my eyes, I was so strongly impressed with what in all nature I might expect that as I dozed the very air I breathed seemed to warn me of danger. My senses heard "*Spray* ahoy!" shouted in warning. I sprang to the deck, wondering who could be there that knew the *Spray* so well as to call out her name passing in the dark; for it was now the blackest of nights all around, except away in the southwest where rose the old familiar white arch, the terror of Cape Horn, rapidly pushed up by a southwest gale. I had only a moment to douse sail and lash all solid when it struck like a shot from a cannon, and for the first halfhour it was something to be remembered by way of a gale. For thirty hours it kept on blowing hard. The sloop could carry no more than a three-reefed mainsail and forestaysail; with these she held on stoutly and was not blown out of the strait. In the height of the squalls in this gale she doused all sail, and this occurred often enough.

After this gale followed only a smart breeze, and the *Spray*, passing through the narrows without mishap, cast anchor at Sandy Point on February 14, 1896.

Sandy Point (Punta Arenas) is a Chilean coaling station, and boasts about two thousand inhabitants, of mixed nationality, but mostly Chileans. What with sheepfarming, goldmining, and hunting, the settlers in this dreary land seemed not the worst off in the world. But the natives, Patagonian and Fuegian, on the other hand, were as squalid as contact with unscrupulous traders could make them. A large percentage of the business there was traffic in "firewater." If there was a law against selling the poisonous stuff to the natives, it was not enforced. Fine specimens of the Patagonian race, looking smart in the morning when they came into town, had repented before night of ever having seen a white man, so beastly drunk were they, to say nothing about the peltry of which they had been robbed.

The port at that time was free, but a customhouse was in course of construction, and when it is finished, port and tariff dues are to be collected. A soldier police guarded the place, and a sort of vigilante force besides took down its guns now and then; but as a general thing, to my mind, whenever an execution was made they killed the wrong man. Just previous to my arrival the governor, himself of a jovial turn of mind, had sent a party of young bloods to foray a Fuegian settlement and wipe out what they could of it on account of the recent massacre of a schooner's crew somewhere else. Altogether the place was quite newsy and supported two papers— dailies, I think. The port captain, a Chilean naval— officer, advised me to ship hands to fight Indians in the strait farther west, and spoke of my stopping until a gunboat should be going through, which would give me a tow. After canvassing the place, however, I found only one man willing to embark, and he on condition that I should ship another "mon and a doog." But as no one else was willing to come along, and as I drew the line at dogs, I said no more about the matter, but simply loaded my guns. At this point in my dilemma Captain Pedro Samblich, a good

Austrian of large experience, coming along, gave me a bag of carpet-tacks, worth more than all the fighting men and dogs of Tierra del Fuego. I protested that I had no use for carpet-tacks on board. Samblich smiled at my want of experience, and maintained stoutly that I would have use for them. "You must use them with discretion," he said; "that is to say, don't step on them yourself." With this remote hint about the use of the tacks I got on all right, and saw the way to maintain clear decks at night without the care of watching.

Samblich was greatly interested in my voyage, and after giving me the tacks he put on board bags of biscuits and a large quantity of smoked venison. He declared that my bread, which was ordinary sea-biscuits and easily broken, was not nutritious as his, which was so hard that I could break it only with a stout blow from a maul. Then he gave me, from his own sloop, a compass which was certainly better than mine, and offered to unbend her mainsail for me if I would accept it. Last of all, this largehearted man brought out a bottle of Fuegian golddust from a place where it had been *cached* and begged me to help myself from it, for use farther along on the voyage. But I felt sure of success without this draft on a friend, and I was right. Samblich's tacks, as it turned out, were of more value than gold.

The port captain, finding that I was resolved to go, even alone, since there was no help for it, set up no further objections, but advised me, in case the savages tried to surround me with their canoes, to shoot straight, and begin to do it in time, but to avoid killing them if possible, which I heartily agreed to do. With these simple injunctions the officer gave me my port clearance free of charge, and I sailed on the same day, February 19, 1896. It was not without thoughts of strange and stirring adventure beyond all I had yet encountered that I now sailed into the country and very core of the savage Fuegians.

A fair wind from Sandy Point brought me on the first day to St. Nicholas Bay, where, so I was told, I might expect to meet savages; but seeing no signs of life, I came to anchor in eight fathoms of water, where I lay all night under a high mountain. Here I had my first experience with the terrific squalls, called williwaws, which extended from this point on through the strait to the Pacific. They were compressed gales of wind that Boreas handed down over the hills in chunks. A fullblown williwaw will throw a ship, even without sail on, over on her beam ends; but, like other gales, they cease now and then, if only for a short time.

February 20 was my birthday, and I found myself alone, with hardly so much as a bird in sight, off Cape Froward, the southernmost point of the continent of America. By daylight in the morning I was getting my ship under way for the bout ahead.

The sloop held the wind fair while she ran thirty miles farther on her course, which brought her to Fortescue Bay, and at once among the natives' signalfires, which blazed up now on all sides. Clouds flew over the mountain from the west all day; at night my good east wind failed, and in its stead a gale from the west soon came on. I gained anchorage at twelve o'clock that night, under the lee of a little island, and then prepared myself a cup of coffee, of which I was sorely in need; for, to tell the truth, hard beating in the heavy squalls and against the current had told on my strength. Finding that the anchor held, I drank my beverage, and named the place Coffee Island. It lies to the south of Charles Island, with only a narrow channel between.

By daylight the next morning the *Spray* was again under way, beating hard; but she came to in a cove in Charles Island, two and a half miles along on her course. Here she remained undisturbed two days, with both anchors down in a bed of kelp. Indeed, she might have remained undisturbed indefinitely had not the wind moderated; for during these two days it blew so hard that no boat could venture out on the strait, and the natives being away to other huntinggrounds, the island anchorage was safe. But at the end of the fierce windstorm fair weather came; then I got my anchors, and again sailed out upon the strait.

Canoes manned by savages from Fortescue now came in pursuit. The wind falling light they gained on me rapidly till coming within hail, when they ceased paddling, and a bow-legged savage stood up and called to me, "Yammerschooner! yammerschooner!" which is their begging term. I said, "No!" Now, I was not for letting on that I was alone, and so I stepped into the cabin, and, passing through the hold, came out at the fore-scuttle, changing my clothes as I went along.

That made two men. Then the piece of bowsprit which I had sawed off at Buenos Aires, and which I had still on board, I arranged forward on the outlook, dressed as a seaman, attaching a line by which I could pull it into motion. That made three of us, and we didn't want to "yammerschooner"; but for all that the savages came on faster than before. I saw that besides four at the paddles in the canoe nearest to me, there were others in the bottom, and that they were shifting hands often. At eighty yards I fired a shot across the bows of the nearest canoe, at which they all stopped, but only for a moment. Seeing that they persisted in coming nearer, I fired the second shot so close to the chap who wanted to "yammerschooner" that he changed his mind quickly enough and bellowed with fear, "Bueno jo via Isla," and sitting down in his canoe, he rubbed his starboard cathead for some time. I was thinking of the good port captain's advice when I pulled the trigger, and must have aimed pretty straight; however, a miss was as good as a mile for Mr. "Black Pedro," as he it was, and no other, a leader in several bloody massacres. He made for the island now, and the others followed him. I knew by his Spanish lingo and by his full beard that he was the villain I had named, a renegade mongrel, and the worst murderer in Tierra del Fuego. The authorities had been in search of him for two years. The Fuegians are not bearded.

So much for the first day among the savages. I came to anchor at midnight in Three Island Cove, about twenty miles along from Fortescue Bay. I saw on the opposite side of the strait signalfires, and heard the barking of dogs, but where I lay it was quite deserted by natives. I have always taken it as a sign that where I found birds sitting about, or seals on the rocks, I should not find savage Indians. Seals are never plentiful in these waters, but in Three Island Cove I saw one on the rocks, and other signs of the absence of savage men.

On the next day the wind was again blowing a gale, and although she was in the lee of the land, the sloop dragged her anchors, so that I had to get her under way and beat farther into the cove, where I came to in a landlocked pool. At another time or place this would have been a rash thing to do, and it was safe now only from the fact that the gale which drove me to shelter would keep the Indians from crossing the strait. Seeing this was the case, I went ashore with gun and axe on an island, where I could not in any event be surprised, and there felled trees and split about a cord of fire-wood, which loaded my small boat several times.

While I carried the wood, though I was morally sure there were no savages near, I never once went to or from the skiff without my gun. While I had that and a clear field of over eighty yards about me I felt safe.

The trees on the island, very scattering, were a sort of beech and a stunted cedar, both of which made good fuel. Even the green limbs of the beech, which seemed to possess a resinous quality, burned readily in my great drumstove. I have described my method of wooding up in detail, that the reader who has kindly borne with me so far may see that in this, as in all other particulars of my voyage, I took great care against all kinds of surprises, whether by animals or by the elements. In the Strait of Magellan the greatest vigilance was necessary. In this instance I reasoned that I had all about me the greatest danger of the whole voyage—the treachery of cunning savages, for which I must be particularly on the alert.

The *Spray* sailed from Three Island Cove in the morning after the gale went down, but was glad to return for shelter from another sudden gale. Sailing again on the following day, she fetched Borgia Bay, a few miles on her course, where vessels had anchored from time to time and had nailed boards on the trees ashore with name and date of harbouring carved or painted. Nothing else could I see to indicate the civilized man had ever been before. I had taken a survey of the gloomy place with my spyglass, and was getting my boat out to land and take notes, when the Chilean gunboat *Huemel* came in, and officers, coming on board, advised me to leave the place at once, a thing that required little eloquence to persuade me to do. I accepted the captain's kind offer of a tow to the next anchorage, at the place called Notch Cove, eight miles farther along, where I should be clear of the worst of the Fuegians.

We made anchorage at the cove about dark that night, while the wind came down in fierce williwaws from the mountains. An instance of Magellan weather was afforded when the *Huemel*, a wellappointed gunboat of great power, after attempting on the following day to proceed on her voyage, was obliged by sheer force of the wind to return and take up anchorage again and remain till the gale abated; and lucky she was to get back!

Meeting this vessel was a little godsend. She was commanded and officered by highclass sailors and educated gentlemen. An entertainment that was gotten up on her, impromptu, at the Notch would be hard to beat anywhere. One of her midshipmen sang popular songs in French, German, and Spanish, and one (so he said) in Russian. If the audience did not know the lingo of one song from another, it was no drawback to the merriment.

I was left alone the next day, for then the *Huemel* put out on her voyage, the gale having abated. I spent a day taking in wood and water; by the end of that time the weather was fine. Then I sailed from the desolate place.

There is little more to be said concerning the *Spray*'s first passage through the strait that would differ from what I have already recorded. She anchored and weighed many times, and beat many days against the current, with now and then a "slant" for a few miles, till finally she gained anchorage and shelter for the night at Port Tamar, with Cape Pillar in sight to the west. Here I felt the throb of the great ocean that lay before me. I knew now that I had put a world behind me, and that I was opening out another world ahead. I had passed the haunts of savages. Great piles of granite mountains of bleak and lifeless aspect were now astern; on some of them not even a speck of moss had ever grown. There was an unfinished newness all about the land. On the hill back of Port Tamar a small beacon had been thrown up showing that some man had been there. But how could one tell but that he had died of loneliness and grief? In a bleak land is not the place to enjoy solitude.

Throughout the whole of the strait west of Cape Froward I saw no animals except dogs owned by savages. These I saw often enough, and heard them yelping night and day. Birds were not plentiful. The scream of a wild fowl, which I took for a loon, sometimes startled me with its piercing cry. The steamboat duck, so called because it propels itself over the sea with its wings, and resembles a miniature sidewheel steamer in its motion, was sometimes seen scurrying on out of danger. It never flies, but, hitting the water instead of the air with its wings, it moves faster than a rowboat or a canoe. The few fur-seals I saw were very shy; and of fishes I saw next to none at all. I did not catch one; indeed, I seldom or never put a hook over during the whole voyage. Here in the strait I found great abundance of mussels of an excellent quality. I fared sumptu-ously on them. There was a sort of swan, smaller than a Muscovy duck, which might have been brought down with the gun, but in the loneliness of life about the dreary country I found myself in no mood to make one life less, except in selfdefence.

# Young Ironsides

*James Fenimore Cooper*

THE SECOND CRUISE OF OLD IRONSIDES COMMENCED IN August, 1799. Her orders were to go off Cayenne, in the first place, where she was to remain until near the close of September, when she was to proceed via Guadaloupe to Cape Francois, at which point, Talbot was to assume the command of all the vessels he found on the station. In the course of the season, this squadron grew to be six sail, three frigates and as many sloops, or brigs.

Two incidents occurred to Old Ironsides, while on the St. Domingo station, that are worthy of being noticed, the first being of an amicable, and the second of a particularly hostile character.

While cruising to windward the island, a strange sail was made, which, on closing, proved to be the English frigate, the _____. The commander of this ship and Com. Talbot were acquaintances, and the Englishman had the curiosity to take a full survey of the new Yankee craft. He praised her, as no unprejudiced seaman could fail to do, but insisted that his own ship could beat her on a wind. After some pleasantry on the subject, the English captain made the following proposition; he had touched at Madeira on his way out, and taken on board a few casks of wine for his own use. This wine stood him in so much a cask—now, he was going into port to refit, and clean his bottom, which was a little foul; but, if he could depend on finding the *Constitution* on that station, a few weeks later he would join her, when there should be a trial of speed between the two ships, the loser to pay a cask of the wine, or its price to the winner.

The bet was made, and the vessels parted. At the appointed time, the _____ reappeared; her rigging overhauled, new sails bent, her sides painted, her bottom cleaned. And, as Jack expressed it, looking like a new fiddle. The two frigates closed, and their commanders dined together, arranging the terms of the cartel for the next day's proceedings. That night, the vessels kept near each other, on the same line of sailing, and under short canvas. The following morning, as the day dawned, the *Constitution* and the _____ each turned up their hands, in readiness for what was to follow.

Just as the lower limb of the sun rose clear of the waves, each fired a gun, and made sail on a bowline. Throughout the whole of that day, did these two gallant ships continue turning to windward, on tacks of a few leagues in length, and endeavoring to avail themselves of every advantage which skill could confer on seamen. Hull sailed the *Constitution* on this interesting occasion and the admirable manner in which he did it, was long the subject of eulogy.

All hands were kept on deck all day, and there were tacks on which the people were made to place themselves to windward, in order to keep the vessel as near upright as possible, so as to hold a better wind. Just as the sun dipped, in the evening, the *Constitution* fired a gun, as did her competitor. At that moment the English frigate was precisely hull down dead to leeward; so much having Old Ironsides, or young Ironsides, as she was then, gained in the race, which lasted about eleven hours! The manner in which the *Constitution* beat her competitor out of the wind, was not the least striking feature of this trial, and it must in great degree be ascribed to Hull, whose dexterity in handling a craft under her canvas, was ever remarkable. In this particular, he was perhaps one of the most skilful seamen of his time, as he was also for coolness in moments of hazard. When the evening gun was fired and acknowledged, the *Constitution* put up her helm, and squared away to join her friend. The vessels joined a little after dark, the Englishman as the leeward ship, first rounding to. The *Constitution* passed under her lee, and threw her maintopsail to the mast. There was a boat out from the _____, which soon came alongside, and in it was the English Captain and his cask of wine; the former being just as prompt to "pay" as to "play."

The other occurrence was the cutting out of the *Sandwich*, a French letter of marque, which was lying in Port Platte, a small harbor on the Spanish side of St. Domingo. While cruising along the coast, the *Constitution* had seized an American sloop called the *Sally*, which had been selling supplies to the enemy.

Hearing that the *Sandwich*, formerly an English packet, but which had fallen into the hands of the French, was filling up with coffee, and was nearly full, Talbot determined to send Hull in, with the *Sally*, in order to cut her out. The sloop had not long before come out of that very haven, with an avowed intention to return, and offered every desirable facility to the success of the enterprise. The great and insuperable objection to its ultimate advantage, was the material circumstance that the Frenchman was lying in a neutral port, as respects ourselves, though watchful of the English who were swarming in those seas.

The *Constitution* manned the *Sally* at sea, near sunset, on the tenth of May, 1800, a considerable distance from Port Platte, and the vessels separated, Hull so timing his movements, as to reach his point of destination about midday of a Sunday, when it was rightly enough supposed many of the French, officers as well as men, would be ashore keeping holiday. Short sail was carried that night on board the *Sally*, and while she was quietly jogging along, thinking no harm, a gun was suddenly heard, and a shot came whistling over the sloop.

On looking around, a large ship was seen in chase, and so near, as to render escape impossible. The *Sally* rounded to, and presently, an English frigate ranged alongside. The boarding Officer was astonished when he found himself among ninety armed men, with officers in naval uniform at their head. On demanding an explanation, Hull told him his business, when the English lieutenant expressed his disappointment, candidly acknowledging that his own ship was waiting on the coast to let the *Sandwich* fill up, and get her sails bent, in order to send a party in, also, in order to cut her out! It was too late, however, as the *Sally* could not be, and would not be, detained, and Hull proceeded.

There have been many more brilliant exploits than this of the *Constitution* in sending in a party against the *Sandwich*, but very few that were more neatly executed, or ingeniously planned. The *Sally* arrived off the port, at the appointed hour, and stood directly in, showing the customary number of hands on deck, until coming near the letter of marque, she ran her aboard forward, and the *Constitution*'s clambered in over the *Sandwich*'s bows, led by Hull in person. In two minutes, the Americans had possession of their prize, a smart brig, armed with four sixes and two nines, with a pretty strong crew, without the loss of a man. A party of marines, led by Capt. Cormick, landed, drove the Spaniards from a battery that commanded the anchorage, and spiked the guns.

All this was against law and right, but it was very ingeniously arranged, and as gallantly executed. The most serious part of the affair remained to be achieved. The *Sandwich* was stripped to a girt line, and the wind blew directly into the harbor. As it was unsafe for the marines to remain in the battery any time, it was necessarily abandoned, leaving to the people of the place every opportunity of annoying their invaders by all the means they possessed.

The battery was reoccupied, and the guns cleared of the spikes as well and as fast as they could be, while the Americans set about swaying up topmasts and yards and bending sails. After some smart exertion, the brig got royal yards across, and, at sunset, after remaining several hours in front of the town, Hull scaled his guns, by way of letting it be known they could be used, weighed, and began to beat out of the harbor. The Spaniards fired a few shots after him, but with no effect.

Although this was one of the best executed enterprises of the sort on record, and did infinite credit to the coolness and spirit of all concerned, it was not quite an illustration of international law or of justice in general. This was the first victory of Old Ironsides in a certain sense, but all men must regret it was ever achieved, since it was a wrong act, committed with an exaggerated, if not an altogether mistaken notion of duty. America was not even at war with France, in the more formal meaning of the term, nor were all the legal consequences of war connected with the peculiar hostilities that certainly did exist; but with Spain she had no quarrel whatever, and the *Sandwich* was entitled to receive all the protection and immunities that of right belonged to her anchored in the neutral harbor of Portau-Platte. In the end not only was the condemnation of the *Sandwich* resisted successfully, but all the other prizemoney made by Old Ironsides in the cruise went to pay damages. The reason why the exploit itself never received the public commendation to which, as a mere military achievement, it was so justly entitled, was connected with the illegality and reckless-ness of the enterprise in its inception.

It follows that this, which may be termed the *Constitution*'s earliest victory, was obtained in the face of law and right. For-tunately the old craft has lived long enough to atone for this error of her youth by many a noble deed achieved in defence of principles and rights that the most fastidious will not hesitate to defend. The *Constitution* returned to Boston in Aug. 1800, her cruise being up, not only on account of her orders, but on account of the short period for which men were then enlisted in the navy, which was one year.

On the 18th Nov., however, she was ordered to sail again for the old station, still wearing the broad pennant of Talbot. Nothing occurred of interest in the course of this cruise; and, early in the spring, orders were sent to recall all the cruisers from the West Indies, in consequence of an arrangement of the difficulties with France.

# Rounding Cape Horn

## *Herman Melville*

AND NOW, THROUGH DRIZZLING FOGS AND VAPORS, AND under damp, doublereefed topsails, our wetdecked frigate drew nearer and nearer to the squally Cape. Who has not heard of it? Cape Horn, Cape Horn—a *horn* indeed, that has tossed many a good ship. Was the descent of Orpheus, Ulysses, or Dante into Hell, one whit more hardy and sublime than the first navigator's weathering of that terrible Cape?

Turned on her heel by a fierce West Wind, many an outward-bound ship has been driven across the Southern Ocean to the Cape of Good Hope—*that* way to seek a passage to the Pacific. And that stormy Cape, I doubt not, has sent many a fine craft to the bottom, and told no tales. At those ends of the earth are no chronicles. What signify the broken spars and shrouds that, day after day, are driven before the prows of more fortunate vessels? or the tall masts, imbedded in icebergs, that are found floating by? They but hint the old story—of ships that have sailed from their port, and never more have been heard of.

Impracticable Cape! You may approach it from this direction or that—in any way you please—from the East or from the West; with the wind astern, or abeam, or on the quarter; and still Cape Horn is Cape Horn. Cape Horn it is that takes the conceit out of freshwater sailors, and steeps in a still salter brine the saltest. Woe betide the tyro; the foolhardy, Heaven preserve!

Your Mediterranean captain, who with a cargo of oranges has hitherto made merry runs across the Atlantic, without so much as furling a t'-gallant-sail, oftentimes, off Cape Horn, receives a lesson which he carries to the grave; though the grave—as is too often the case—follows so hard on the lesson that no benefit comes from the experience.

Other strangers who draw nigh to this Patagonia termination of our Continent, with their souls full of its shipwrecks and disasters—top-sails cautiously reefed, and everything guardedly snug—these strangers at first unexpectedly encountering a tolerably smooth sea, rashly conclude that the Cape, after all, is but a bugbear; they have been imposed upon by fables, and founderings and sinkings hereabouts are all cock-and-bull stories.

"Out reefs, my hearties; fore and aft set t'gallantsails! stand by to give her the foretopmast stun'-sail!"

But, Captain Rash, those sails of yours were much safer in the sailmaker's loft. For now, while the heedless craft is bounding over the billows, a black cloud rises out of the sea; the sun drops down from the sky; a horrible mist far and wide spreads over the water.

"Hands by the halyard! Let go! Clew up!"

Too late.

For ere the ropes' ends can be cast off from the pins, the tornado is blowing down to the bottom of their throats. The masts are willows, the sails ribbons, the cordage wool; the whole ship is brewed into the yeast of the gale.

And now, if, when the first green sea breaks over him, Captain Rash is not swept overboard, he has his hands full to be sure. In all probability his three masts have gone by the board, and, raveled into list, his sails are floating in the air. Or, perhaps, the ship *broaches to*, or is *brought by the lee*. In either case, Heaven help the sailors, their wives and their little ones; and Heaven help the underwriters.

Familiarity with danger makes a brave man braver, but less daring. Thus with seamen: he who goes the oftenest round Cape Horn goes the most circumspectly. A veteran mariner is never deceived by the treacherous breezes which sometimes waft him pleasantly toward the latitude of the Cape. No sooner does he come within a certain distance of it—previously fixed in his own mind—than all hands are turned to setting the ship in storm-trim; and never mind how light the breeze, down come his t'gallantyards. He "bends" his strongest storm-sails, and lashes everything on deck securely. The ship is then ready for the worst; and if, in reeling round the headland, she receives a broadside, it generally goes well with her. If ill, all hands go to the bottom with quiet consciences.

Among seacaptains, there are some who seem to regard the genius of the Cape as a wilful, capricious jade, that must be courted and coaxed into complaisance. First, they come along under easy sails; do not steer boldly for the headland, but tack this way and that—sidling up to it. Now they woo the Jezebel with a t'-gallant studdingsail; anon, they deprecate her wrath with doublereefed topsails. When, at length, her unappeasable fury is fairly aroused, and all round the dismantled ship the storm howls and howls for days together, they still persevere in their efforts. First, they try unconditional submission; furling every rag and *heaving to*; laying like a log, for the tempest to toss wheresoever it pleases.

This failing, they set a *spencer* or *trysail*, and shift on the other tack. Equally vain! The gale sings as hoarsely as before. At last, the wind comes round fair; they drop the fore-sail; square the yards, and scud before it; their implacable foe chasing them with tornadoes, as if to show her insensibility to the last.

Other ships, without encountering these terrible gales, spend week after week endeavoring to turn this boisterous world-corner against a continual headwind. Tacking hither and thither, in the language of sailors they *polish* the Cape by beating about its edges so long.

Le Mair and Schouten, two Dutchmen, were the first navigators who weathered Cape Horn. Previous to this, passages had been made to the Pacific by the Straits of Magellan; nor, indeed, at that period, was it known to a certainty that there was any other route, or that the land now called Tierra del Fuego was an island. A few leagues southward from Tierra del

Fuego is a cluster of small islands, the Diegoes; between which and the former island are the Straits of Le Mair, so called in honor of their discoverer, who first sailed through them into the Pacific. Le Mair and Schouten, in their small, clumsy vessels, encountered a series of tremendous gales, the prelude to the long train of similar hardships which most of their followers have experienced. It is a significant fact, that Schouten's vessel, the *Horne*, which gave its name to the Cape, was almost lost in weathering it.

The next navigator round the Cape was Sir Francis Drake, who, on Raleigh's Expedition, beholding for the first time, from the Isthmus of Darien, the "goodlie south Sea," like a trueborn Englishman, vowed, please God, to sail an English ship thereon; which the gallant sailor did, to the sore discomfiture of the Spaniards on the coasts of Chili and Peru.

But perhaps the greatest hardships on record, in making this celebrated passage, were those experienced by Lord Anson's squadron in 1736. Three remarkable and most interesting narratives record their disasters and sufferings. The first, jointly written by the carpenter and gunner of the *Wager*; the second by young Byron, a midshipman in the same ship; the third, by the chaplain of the *Centurion*. White-Jacket has them all; and they are fine reading of a boisterous March night, with the casement rattling in your ear, and the chimney-stacks blowing down upon the pavement, bubbling with raindrops.

But if you want the best idea of Cape Horn, get my friend Dana's unmatchable "Two Years Before the Mast." But you can read, and so you must have read it. His chapters describing Cape Horn must have been written with an icicle.

At the present day the horrors of the Cape have somewhat abated. This is owing to a growing familiarity with it; but, more than all, to the improved condition of ships in all respects, and the means now generally in use of preserving the health of the crews in times of severe and prolonged exposure.

Colder and colder; we are drawing nigh to the Cape. Now gregoes, pea jackets, monkey jackets, reefing jackets, storm jackets, oil jackets, paint jackets, round jackets, short jackets, long jackets, and all manner of jackets, are the order of the day, not excepting the immortal white jacket, which begins to be sturdily buttoned up to the throat, and pulled down vigorously at the skirts, to bring them well over the loins.

But, alas! those skirts were lamentably scanty; and though, with its quiltings, the jacket was stuffed out about the breasts like a Christmas turkey, and of a dry cold day kept the wearer warm enough in that vicinity, yet about the loins it was shorter than a ballet-dancer's skirts; so that while my chest was in the temperate zone close adjoining the torrid, my hapless thighs were in Nova Zembla, hardly an icicle's toss from the Pole.

Then, again, the repeated soakings and dryings it had undergone, had by this time made it shrink woefully all over, especially in the arms, so that the wristbands had gradually crawled up near to the elbows; and it required an energetic thrust to push the arm through, in drawing the jacket on.

I endeavored to amend these misfortunes by sewing a sort of canvas ruffle round the skirts, by way of a continuation or supplement to the original work, and by doing the same with the wristbands.

This is the time for oil-skin suits, dreadnaughts, tarred trousers and overalls, sea-boots, comforters, mittens, woolen socks, Guernsey frocks, Havre shirts, buffalo-robe shorts, and mooseskin drawers. Every man's jacket is his wigwam, and every man's hat his caboose.

Perfect license is now permitted to the men respecting their clothing. Whatever they can rake and scrape together they put on—swaddling themselves in old sails, and drawing old socks over their heads for nightcaps. This is the time for smiting your chest with your hand, and talking loud to keep up the circulation.

Colder, and colder, and colder, till at last we spoke a fleet of icebergs bound North. After that, it was one incessant "*cold snap*," that almost snapped off our fingers and toes. Cold! It was cold as *Blue Flujin*, where sailors say fire freezes.

And now coming up with the latitude of the Cape, we stood southward to give it a wide berth, and while so doing were becalmed; ay, becalmed off Cape Horn, which is worse, far worse, than being becalmed on the Line.

Here we lay fortyeight hours, during which the cold was intense. I wondered at the liquid sea, which refused to freeze in such a temperature. The clear, cold sky overhead looked like a steelblue cymbal, that might ring, could you smite it. Our breath came and went like puffs of smoke from pipebowls. At first there was a long gauky swell, that obliged us to furl most of the sails, and even send down t'gallantyards, for fear of pitching them overboard.

Out of sight of land, at this extremity of both the inhabitable and uninhabitable world, our peopled frigate, echoing with the voices of men, the bleating of lambs, the cackling of fowls, the grunting of pigs, seemed like Noah's old ark itself, becalmed at the climax of the Deluge.

There was nothing to be done but patiently to await the pleasure of the elements, and "whistle for a wind," the usual practice of seamen in a calm. No fire was allowed, except for the indispensable purpose of cooking, and heating bottles of water to toast Selvagee's feet. He who possessed the largest stock of vitality, stood the best chance to escape freezing. It was horrifying.

In such weather any man could have undergone amputation with great ease, and helped take up the arteries himself.

Indeed, this state of affairs had not lasted quite twenty-four hours, when the extreme frigidity of the air, united to our increased tendency to inactivity, would very soon have rendered some of us subjects for the surgeon and his mates, had not a humane proceeding of the Captain suddenly impelled us to rigorous exercise.

And here be it said, that the appearance of the Boatswain, with his silver whistle to his mouth, at the main hatchway of the gundeck, is always regarded by the crew with the utmost curiosity, for this betokens that some general order is about to be promulgated through the ship. What now? is the question that runs on from man to man. A short preliminary whistle is then given by "Old Yarn," as they call him, which whistle serves to collect round him, from their various stations, his four mates. Then Yarn, or Pipes, as leader of the orchestra, begins a peculiar call, in which his assistants join. This over, the order, whatever it may be, is loudly sung out and prolonged, till the remotest corner echoes again. The Boatswain and his mates are the towncriers of a manofwar.

The calm had commenced in the afternoon: and the following morning the ship's company were electrified by a general order, thus set forth and declared: *"D'ye hear there, fore and aft! all hands skylark!"*

This mandate, nowadays never used except upon very rare occasions, produced the same effect upon the men that Exhilarating Gas would have done, or an extra allowance of "grog." For a time, the wonted discipline of the ship was broken through, and perfect license allowed. It was a Babel here, a Bedlam there, and a Pandemonium everywhere. The Theatricals were nothing compared with it. Then the faint-hearted and timorous crawled to their hidingplaces, and the lusty and bold shouted forth their glee. Gangs of men, in all sorts of outlandish habiliments, wild as those worn at some crazy carnival, rushed to and fro, seizing upon whomsoever they pleased—warrant-officers and dangerous pugilists excepted—pulling and hauling the luckless tars about, till fairly baited into a genial warmth. Some were made fast to and hoisted aloft with a will: others, mounted upon oars, were ridden fore and aft on a rail, to the boisterous mirth of the spectators, any one of whom might be the next victim. Swings were rigged from the tops, or the masts; and the most reluctant wights being purposely selected, in spite of all struggles, were swung from East to West, in vast arcs of circles, till almost breathless. Hornpipes, fandangoes, Donnybrook-jibs, reels, and quadrilles, were danced under the very nose of the most mighty captain, and upon the very quarterdeck and poop. Sparring and wrestling, too, were all the vogue; *Kentucky bites* were given, and the *Indian hug* exchanged. The din frightened the seafowl, that flew by with accelerated wing.

It is worth mentioning that several casualties occurred, of which, however, I will relate but one. While the "skylarking" was at its height, one of the foretopmen—an ugly-tempered devil of a Portuguese, looking on—swore that he would be the death of any man who laid violent hands upon his inviolable person. This threat being overhead, a band of desperadoes, coming up from behind, tripped him up in an instant, and in the twinkling of an eye the Portuguese was straddling an oar, borne aloft by an uproarious multitude, who rushed him along the deck at a railroad gallop. The living mass of arms all round and beneath him was so dense, that every time he inclined one side he was instantly pushed upright, but only to fall over again, to receive another push from the contrary direction. Presently, disengaging his hands from those who held them, the enraged seaman drew from his bosom an iron belayingpin, and recklessly laid about him to right and left. Most of his persecutors fled; but some eight or ten still stood their ground, and, while bearing him aloft, endeavored to wrest the weapon from his hands. In this attempt, one man was stuck on the head, and dropped insensible. He was taken up for dead, and carried below to Cuticle, the surgeon, while the Portuguese was put under guard. But the wound did not prove very serious; and in a few days the man was walking about the deck, with his head well bandaged.

This occurrence put an end to the "skylarking," further headbreaking being strictly prohibited. In due time the Portuguese paid the penalty of his rashness at the gangway; while once again the officers *shipped their quarterdeck faces*.

Ere the calm had yet left us, a sail had been discerned from the foretop-mast-head, at a great distance, probably three leagues or more. At first it was a mere speck, altogether out of sight from the deck. By the force of attraction or something else equally inscrutable, two ships in a calm, and equally affected by the currents, will always approximate, more or less. Though there was not a breath of wind, it was not a great while before the strange sail was described from our bulwarks; gradually, it drew still nearer.

What was she, and whence? There is no object which so excites interest and conjecture, and, at the same time, baffles both, as a sail, seen as a mere speck on these remote seas off Cape Horn.

A breeze! a breeze! for lo! the stranger is now percepti-bly nearing the frigate; the officer's spyglass pronounced her a fullrigged ship, with all sail set, and coming right down to us, though in our own vicinity the calm still reigns.

She is bringing the wind with her. Hurrah! Ay, there it is! Behold how mincingly it creeps over the sea, just ruffling and crisping it.

Our top-men were at once sent aloft to loose the sails, and presently they faintly began to distend. As yet we hardly had steerage-way. Toward sunset the stranger bore down before the wind, a complete pyramid of canvas. Never before, I venture to say, was Cape Horn so audaciously insulted. Stun'-sails alow and aloft; royals, moonsails, and everything else. She glided under our stern, within hailing distance, and the signalquartermaster ran up our ensign to the gaff.

"Ship ahoy!" cried the Lieutenant of the Watch, through his trumpet.

"Halloa!" bawled an old fellow in a green jacket, clapping one hand to his mouth, while he held on with the other to the mizzenshrouds.

"What ship's that?"

"The *Sultan*, Indiaman, from New York, and bound to Cal-lao and Canton, sixty days out, all well. What frigate's that?"

"The United States ship *Neversink*, homeward bound."

"Hurrah! hurrah! hurrah!" yelled our enthusiastic country-man, transported with patriotism.

By this time the *Sultan* had swept past, but the Lieutenant of the Watch could not withhold a parting admonition.

"D'ye hear? You'd better take in some of your flying-kites there. Look out for Cape Horn!"

But the friendly advice was lost in the now increasing wind. With a suddenness by no means unusual in these latitudes, the light breeze soon became a succession of sharp squalls, and our sailproud braggadocio of an Indiaman was observed to let everything go by the run, his t'-gallant stun'sails and flyingjib taking quick leave of the spars; the flying-jib was swept into the air, rolled together for a few minutes, and tossed about in the squalls like a football. But the wind played no such pranks with the more prudently managed canvas of the *Neversink*, though before many hours it was stirring times with us.

About midnight, when the starboard watch, to which I belonged, was below, the boatswain's whistle was heard, followed by the shrill cry of "*All hands take in sail!* Jump, men, and save ship!"

Springing from our hammocks, we found the frigate leaning over to it so steeply, that it was with difficulty we could climb the ladders leading to the upper deck.

Here the scene was awful. The vessel seemed to be sailing on her side. The maindeck guns had several days previous been run in and housed, and the portholes closed, but the lee carronades on the quarter-deck and forecastle were plunging through the sea, which undulated over them in milk-like billows of foam. With every lurch to leeward the yard-arm-ends seemed to dip in the sea, while forward the spray dashed over the bows in cataracts, and drenched the men who were on the foreyard. By this time the deck was alive with the whole strength of the ship's company, five hundred men, officers and all, mostly clinging to the weather bulwarks. The occasional phosphorescence of the yeasting sea cast a glare upon their uplifted faces, as a night fire in a populous city lights up the panicstricken crowd.

In a sudden gale, or when a large quantity of sail is suddenly to be furled, it is the custom for the First Lieutenant to take the trumpet from whoever happens then to be officer of the deck. But Mad Jack had the trumpet that watch; nor did the First Lieutenant now seek to wrest it from his hands. Every eye was upon him, as if we had chosen him from among us all, to decide this battle with the elements, by single combat with the spirit of the Cape; for Mad Jack was the saving genius of the ship, and so proved himself that night. I owe this right hand, that is this moment flying over my sheet, and all my present being to Mad Jack. The ship's bows were now butting, battering, ramming, and thundering over and upon the head seas, and with a horrible wallowing sound our whole hull was rolling in the trough of the foam. The gale came athwart the deck, and every sail seemed bursting with its wild breath.

All the quartermasters, and several of the forecastlemen, were swarming round the double-wheel on the quarter-deck. Some jumping up and down, with their hands upon the spokes;

for the whole helm and galvanized keel were fiercely feverish, with the life imparted to them by the wild tempest.

"Hard up the helm!" shouted Captain Claret, bursting from his cabin like a ghost in his nightdress.

"Damn you!" raged Mad Jack to the quarter-masters; "hard *down*—hard *down*, I say, and be damned to you!"

Contrary orders! but Mad Jack's were obeyed. His object was to throw the ship into the wind, so as the better to admit of close-reefing the topsails, but though the halyards were let go, it was impossible to clew down the yards, owing to the enormous horizontal strain on the canvas. It now blew a hurricane. The spray flew over the ship in floods. The gigantic masts seemed about to snap under the world-wide strain of the three entire topsails.

"Clew down! Clew down!" shouted Mad Jack, husky with excitement, and in a frenzy, beating his trumpet against one of the shrouds. But, owing to the slant of the ship, the thing could not be done. It was obvious that before many minutes something must go—either sails, rigging, or sticks; perhaps the hull itself, and all hands.

Presently a voice from the top exclaimed that there was a rent in the maintop-sail. And instantly we heard a report like two or three muskets discharged together; the vast sail was rent up and down like the Veil of the Temple. This saved the main-mast; for the yard was now clewed down with comparative ease, and the topmen laid out to stow the shattered canvas. Soon, the two remaining top-sails were also clewed down and close-reefed.

Above all the roar of the tempest and the shouts of the crew, was heard the dismal tolling of the ship's bell—almost as large as that of a village church—which the violent rolling of the ship was occasioning. Imagination cannot conceive the horror of such a sound in a nighttempest at sea.

"Stop that ghost!" roared Mad Jack; "away, one of you, and wrench off the clapper!"

But no sooner was this ghost gagged, than a still more appalling sound was heard, the rolling to and fro of the heavy shot, which, on the gundeck, had broken loose from the gun-racks, and converted that part of the ship into an immense bowlingalley. Some hands were sent down to secure them; but it was as much as their lives were worth. Several were maimed; and the midshipmen who were ordered to see the duty performed reported it impossible, until the storm abated.

The most terrific job of all was to furl the main-sail, which, at the commencement of the squalls, had been clewed up, coaxed and quieted as much as possible with the bunt-lines and slab lines. Mad Jack waited some time for a lull, ere he gave an order so perilous to be executed. For to furl this enormous sail, in such a gale, required at least fifty men on the yard; whose weight, superadded to that of the ponderous stick itself, still further jeopardized their lives. But there was no prospect of a cessation of the gale, and the order was at last given.

At this time a hurricane of slanting sleet and hail was descending upon us; the rigging was coated with a thin glare of ice, formed within the hour.

"Aloft, main-yard-men! and all you maintop-men! and furl the mainsail!" cried Mad Jack.

I dashed down my hat, slipped out of my quilted jacket in an instant, kicked the shoes from my feet, and, with a crowd of others, sprang for the rigging. Above the bulwarks (which in a frigate are so high as to afford much protection to those on deck) the gale was horrible. The sheer force of the wind flattened us to the rigging as we ascended, and every hand seemed congealing to the icy shrouds by which we held.

"Up—up, my brave hearties!" shouted Mad Jack; and up we got, some way or other, all of us, and groped our way out on the yard-arms.

"Hold on, every mother's son!" cried an old quartergunner at my side. He was bawling at the top of his compass, but in the gale, he seemed to be whispering; and I only heard him from his being right to windward of me.

But his hint was unnecessary; I dug my nails into the *Jack-stays*, and swore that nothing but death should part me and them until I was able to turn round and look to windward. As yet, this was impossible; I could scarcely hear the man to leeward at my elbow; the wind seemed to snatch the words from his mouth and fly away with them to the South Pole.

All this while the sail itself was flying about, sometimes catching over our heads, and threatening to tear us from the yard in spite of all our hugging. For about three quarters of an hour we thus hung suspended right over the rampant billows, which curled their very crests under the feet of some four or five of us clinging to the leeyardarm, as if to float us from our place.

Presently, the word passed along the yard from windward that we were ordered to come down and leave the sail to blow; since it could not be furled. A midshipman, it seemed, had been sent up by the officer of the deck to give the order, as no trumpet could be heard where we were.

Those on the weather yard-arm managed to crawl upon the spar and scramble down the rigging; but with us, upon the extreme leeward side, this feat was out of the question; it was, literally, like climbing a precipice to get to windward in order to reach the shrouds; besides, the entire yard was now encased in ice, and our hands and feet were so numb that we dared not trust our lives to them. Nevertheless, by assisting each other, we contrived to throw ourselves prostrate along the yard, and embrace it with our arms and legs. In this position, the stun'sail-booms greatly assisted in securing our hold. Strange as it may appear, I do not suppose that, at this moment, the slightest sensation of fear was felt by one man on that yard. We clung to it with might and main; but this was instinct. The truth is, that, in circumstances like these, the sense of fear is annihilated in the unutterable sights that fill all the eye, and the sounds that fill all the ear. You become identified with the tempest; your insignificance is lost in the riot of the stormy universe around.

Below us, our noble frigate seemed thrice its real length— a vast black wedge, opposing its widest end to the combined fury of the sea and wind.

At length the first fury of the gale began to abate, and we at once fell to pounding our hands, as a preliminary operation to going to work; for a gang of men had now ascended to help secure what was left of the sail; we somehow packed it away, at last, and came down.

About noon the next day, the gale so moderated that we shook two reefs out of the top-sails, set new courses, and stood due east, with the wind astern.

Thus, all the fine weather we encountered after first weighing anchor on the pleasant Spanish coast, was but the prelude to this one terrific night; more especially, that treacherous calm immediately preceding it. But how could we reach our long-promised homes without encountering Cape Horn? by what possibility avoid it? And though some ships have weathered it without these perils, yet by far the greater part must encounter them. Lucky it is that it comes about midway in the homeward-bound passage, so that the sailors have time to prepare for it, and time to recover from it after it is astern.

But, sailor or landsman, there is some sort of a Cape Horn for all. Boys! beware of it; prepare for it in time. Greybeards! thank God it is passed. And ye lucky livers, to whom, by some rare fatality, your Cape Horns are placid as Lake Lemans, flatter not yourselves that good luck is judgment and discretion; for all the yolk in your eggs, you might have foundered and gone down, had the Spirit of the Cape said the word.

# Loss of a Man—Superstition

### *Richard Henry Dana*

MONDAY, NOV. 19TH. THIS WAS A BLACK DAY IN OUR CALENDAR. At seven o'clock in the morning, it being our watch below, we were aroused from a sound sleep by the cry of "All hands ahoy! a man overboard!" This unwonted cry sent a thrill through the heart of every one, and hurrying on deck we found the vessel hove flat aback, with all her studdingsails set; for the boy who was at the helm left it to throw something overboard, and the carpenter, who was an old sailor, knowing that the wind was light, put the helm down and hove her aback.

The watch on deck were lowering away the quarter-boat, and I got on deck just in time to heave myself into her as she was leaving the side; but it was not until out upon the wide Pacific, in our little boat, that I knew whom we had lost. It was George Ballmer, a young English sailor, who was prized by the officers as an active lad and willing seaman, and by the crew as a lively, hearty fellow, and a good shipmate.

He was going aloft to fit a strap round the main topmast-head, for ringtail halyards, and had the strap and block, a coil of halyards and a marlinespike about his neck. He fell from the starboard futtock shrouds, and not knowing how to swim, and being heavily dressed, with all those things round his neck, he probably sank immediately. We pulled astern, in the direction in which he fell, and though we knew that there was no hope of saving him, yet no one wished to speak of returning, and we rowed about for nearly an hour, without the hope of doing anything, but unwilling to acknowledge to ourselves that we must give him up. At length we turned the boat's head and made towards the vessel.

Death is at all times solemn, but never so much so as at sea. A man dies on shore; his body remains with his friends, and "the mourners go about the streets"; but when a man falls overboard at sea and is lost, there is a suddenness in the event, and a difficulty in realizing it, which give to it an air of awful mystery. A man dies on shore—you follow his body to the grave, and a stone marks the spot. You are often prepared for the event. There is always something which helps you to realize it when it happens, and to recall it when it has passed.

A man is shot down by your side in battle, and the mangled body remains an object, and a real evidence; but at sea, the man is near you—at your side—you hear his voice, and in an instant he is gone, and nothing but a vacancy shows his loss. Then, too, at sea—to use a homely but expressive phrase—you miss a man so much. A dozen men are shut up together in a little bark, upon the wide, wide sea, and for months and months see no forms and hear no voices but their own, and one is taken suddenly from among them, and they miss him at every turn. It is like losing a limb. There are no new faces or new scenes to fill up the gap. There is always an empty berth in the forecastle, and one man wanting when the small night watch is mustered. There is one less to take the wheel, and one less to lay out with you upon the yard. You miss his form, and the sound of his voice, for habit had made them almost necessary to you, and each of your senses feels the loss.

All these things make such a death peculiarly solemn, and the effect of it remains upon the crew for some time. There is more kindness shown by the officers to the crew, and by the crew to one another. There is more quietness and seriousness. The oath and the loud laugh are gone. The officers are more watchful, and the crew go more carefully aloft. The lost man is seldom mentioned, or is dismissed with a sailor's rude eulogy—"Well, poor George is gone! His cruise is up soon! He knew his work, and did his duty, and was a good shipmate." Then usually follows some allusion to another world, for sailors are almost all believers; but their notions and opinions are unfixed and at loose ends. They say,—"God won't be hard upon the poor fellow," and seldom get beyond the common phrase which seems to imply that their sufferings and hard treatment here will excuse them hereafter,— "To work hard, live hard, die hard, and go to hell after all, would be hard indeed!" Our cook, a simplehearted old African, who had been through a good deal in his day, and was rather seriously inclined, always going to church twice a day

113

when on shore, and reading his Bible on a Sunday in the galley, talked to the crew about spending their Sabbaths badly, and told them that they might go as suddenly as George had, and be as little prepared.

Yet a sailor's life is, at best, but a mixture of a little good with much evil, and a little pleasure with much pain. The beautiful is linked with the revolting, the sublime with the commonplace, and the solemn with the ludicrous. We had hardly returned on board with our sad report, before an auction was held of the poor man's clothes. The captain had first, however, called all hands aft and asked them if they were satisfied that everything had been done to save the man, and if they thought there was any use in remaining there longer. The crew all said that it was in vain, for the man did not know how to swim, and was very heavily dressed. So we then filled away and kept her off to her course.

The laws regulating navigation make the captain answerable for the effects of a sailor who dies during the voyage, and it is either a law or a universal custom, established for convenience, that the captain should immediately hold an auction of his things, in which they are bid off by the sailors, and the sums which they give are deducted from their wages at the end of the voyage. In this way the trouble and risk of keeping his things through the voyage are avoided, and the clothes are usually sold for more than they would be worth on shore.

Accordingly, we had no sooner got the ship before the wind, than his chest was brought up upon the forecastle, and the sale began. The jackets and trowsers in which we had seen him dressed but a few days before, were exposed and bid off while the life was hardly out of his body, and his chest was taken aft and used as a store-chest, so that there was nothing left which could be called his. Sailors have an unwillingness to wear a dead man's clothes during the same voyage, and they seldom do so unless they are in absolute want.

As is usual after a death, many stories were told about George. Some had heard him say that he repented never having learned to swim, and that he knew that he should meet his death by drowning. Another said that he never knew any good to come of a voyage made against the will, and the deceased man shipped and spent his advance and was afterwards very unwilling to go, but not being able to refund, was obliged to sail with us. A boy, too, who had become quite attached to him, said that George talked to him during most of the watch on the night before, about his mother and family at home, and this was the first time that he had mentioned the subject during the voyage.

The night after this event, when I went to the galley to get a light, I found the cook inclined to be talkative, so I sat down on the spars, and gave him an opportunity to hold a yarn. I was the more inclined to do so, as I found that he was full of the superstitions once more common among seamen, and which the recent death had waked up in his mind. He talked about George's having spoken of his friends, and said he believed few men died without having a warning of it, which he supported by a great many stories of dreams, and the unusual behavior of men before death. From this he went on to other superstitions, the Flying Dutchman, etc., and talked rather mysteriously, having something evidently on his mind.

At length he put his head out of the galley and looked carefully about to see if any one was within hearing, and being satisfied on that point, asked me in a low tone—

"I say! you know what countryman 'e carpenter be?"

"Yes," said I; "he's a German."

"What kind of a German?" said the cook.

"He belongs to Bremen," said I.

"Are you sure o' dat?" said he.

I satisfied him on that point by saying that he could speak no language but the German and English.

"I'm plaguy glad o' dat," said the cook. "I was mighty 'fraid he was a Fin. I tell you what, I been plaguy civil to that man all the voyage."

I asked him the reason of this, and found that he was fully possessed with the notion that Fins are wizards, and especially have power over winds and storms. I tried to reason with him about it, but he had the best of all arguments, that from experience, at hand, and was not to be moved. He had been in a vessel at the Sandwich Islands, in which the sail-maker was a Fin, and could do anything he was of a mind to. This sailmaker kept a junk bottle in his berth, which was always just half full of rum, though he got drunk upon it nearly every day. He had seen him sit for hours together, talking to this bottle, which he stood up before him on the table. The same man cut his throat in his berth, and everybody said he was possessed.

He had heard of ships, too, beating up the gulf of Finland against a head wind, and having a ship heave in sight astern, overhaul and pass them, with as fair a wind as could blow, and all studdingsails out, and find she was from Finland.

"Oh ho!" said he; "I've seen too much of them men to want to see 'em 'board a ship. If they can't have their own way, they'll play the d—l with you."

As I still doubted, he said he would leave it to John, who was the oldest seaman aboard, and would know, if anybody did. John, to be sure, was the oldest, and at the same time the most ignorant, man in the ship; but I consented to have him called. The cook stated the matter to him, and John, as I anticipated, sided with the cook, and said that he himself had been in a ship where they had a head wind for a fortnight, and the captain found out at last that one of the men, whom he had had some hard words with a short time before, was a Fin, and immediately told him if he didn't stop the head wind he would shut him down in the fore peak, and would not give him anything to eat. The Fin held out for a day and a half, when he could not stand it any longer, and did something or other which brought the wind round again, and they let him up.

"There," said the cook, "what do you think o' dat?"

I told him I had no doubt it was true, and that it would have been odd if the wind had not changed in fifteen days, Fin or no Fin.

"Oh," said he, "go 'way! You think, 'cause you been to college, you know better than anybody. You know better than them as 'as seen it with their own eyes. You wait till you've been to sea as long as I have, and you'll know."

# Mal de Mer

## *Jerome K. Jerome*

WE SAT THERE FOR HALFANHOUR, DESCRIBING TO EACH other our maladies. I explained to George and William Harris how I felt when I got up in the morning, and William Harris told us how he felt when he went to bed; and George stood on the hearth-rug, and gave us a clever and powerful piece of acting, illustrative of how he felt in the night.

George FANCIES he is ill; but there's never anything really the matter with him, you know.

At this point, Mrs. Poppets knocked at the door to know if we were ready for supper. We smiled sadly at one another, and said we supposed we had better try to swallow a bit. Harris said a little something in one's stomach often kept the disease in check; and Mrs. Poppets brought the tray in, and we drew up to the table, and toyed with a little steak and onions, and some rhubarb tart.

I must have been very weak at the time; because I know, after the first halfhour or so, I seemed to take no interest whatever in my food—an unusual thing for me—and I didn't want any cheese.

This duty done, we refilled our glasses, lit our pipes, and resumed the discussion upon our state of health. What it was that was actually the matter with us, we none of us could be sure of; but the unanimous opinion was that it—whatever it was—had been brought on by overwork.

"What we want is rest," said Harris.

"Rest and a complete change," said George. "The overstrain upon our brains has produced a general depression throughout the system. Change of scene, and absence of the necessity for thought, will restore the mental equilibrium."

George has a cousin, who is usually described in the chargesheet as a medical student, so that he naturally has a somewhat familyphysicianary way of putting things.

I agreed with George, and suggested that we should seek out some retired and oldworld spot, far from the madding crowd, and dream away a sunny week among its drowsy lanes—some halfforgotten nook, hidden away by the fairies, out of reach of the noisy world—some quaint-perched eyrie on the cliffs of Time, from whence the surging waves of the nineteenth century would sound far-off and faint.

Harris said he thought it would be humpy. He said he knew the sort of place I meant; where everybody went to bed at eight o'clock, and you couldn't get a REFEREE for love or money, and had to walk ten miles to get your baccy.

"No," said Harris, "if you want rest and change, you can't beat a sea trip."

I objected to the sea trip strongly. A sea trip does you good when you are going to have a couple of months of it, but, for a week, it is wicked. You start on Monday with the idea implanted in your bosom that you are going to enjoy yourself. You wave an airy adieu to the boys on shore, light your biggest pipe, and swagger about the deck as if you were Captain Cook, Sir Francis Drake, and Christopher Columbus all rolled into one. On Tuesday, you wish you hadn't come. On Wednesday, Thursday, and Friday, you wish you were dead. On Saturday, you are able to swallow a little beef tea, and to sit up on deck, and answer with a wan, sweet smile when kindhearted people ask you how you feel now. On Sunday, you begin to walk about again, and take solid food. And on Monday morning, as, with your bag and umbrella in your hand, you stand by the gunwale, waiting to step ashore, you begin to thoroughly like it.

I remember my brotherin-law going for a short sea trip once, for the benefit of his health. He took a return berth from London to Liverpool; and when he got to Liverpool, the only thing he was anxious about was to sell that return ticket.

It was offered round the town at a tremendous reduction, so I am told; and was eventually sold for eighteenpence to a biliouslooking youth who had just been advised by his medical men to go to the sea-side, and take exercise.

"Sea-side!" said my brotherinlaw, pressing the ticket affectionately into his hand; "why, you'll have enough to last you a lifetime; and as for exercise! why, you'll get more exercise, sitting down on that ship, than you would turning somersaults on dry land."

He himself—my brotherinlaw—came back by train. He said the North-Western Railway was healthy enough for him.

Another fellow I knew went for a week's voyage round the coast, and, before they started, the steward came to him to ask whether he would pay for each meal as he had it, or arrange beforehand for the whole series.

The steward recommended the latter course, as it would come so much cheaper. He said they would do him for the whole week at two pounds five. He said for breakfast there would be fish, followed by a grill. Lunch was at one, and consisted of four courses. Dinner at six—soup, fish, entree, joint, poultry, salad, sweets, cheese, and dessert. And a light meat supper at ten. My friend thought he would close on the two-pound-five job (he is a hearty eater), and did so.

Lunch came just as they were off Sheerness. He didn't feel so hungry as he thought he should, and so contented himself with a bit of boiled beef, and some strawberries and cream. He pondered a good deal during the afternoon, and at one time it seemed to him that he had been eating nothing but boiled beef for weeks, and at other times it seemed that he must have been living on strawberries and cream for years.

Neither the beef nor the strawberries and cream seemed happy, either—seemed discontented like.

At six, they came and told him dinner was ready. The announcement aroused no enthusiasm within him, but he felt that there was some of that twopoundfive to be worked off, and he held on to ropes and things and went down. A pleasant odour of onions and hot ham, mingled with fried fish and greens, greeted him at the bottom of the ladder; and then the steward came up with an oily smile, and said:

"What can I get you, sir?"

"Get me out of this," was the feeble reply.

And they ran him up quick, and propped him up, over to leeward, and left him.

For the next four days he lived a simple and blameless life on thin captain's biscuits (I mean that the biscuits were thin, not the captain) and sodawater; but, towards Saturday, he got uppish, and went in for weak tea and dry toast, and on Monday he was gorging himself on chicken broth. He left the ship on Tuesday, and as it steamed away from the landing-stage he gazed after it regretfully.

"There she goes," he said, "there she goes, with two pounds' worth of food on board that belongs to me, and that I haven't had."

He said that if they had given him another day he thought he could have put it straight.

So I set my face against the sea trip. Not, as I explained, upon my own account. I was never queer. But I was afraid for George. George said he should be all right, and would rather like it, but he would advise Harris and me not to think of it, as he felt sure we should both be ill. Harris said that, to himself, it was always a mystery how people managed to get sick at sea—said he thought people must do it on purpose, from affectation—said he had often wished to be, but had never been able.

Then he told us anecdotes of how he had gone across the Channel when it was so rough that the passengers had to be tied into their berths, and he and the captain were the only two living souls on board who were not ill. Sometimes it was he and the second mate who were not ill; but it was generally he and one other man. If not he and another man, then it was he by himself.

It is a curious fact, but nobody ever is sea-sick—on land. At sea, you come across plenty of people very bad indeed, whole boatloads of them; but I never met a man yet, on land, who had ever known at all what it was to be seasick. Where the thousands upon thousands of bad sailors that swarm in every ship hide themselves when they are on land is a mystery.

If most men were like a fellow I saw on the Yarmouth boat one day, I could account for the seeming enigma easily enough. It was just off Southend Pier, I recollect, and he was leaning out through one of the portholes in a very dangerous position. I went up to him to try and save him.

"Hi! come further in," I said, shaking him by the shoulder. "You'll be overboard."

"Oh my! I wish I was," was the only answer I could get; and there I had to leave him.

Three weeks afterwards, I met him in the coffeeroom of a Bath hotel, talking about his voyages, and explaining, with enthusiasm, how he loved the sea.

"Good sailor!" he replied in answer to a mild young man's envious query; "well, I did feel a little queer ONCE, I confess. It was off Cape Horn. The vessel was wrecked the next morning." I said:

"Weren't you a little shaky by Southend Pier one day, and wanted to be thrown overboard?"

"Southend Pier!" he replied, with a puzzled expression.

"Yes; going down to Yarmouth, last Friday three weeks."

"Oh, ah—yes," he answered, brightening up; "I remember now. I did have a headache that afternoon. It was the pickles, you know. They were the most disgraceful pickles I ever tasted in a respectable boat. Did you have any?"

For myself, I have discovered an excellent preventive against sea-sickness, in balancing myself. You stand in the centre of the deck, and, as the ship heaves and pitches, you move your body about, so as to keep it always straight. When the front of the ship rises, you lean forward, till the deck almost touches your nose; and when its back end gets up, you lean backwards. This is all very well for an hour or two; but you can't balance yourself for a week. George said:

"Let's go up the river."

He said we should have fresh air, exercise and quiet; the constant change of scene would occupy our minds (including what there was of Harris's); and the hard work would give us a good appetite, and make us sleep well. Harris said he didn't think George ought to do anything that would have a tendency to make him sleepier than he always was, as it might be dangerous.

He said he didn't very well understand how George was going to sleep any more than he did now, seeing that there were only twenty-four hours in each day, summer and winter alike; but thought that if he DID sleep any more, he might just as well be dead, and so save his board and lodging.

Harris said, however, that the river would suit him to a "T." I don't know what a "T" is (except a sixpenny one, which includes bread-and-butter and cake AD LIB., and is cheap at the price, if you haven't had any dinner). It seems to suit everybody, however, which is greatly to its credit.

It suited me to a "T" too, and Harris and I both said it was a good idea of George's; and we said it in a tone that seemed to somehow imply that we were surprised that George should have come out so sensible.

The only one who was not struck with the suggestion was Montmorency. He never did care for the river, did Montmorency.

"It's all very well for you fellows," he says; "you like it, but I don't. There's nothing for me to do. Scenery is not in my line, and I don't smoke. If I see a rat, you won't stop; and if I go to sleep, you get fooling about with the boat, and slop me overboard. If you ask me, I call the whole thing bally foolishness."

We were three to one, however, and the motion was carried.

# MS. Found in a Bottle

## *Edgar Allan Poe*

*Qui n'a plus qu'un moment a vivre*
*N'a plus rien a dissimuler.*

—QUINAULT—ATYS.

OF MY COUNTRY AND OF MY FAMILY I HAVE LITTLE TO SAY. Ill usage and length of years have driven me from the one, and estranged me from the other. Hereditary wealth afforded me an education of no common order, and a contemplative turn of mind enabled me to methodize the stores which early study very diligently garnered up. Beyond all things, the study of the German moralists gave me great delight; not from any illadvised admiration of their eloquent madness, but from the ease with which my habits of rigid thought enabled me to detect their falsities. I have often been reproached with the aridity of my genius; a deficiency of imagination has been imputed to me as a crime; and the Pyrrhonism of my opinions has at all times rendered me notorious. Indeed, a strong relish for physical philosophy has, I fear, tinctured my mind with a very common error of this age—I mean the habit of referring occurrences, even the least susceptible of such reference, to the principles of that science. Upon the whole, no person could be less liable than myself to be led away from the severe precincts of truth by the *ignes fatui* of superstition. I have thought proper to premise thus much, lest the incredible tale I have to tell should be considered rather the raving of a crude imagination, than the positive experience of a mind to which the reveries of fancy have been a dead letter and a nullity.

After many years spent in foreign travel, I sailed in the year 18__, from the port of Batavia, in the rich and populous island of Java, on a voyage to the Archipelago of the Sunda islands. I went as passenger—having no other inducement than a kind of nervous restlessness which haunted me as a fiend. Our vessel was a beautiful ship of about four hundred tons, copperfastened, and built at Bombay of Malabar teak. She was freighted with cottonwool and oil, from the Lachadive islands. We had also on board coir, jaggeree, ghee, cocoanuts, and a few cases of opium. The stowage was clumsily done, and the vessel consequently crank.

We got under way with a mere breath of wind, and for many days stood along the eastern coast of Java, without any other incident to beguile the monotony of our course than the occasional meeting with some of the small grabs of the Archipelago to which we were bound.

One evening, leaning over the taffrail, I observed a very singular, isolated cloud, to the N.W. It was remarkable, as well for its color, as from its being the first we had seen since our departure from Batavia. I watched it attentively until sunset, when it spread all at once to the eastward and westward, girting in the horizon with a narrow strip of vapor, and looking like a long line of low beach. My notice was soon afterwards attracted by the duskyred appearance of the moon, and the peculiar character of the sea. The latter was undergoing a rapid change, and the water seemed more than usually transparent. Although I could distinctly see the bottom, yet, heaving the lead, I found the ship in fifteen fathoms. The air now became intolerably hot, and was loaded with spiral exhalations similar to those arising from heat iron. As night came on, every breath of wind died away, and more entire calm it is impossible to conceive. The flame of a candle burned upon the poop without the least perceptible motion, and a long hair, held between the finger and thumb, hung without the possibility of detecting a vibration. However, as the captain said he could perceive no indication of danger, and as we were drifting in bodily to shore, he ordered the sails to be furled, and the anchor let go. No watch was set, and the crew, consisting principally of Malays, stretched themselves deliberately upon deck. I went below—not without a full presentiment of evil. Indeed, every appearance warranted me in apprehending a Simoom. I told the captain my fears; but he paid no attention to what I said, and left me without deigning to give a reply. My uneasiness, however, prevented me from sleeping, and about midnight I went upon deck. As I placed my foot upon the upper step of the companion-ladder, I was startled by a loud, humming noise, like that occasioned by the rapid revolution of a mill-wheel, and before I could ascertain its meaning, I found the ship quivering to its centre. In the next instant, a wilderness of foam hurled us upon our beam-ends, and, rushing over us fore and aft, swept the entire decks from stem to stern.

The extreme fury of the blast proved, in a great measure, the salvation of the ship. Although completely waterlogged, yet, as her masts had gone by the board, she rose, after a minute, heavily from the sea, and, staggering awhile beneath the immense pressure of the tempest, finally righted.

By what miracle I escaped destruction, it is impossible to say. Stunned by the shock of the water, I found myself, upon recovery, jammed in between the stern-post and rudder. With great difficulty I gained my feet, and looking dizzily around, was, at first, struck with the idea of our being among breakers; so terrific, beyond the wildest imagination, was the whirlpool of mountainous and foaming ocean within which we were engulfed. After a while, I heard the voice of an old Swede, who had shipped with us at the moment of our leaving port. I hallooed to him with all my strength, and presently he came reeling aft. We soon discovered that we were the sole survivors of the accident. All on deck, with the exception of ourselves, had been swept overboard; the captain and mates must have perished as they slept, for the cabins were deluged with water. Without assistance, we could expect to do little for the security of the ship, and our exertions were at first paralyzed by the momentary expectation of going down. Our cable had, of course, parted like packthread, at the first breath of the hurricane, or we should have been instantaneously overwhelmed. We scudded with frightful velocity before the sea, and the water made clear breaches over us. The framework of our stern was shattered excessively, and, in almost every respect, we had received considerable injury; but to our extreme joy we found the pumps unchoked, and that we had made no great shifting of our ballast. The main fury of the blast had already blown over, and we apprehended little danger from the violence of the wind; but we looked forward to its total cessation with dismay; well believing, that, in our shattered condition, we should inevitably perish in the tremendous swell which would ensue. But this very just apprehension seemed by no means likely to be soon verified. For five entire days and nights—during which our only subsistence was a small quantity of jaggeree, procured with great difficulty from the forecastle—the hulk flew at a rate defying computation, before rapidly succeeding flaws of wind, which, without equalling the first violence of the Simoom, were still more terrific than any tempest I had before encountered. Our course for the first four days was, with trifling variations, S.E. and by S.; and we must have run down the coast of New Holland. On the fifth day the cold became extreme, although the wind had hauled round a point more to the northward. The sun arose with a sickly yellow lustre, and clambered a very few degrees above the horizon—emitting no decisive light. There were no clouds apparent, yet the wind was upon the increase, and blew with a fitful and unsteady fury. About noon, as nearly as we could guess, our attention was again arrested by the appearance of the sun. It gave out no light, properly so called, but a dull and sullen glow without reflection, as if all its rays were polarized. Just before sinking within the turgid sea, its central fires suddenly went out, as if hurriedly extinguished by some unaccountable power. It was a dim, sliverlike rim, alone, as it rushed down the unfathomable ocean.

We waited in vain for the arrival of the sixth day—that day to me has not arrived—to the Swede, never did arrive. Thenceforward we were enshrouded in patchy darkness, so that we could not have seen an object at twenty paces from the ship. Eternal night continued to envelop us, all unrelieved by the phosphoric sea-brilliancy to which we had been accustomed in the tropics. We observed too, that, although the tempest continued to rage with unabated violence, there was no longer to be discovered the usual appearance of surf, or foam, which had hitherto attended us. All around were horror, and thick gloom, and a black sweltering desert of ebony. Superstitious terror crept by degrees into the spirit of the old Swede, and my own soul was wrapped up in silent wonder. We neglected all care of the ship, as worse than useless, and securing ourselves, as well as possible, to the stump of the mizen-mast, looked out bitterly into the world of ocean. We had no means of calculating time, nor could we form any guess of our situation. We were, however, well aware of having made farther to the southward than any previous navigators, and felt great amazement at not meeting with the usual impediments of ice. In the meantime every moment threatened to be our last—every mountainous billow hurried to overwhelm us. The swell surpassed anything I had imagined possible, and that we were not instantly buried is a miracle. My companion spoke of the lightness of our cargo, and reminded me of the excellent qualities of our ship; but I could not help feeling the utter hopelessness of hope itself, and prepared myself gloomily for that death which I thought nothing could defer beyond an hour, as, with every knot of way the ship made, the swelling of the black stupendous seas became more dismally appalling. At times we gasped for breath at an elevation beyond the albatross—at times became dizzy with the velocity of our descent into some watery hell, where the air grew stagnant, and no sound disturbed the slumbers of the kraken.

We were at the bottom of one of these abysses, when a quick scream from my companion broke fearfully upon the night. "See! see!" cried he, shrieking in my ears, "Almighty God! see! see!" As he spoke, I became aware of a dull, sullen glare of red light which streamed down the sides of the vast chasm where we lay, and threw a fitful brilliancy upon our deck. Casting my eyes upwards, I beheld a spectacle which froze the current of my blood. At a terrific height directly above us, and upon the very verge of the precipitous descent, hovered a gigantic ship of, perhaps, four thousand tons. Although upreared upon the summit of a wave more than a hundred times her own altitude, her apparent size exceeded that of any ship of the line or East Indiaman in existence. Her huge hull was of a deep dingy black, unrelieved by any of the customary carvings of a ship. A single row of brass cannon protruded from her open ports, and dashed from their polished surfaces the fires of innumerable battlelanterns, which swung to and fro about her rigging. But what mainly inspired us with horror and astonishment, was that she bore up under a press of sail in the very teeth of that supernatural sea, and of that ungovernable hurricane. When we first discovered her, her bows were alone to be seen, as she rose slowly from the dim and horrible gulf beyond her. For a moment of intense terror she paused upon the giddy pinnacle, as if in contemplation of her own sublimity, then trembled and tottered, and—came down.

At this instant, I know not what sudden self-possession came over my spirit. Staggering as far aft as I could, I awaited fearlessly the ruin that was to overwhelm. Our own vessel was at length ceasing from her struggles, and sinking with her head to the sea. The shock of the descending mass struck her, consequently, in that portion of her frame which was already under water, and the inevitable result was to hurl me, with irresistible violence, upon the rigging of the stranger.

As I fell, the ship hove in stays, and went about; and to the confusion ensuing I attributed my escape from the notice of the crew. With little difficulty I made my way unperceived to the main hatchway, which was partially open, and soon found an opportunity of secreting myself in the hold. Why I did so I can hardly tell. An indefinite sense of awe, which at first sight of the navigators of the ship had taken hold of my mind, was perhaps the principle of my concealment. I was unwilling to trust myself with a race of people who had offered, to the cursory glance I had taken, so many points of vague novelty, doubt, and apprehension. I therefore thought proper to contrive a hiding-place in the hold. This I did by removing a small portion of the shiftingboards, in such a manner as to afford me a convenient retreat between the huge timbers of the ship.

I had scarcely completed my work, when a footstep in the hold forced me to make use of it. A man passed by my place of concealment with a feeble and unsteady gait. I could not see his face, but had an opportunity of observing his general appearance. There was about it an evidence of great age and infirmity. His knees tottered beneath a load of years, and his entire frame quivered under the burthen. He muttered to himself, in a low broken tone, some words of a language which I could not understand, and groped in a corner among a pile of singularlooking instruments, and decayed charts of navigation. His manner was a wild mixture of the peevishness of second childhood, and the solemn dignity of a God. He at length went on deck, and I saw him no more.

~

A feeling, for which I have no name, has taken possession of my soul—a sensation which will admit of no analysis, to which the lessons of bygone times are inadequate, and for which I fear futurity itself will offer me no key. To a mind constituted like my own, the latter consideration is an evil. I shall never—I know that I shall never—be satisfied with regard to the nature of my conceptions. Yet it is not wonderful that these conceptions are indefinite, since they have their origin in sources so utterly novel. A new sense—a new entity is added to my soul.

~

It is long since I first trod the deck of this terrible ship, and the rays of my destiny are, I think, gathering to a focus. Incomprehensible men! Wrapped up in meditations of a kind which I cannot divine, they pass me by unnoticed. Concealment is utter folly on my part, for the people will not see. It was but just now that I passed directly before the eyes of the mate—it was no long while ago that I ventured into the captain's own private cabin, and took thence the materials with which I write, and have written. I shall from time to time continue this Journal. It is true that I may not find an opportunity of transmitting it to the world, but I will not fail to make the endeavour. At the last moment I will enclose the MS. in a bottle, and cast it within the sea.

---

An incident has occurred which has given me new room for meditation. Are such things the operation of ungoverned Chance? I had ventured upon deck and thrown myself down, without attracting any notice, among a pile of ratlin-stuff and old sails in the bottom of the yawl. While musing upon the singularity of my fate, I unwittingly daubed with a tarbrush the edges of a neatlyfolded studding-sail which lay near me on a barrel. The studdingsail is now bent upon the ship, and the thoughtless touches of the brush are spread out into the word DISCOVERY.

I have made many observations lately upon the structure of the vessel. Although well armed, she is not, I think, a ship of war. Her rigging, build, and general equipment, all negative a supposition of this kind. What she is not, I can easily perceive—what she is I fear it is impossible to say. I know not how it is, but in scrutinizing her strange model and singular cast of spars, her huge size and overgrown suits of canvas, her severely simple bow and antiquated stern, there will occasionally flash across my mind a sensation of familiar things, and there is always mixed up with such indistinct shadows of recollection, an unaccountable memory of old foreign chronicles and ages long ago.

---

I have been looking at the timbers of the ship. She is built of a material to which I am a stranger. There is a peculiar character about the wood which strikes me as rendering it unfit for the purpose to which it has been applied. I mean its extreme porousness, considered independently by the worm-eaten condition which is a consequence of navigation in these seas, and apart from the rottenness attendant upon age. It will appear perhaps an observation somewhat overcurious, but this wood would have every characteristic of Spanish oak, if Spanish oak were distended by any unnatural means.

In reading the above sentence a curious apothegm of an old weatherbeaten Dutch navigator comes full upon my recollection. "It is as sure," he was wont to say, when any doubt was entertained of his veracity, "as sure as there is a sea where the ship itself will grow in bulk like the living body of the seaman."

❦

About an hour ago, I made bold to thrust myself among a group of the crew. They paid me no manner of attention, and, although I stood in the very midst of them all, seemed utterly unconscious of my presence. Like the one I had at first seen in the hold, they all bore about them the marks of a hoary old age. Their knees trembled with infirmity; their shoulders were bent double with decrepitude; their shriveled skins rattled in the wind; their voices were low, tremulous and broken; their eyes glistened with the rheum of years; and their gray hairs streamed terribly in the tempest. Around them, on every part of the deck, lay scattered mathematical instruments of the most quaint and obsolete construction.

<hr>

I mentioned some time ago the bending of a studdingsail. From that period the ship, being thrown dead off the wind, has continued her terrific course due south, with every rag of canvas packed upon her, from her trucks to her lower studdingsail booms, and rolling every moment her topgallant yardarms into the most appalling hell of water which it can enter into the mind of a man to imagine. I have just left the deck, where I find it impossible to maintain a footing, although the crew seem to experience little inconvenience. It appears to me a miracle of miracles that our enormous bulk is not swallowed up at once and forever. We are surely doomed to hover continually upon the brink of Eternity, without taking a final plunge into the abyss. From billows a thousand times more stupendous than any I have ever seen, we glide away with the facility of the arrowy seagull; and the colossal waters rear their heads above us like demons of the deep, but like demons confined to simple threats and forbidden to destroy. I am led to attribute these frequent escapes to the only natural cause which can account for such effect. I must suppose the ship to be within the influence of some strong current, or impetuous undertow.

<hr>

I have seen the captain face to face, and in his own cabin—but, as I expected, he paid me no attention. Although in his appearance there is, to a casual observer, nothing which might bespeak him more or less than man—still a feeling of irrepressible reverence and awe mingled with the sensation of wonder with which I regarded him. In stature he is nearly my own height; that is, about five feet eight inches. He is of a wellknit and compact frame of body, neither robust nor remarkably otherwise. But it is the singularity of the expression which reigns upon the face—it is the intense, the wonderful, the thrilling evidence of old age, so utter, so extreme, which excites within my spirit a sense—a sentiment ineffable. His forehead, although little wrinkled, seems to bear upon it the stamp of a myriad of years. His gray hairs are records of the past, and his grayer eyes are Sybils of the future. The cabin floor was thickly strewn with strange, ironclasped folios, and mouldering instruments of science, and obsolete longforgotten charts. His head was bowed down upon his hands, and he pored, with a fiery unquiet eye, over a paper which I took to be a commission, and which, at all events, bore the signature of a monarch. He muttered to himself, as did the first seaman whom I saw in the hold, some low peevish syllables of a foreign tongue, and although the speaker was close at my elbow, his voice seemed to reach my ears from the distance of a mile.

The ship and all in it are imbued with the spirit of Eld. The crew glide to and fro like the ghosts of buried centuries; their eyes have an eager and uneasy meaning; and when their fingers fall athwart my path in the wild glare of the battle-lanterns, I feel as I have never felt before, although I have been all my life a dealer in antiquities, and have imbibed the shadows of fallen columns at Balbec, and Tadmor, and Persepolis, until my very soul has become a ruin.

⁓

When I look around me I feel ashamed of my former apprehensions. If I trembled at the blast which has hitherto attended us, shall I not stand aghast at a warring of wind and ocean, to convey any idea of which the words tornado and simoom are trivial and ineffective? All in the immediate vicinity of the ship is the blackness of eternal night, and a chaos of foamless water; but, about a league on either side of us, may be seen, indistinctly and at intervals, stupendous ramparts of ice, towering away into the desolate sky, and looking like the walls of the universe.

⁓

As I imagined, the ship proves to be in a current; if that appellation can properly be given to a tide which, howling and shrieking by the white ice, thunders on to the southward with a velocity like the headlong dashing of a cataract.

⁓

To conceive the horror of my sensations is, I presume, utterly impossible; yet a curiosity to penetrate the mysteries of these awful regions, predominates even over my despair, and will reconcile me to the most hideous aspect of death. It is evident that we are hurrying onwards to some exciting knowledge—some never-tobeimparted secret, whose attainment is destruction. Perhaps this current leads us to the southern pole itself. It must be confessed that a supposition apparently so wild has every probability in its favor.

～ ～

The crew pace the deck with unquiet and tremulous step; but there is upon their countenances an expression more of the eagerness of hope than of the apathy of despair.

In the meantime the wind is still in our poop, and, as we carry a crowd of canvas, the ship is at times lifted bodily from out the sea—Oh, horror upon horror! the ice opens suddenly to the right, and to the left, and we are whirling dizzily, in immense concentric circles, round and round the borders of a gigantic amphitheatre, the summit of whose walls is lost in the darkness and the distance. But little time will be left me to ponder upon my destiny—the circles rapidly grow small—we are plunging madly within the grasp of the whirlpool—and amid a roaring, and bellowing, and thundering of ocean and of tempest, the ship is quivering, oh God! and—going down.

～ ～

NOTE. The "MS. Found in a Bottle," was originally published in 1831, and it was not until many years afterwards that I became acquainted with the maps of Mercator, in which the ocean is represented as rushing, by four mouths, into the (northern) Polar Gulf, to be absorbed into the bowels of the earth; the Pole itself being represented by a black rock, towering to a prodigious height.

# The Unfortunate Voyage

## *Master John Hawkins*

THE SHIPS DEPARTED FROM PLYMOUTH THE 2ND DAY OF
October, anno 1567, and had reasonable weather until the sev-
enth day, at which time, forty leagues north from Cape Finis-
terre, there arose an extreme storm which continued four days,
in such sort that the fleet was dispersed and all our great boats
lost, and the *Jesus*, our chief ship, in such case as not thought
able to serve the voyage.

Whereupon in the same storm we set our course homeward, determining to give over the voyage; but the 11th day of
the same month the wind changed, with fair weather, whereby
we were animated to follow our enterprise, and so did, directing
our course to the islands of Grand Canaries, where, according
to an order before prescribed, all our ships, before dispersed,
met in one of those islands, called Gomera, where we took
water, and departed from thence the 4th day of November
towards the coast of Guinea, and arrived at Cape Verde the
18th of November, where we landed one hundred and fifty
men, hoping to obtain some negroes; where we got but few,
and those with great hurt and damage to our men, which

chiefly proceeded from their envenomed arrows; although in the beginning they seemed to be but small hurts, yet there hardly escaped any that had blood drawn of them but died in strange sort, with their mouths shut, some ten days before they died, and after their wounds were whole; where I myself had one of the greatest wounds, yet, thanks be to God, escaped.

From thence we passed the time upon the coast of Guinea, searching with all diligence the rivers from Rio Grande unto Sierra Leone till the 12th of January, in which time we had not gotten together a hundred and fifty negroes: yet, notwithstanding, the sickness of our men and the late time of the year commanded us away: and thus having nothing wherewith to seek the coast of the West Indies, I was with the rest of our company in consultation to go to the coast of the Myne, hoping there to have obtained some gold for our wares, and thereby to have defrayed our charge. But even in that present instant there came to us a negro sent from a king oppressed by other kings, his neighbours, desiring our aid, with promise that as many negroes as by these wars might be obtained, as well of his part as of ours, should be at our pleasure.

Whereupon we concluded to give aid, and sent one hundred and twenty of our men, which the 15th of January assaulted a town of the negroes of our allies' adversaries which had in it 8,000 inhabitants, and very strongly impaled and fenced after their manner, but it was so well defended that our men prevailed not, but lost six men, and forty hurt, so that our men sent forthwith to me for more help; whereupon, considering that the good success of this enterprise might highly further the commodity of our voyage, I went myself, and with the help of the king of our side assaulted the town, both by land and sea, and very hardly with fire (their houses being covered with dry palm leaves) obtained the town, and put the inhabitants to flight, where we took 250 persons, men, women, and children, and by our friend the king of our side there were taken 600 prisoners, whereof we hoped to have our choice, but the negro (in which nation is seldom or never found truth) meant nothing less; for that night he removed his camp and prisoners, so that we were fain to content us with those few which we had gotten ourselves.

Now had we obtained between four and five hundred negroes, wherewith we thought it somewhat reasonable to seek the coast of the West Indies, and there, for our negroes, and other our merchandise, we hoped to obtain whereof to countervail our charges with some gains, whereunto we proceeded with all diligence, furnished our watering, took fuel, and departed the coast of Guinea, the third of February, continuing at the sea with a passage more hard than before hath been accustomed, till the 27th day of March, which day we had sight of an island, called Dominique, upon the coast of the West Indies, in fourteen degrees: from thence we coasted from place to place, making our traffic with the Spaniards as we might, somewhat hardly, because the king had straitly commanded all his governors in those parts by no means to suffer any trade to be made with us; notwithstanding we had reasonable trade, and courteous entertainment, from the Isle of Marguerite and Cartagena, without anything greatly worth the noting, saving at Cape de la Vela, in a town called Rio de la Hacha, from whence come all the pearls.

The treasurer who had the charge there would by no means agree to any trade, or suffer us to take water. He had fortified his town with divers bulwarks in all places where it might be entered, and furnished himself with a hundred harquebusiers, so that he thought by famine to have enforced us to have put on land our negroes, of which purpose he had not greatly failed unless we had by force entered the town; which (after we could by no means obtain his favour) we were enforced to do, and so with two hundred men brake in upon their bulwarks, and entered the town with the loss only of eleven men of our parts, and no hurt done to the Spaniards, because after their volley of shot discharged, they all fled.

Thus having the town, with some circumstance, as partly by the Spaniards' desire of negroes, and partly by friendship of the treasurer, we obtained a secret trade; whereupon the Spaniards resorted to us by night, and bought of us to the number of two hundred negroes: in all other places where we traded the Spaniard inhabitants were glad of us, and traded willingly. At Cartagena, the last town we thought to have seen on the coast, we could by no means obtain to deal with any Spaniard, the governor was so strait, and because our trade was so near finished, we thought not good either to adventure any landing or to detract further time, but in peace departed from thence the 24th of July, hoping to have escaped the time of their storms, which then soon after began to reign, the which they call Furicanos; but passing by the west end of Cuba, towards the coast of Florida, there happened to us, the twelfth day of August, an extreme storm, which continued by the space of four days, which so beat the *Jesus*, that we cut down all her higher buildings; her rudder also was sore shaken, and, withal, was in so extreme a leak, that we were rather upon the point to leave her than to keep her any longer; yet, hoping to bring all to good pass, sought the coast of Florida, where we found no place nor haven for our ships, because of the shallowness of the coast.

Thus, being in greater despair, and taken with a new storm, which continued another three days, we were enforced to take for our succour the port which serveth the city of Mexico, called St. John de Ullua, which standeth in nineteen degrees, in seeking of which port we took in our way three ships, which carried passengers to the number of one hundred, which passengers we hoped should be a means to us the better to obtain victuals for our money and a quiet place for the repairing of our fleet. Shortly after this, the sixteenth of September, we entered the port of St. John de Ullua, and in our entry, the Spaniards thinking us to be the fleet of Spain, the chief officers of the country came aboard us, which, being deceived of their expectation, were greatly dismayed, but immediately, when they saw our demand was nothing but victuals, were recomforted.

I found also in the same port twelve ships, which had in them, by the report, 200,000 livres in gold and silver, all which (being in my possession with the King's island, as also the passengers before in my way thitherward stayed) I set at liberty, without the taking from them the weight of a groat; only, because I would not be delayed of my despatch, I stayed two men of estimation, and sent post immediately to Mexico, which was two hundred miles from us, to the presidents and Council there, showing them of our arrival there by the force of weather, and the necessity of the repair of our ship and victuals, which wants we required, as friends to King Philip, to be furnished of for our money, and that the presidents and council there should, with all convenient speed, take order that at the arrival of the Spanish fleet, which was daily looked for, there might no cause of quarrel rise between us and them, but, for the better maintenance of amity, their commandment might be had in that behalf. This message being sent away the 16th day of September, at night, being the very day of our arrival, in the next morning, which was the sixteenth day of the same month, we saw open of the haven thirteen great ships, and understanding them to be the fleet of Spain, I sent immediately to advertise the general of the fleet of my being there, doing him to understand that, before I would suffer them to enter the port, there should be some order of conditions pass between us for our safe being there and maintenance of peace.

Now, it is to be understood that this port is a little island of stones, not three feet above the water in the highest place, and but a bowshot of length any way. This island standeth from the mainland two bowshots or more. Also it is to be understood that there is not in all this coast any other place for ships to arrive in safety, because the north wind hath there such violence, that, unless the ships be very safely moored, with their anchors fastened upon this island, there is no remedy for these north winds but death; also, the place of the haven was so little, that of necessity the ships must ride one aboard the other, so that we could not give place to them nor they to us; and here I began to bewail the which after followed: "For now," said I, "I am in two dangers, and forced to receive the one of them." That was, either I must have kept out the fleet from entering the port (the which, with God's help, I was very well able to do), or else suffer them to enter in with their accustomed treason, which they never fail to execute where they may have opportunity, or circumvent it by any means. If I had kept them out, then had there been present shipwreck of all the fleet, which amounted in value to six millions, which was in value of our money 1,800,000 livres, which I considered I was not able to answer, fearing the Queen's Majesty's indignation in so weighty a matter. Thus with myself revolving the doubts, I thought rather better to abide the jutt of the uncertainty than the certainty. The uncertain doubt was their treason, which by good policy I hoped might be prevented; and therefore, as choosing the least mischief, I proceeded to conditions.

Now was our first messenger come and returned from the fleet with report of the arrival of a Viceroy, so that he had authority, both in all this province of Mexico (otherwise called Nova Hispania) and in the sea, who sent us word that we should send our conditions, which of his part should (for the better maintenance of amity between the princes) be both favourably granted and faithfully performed, with many fair words how, passing the coast of the Indies, he had understood of our honest behaviour towards the inhabitants, where we had to do as well elsewhere as in the same port, the which I let pass, thus following our demand. We required victual for our money, and licence to sell as much ware as might furnish our wants, and that there might be of either part twelve gentlemen as hostage for the maintenance of peace, and that the island, for our better safety, might be in our own possession during our abode there, and such ordnance as was planted in the same island, which was eleven pieces of brass, and that no Spaniard might land in the island with any kind of weapon.

These conditions at the first he somewhat misliked—chiefly the guard of the island to be in our own keeping; which, if they had had, we had soon known our fate; for with the first north wind they had cut our cables, and our ships had gone ashore; but in the end he concluded to our request, bringing the twelve hostages to ten, which with all speed on either part were received, with a writing from the Viceroy, signed with his hand and sealed with his seal, of all the conditions concluded, and forthwith a trumpet blown, with commandment that none of either part should inviolate the peace upon pain of death; and, further, it was concluded that the two generals of the fleet should meet, and give faith each to other for the performance of the promises, which was so done.

Thus, at the end of three days, all was concluded, and the fleet entered the port, saluting one another as the manner of the sea doth require. Thus, as I said before, Thursday we entered the port, Friday we saw the fleet, and on Monday, at night, they entered the port; then we laboured two days, placing the English ships by themselves, and the Spanish ships by themselves, the captains of each part, and inferior men of their parts, promising great amity of all sides; which, even as with all fidelity was meant of our part, though the Spanish meant nothing less of their parts, but from the mainland had furnished themselves with a supply of men to the number of one thousand, and meant the next Thursday, being the 23rd of September, at dinnertime, to set upon us of all sides. The same Thursday, the treason being at hand, some appearance showed, as shifting of weapons from ship to ship, planting and bending of ordnance from the ship to the island where our men were, passing to and fro of companies of men more than required for their necessary business, and many other ill likelihoods, which caused us to have a vehement suspicion, and therewithal sent to the Viceroy to inquire what was meant by it, which sent immediately straight commandment to unplant all things suspicious, and also sent word that he, in the faith of a Viceroy, would be our defence from all villainies.

Yet we, not being satisfied with this answer, because we suspected a great number of men to be hid in a great ship of nine hundred tons, which was moored next unto the *Minion*, sent again unto the Viceroy the master of the *Jesus*, which had the Spanish tongue, and required to be satisfied if any such thing were or not; on which the Viceroy, seeing that the treason must be discovered, forthwith stayed our master, blew the trumpet, and of all sides set upon us. Our men which were on guard ashore, being stricken with sudden fear, gave place, fled, and sought to recover succour of the ships; the Spaniards, being before provided for the purpose, landed in all places in multitudes from their ships, which they could easily do without boats, and slew all our men ashore without mercy, a few of them escaping aboard the *Jesus*. The great ship which had, by the estimation, three hundred men placed in her secretly, immediately fell aboard the *Minion*, which, by God's appointment, in the time of the suspicion we had, which was only one halfhour, the *Minion* was made ready to avoid, and so, loosing her headfasts, and hailing away by the sternfasts, she was gotten out; thus, with God's help, she defended the violence of the first brunt of these three hundred men.

The *Minion* being passed out, they came aboard the *Jesus*, which also, with very much ado and the loss of many of our men, were defended and kept out. Then were there also two other ships that assaulted the *Jesus* at the same instant, so that she had hard work getting loose; but yet, with some time, we had cut our headfasts, and gotten out by the sternfasts. Now, when the *Jesus* and the *Minion* were gotten two shiplengths from the Spanish fleet, the fight began hot on all sides, so that within one hour the admiral of the Spaniards was supposed to be sunk, their vice-admiral burned, and one other of their principal ships supposed to be sunk, so that the ships were little to annoy us.

Then is it to be understood that all the ordnance upon the island was in the Spaniards' hands, which did us so great annoyance that it cut all the masts and yards of the *Jesus* in such sort, that there was no hope to carry her away; also it sank our small ships, whereupon we determined to place the *Jesus* on that side of the *Minion*, that she might abide all the battery from the land, and so be a defence for the *Minion* till night, and then to take such relief of victual and other necessaries from the *Jesus* as the time would suffer us, and to leave her.

As we were thus determining, and had placed the *Minion* from the shot of the land, suddenly the Spaniards had fired two great ships which were coming directly to us, and having no means to avoid the fire, it bred among our men a marvellous fear, so that some said, "Let us depart with the *Minion*," and others said, "Let us see whether the wind will carry the fire from us." But to be short, the *Minion*'s men, which had always their sails in a readiness, thought to make sure work, and so without either consent of the captain or master, cut their sail, so that very hardly I was received into the *Minion*.

The most part of the men that were left alive in the *Jesus* made shift and followed the *Minion* in a small boat; the rest, which the little boat was not able to receive, were enforced to abide the mercy of the Spaniards (which I doubt was very little); so with the *Minion* only, and the *Judith* (a small barque of fifty tons) we escaped, which barque the same night forsook us in our great misery. We were now removed with the *Minion* from the Spanish ships two bowshots, and there rode all that night. The next morning we recovered an island a mile from the Spaniards, where there took us a north wind, and being left only with two anchors and two cables (for in this conflict we lost three cables and two anchors), we thought always upon death, which ever was present, but God preserved us to a longer time.

The weather waxed reasonable, and the Saturday we set sail, and having a great number of men and little victual, our hope of life waxed less and less. Some desired to yield to the Spaniards, some rather desired to obtain a place where they might give themselves to the infidels; and some had rather abide, with a little pittance, the mercy of God at sea. So thus, with many sorrowful hearts, we wandered in an unknown sea by the space of fourteen days, till hunger enforced us to seek the land; for hides were thought very good meat; rats, cats, mice, and dogs, none escaped that might be gotten; parrots and monkeys, that were had in great prize, were thought there very profitable if they served the turn of one dinner. Thus in the end, on the 8th day of October, we came to the land in the bottom of the same bay of Mexico, in twentythree degrees and a half, where we hoped to have found habitations of the Spaniards, relief of victuals, and place for the repair of our ship, which was so sore beaten with shot from our enemies, and bruised with shooting of our own ordnance, that our weary and weak arms were scarce able to defend and keep out the water. But all things happened to the contrary, for we found neither people, victual, nor haven of relief, but a place where, having fair weather, with some peril we might land a boat. Our people, being forced with hunger, desired to be set aland, whereunto I concluded. And such as were willing to land I put apart, and such as were desirous to go homewards I put apart, so that they were indifferently parted, a hundred of one side and a hundred of the other side. These hundred men we set on land with all diligence, in this little place aforesaid, which being landed, we determined there to refresh our water, and so with our little remain of victuals to take the sea.

The next day, having on land with me fifty of our hundred men that remained, for the speedier preparing of our water aboard, there arose an extreme storm, so that in three days we could by no means repair our ships. The ship also was in such peril that every hour we looked for shipwreck.

But yet God again had mercy on us, and sent fair weather. We got aboard our water, and departed the 16th day of October, after which day we had fair and prosperous weather till the 16th day of November, which day, God be praised, we were clear from the coast of the Indians and out of the channel and gulf of Bahama, which is between the cape of Florida and the islands of Cuba. After this, growing near to the cold country, our men, being oppressed with famine, died continually, and they that were left grew into such weakness that we were scarcely able to manoeuvre our ship, and the wind being always ill for us to recover England, determined to go to Galicia, in Spain, with intent there to relieve our company and other extreme wants. And being arrived the last day of December, in a place near unto Vigo, called Pontevedra, our men, with excess of fresh meat, grew into miserable diseases, and died a great part of them. This matter was borne out as long as it might be, but in the end, although there was none of our men suffered to go on land, yet by access of the Spaniards our feebleness was known to them.

Whereupon they ceased not to seek by all means to betray us, but with all speed possible we departed to Vigo, where we had some help of certain English ships, and twelve fresh men, wherewith we repaired our wants as we might, and departing the 30th day of January, 1568, arrived in Mount's Bay in Cornwall the 25th of the same month, praised be God therefore.

If all the misery and troublesome affairs of this sorrowful voyage should be perfectly and thoroughly written, there should need a painful man with his pen, and as great time as he had that wrote the "Lives and Deaths of the Martyrs."

# The Seige of the Round-House

## *Robert Louis Stevenson*

BUT NOW OUR TIME OF TRUCE WAS COME TO AN END. THOSE on deck had waited for my coming till they grew impatient; and scarce had Alan spoken, when the captain showed face in the open door.

"Stand!" cried Alan, and pointed his sword at him. The captain stood, indeed; but he neither winced nor drew back a foot.

"A naked sword?" says he. "This is a strange return for hospitality."

"Do ye see me?" said Alan. "I am come of kings; I bear a king's name. My badge is the oak. Do ye see my sword? It has slashed the heads off mair Whigamores than you have toes upon your feet. Call up your vermin to your back, sir, and fall on! The sooner the clash begins, the sooner ye'll taste this steel throughout your vitals."

The captain said nothing to Alan, but he looked over at me with an ugly look. "David," said he, "I'll mind this"; and the sound of his voice went through me with a jar.

Next moment he was gone.

"And now," said Alan, "let your hand keep your head, for the grip is coming."

Alan drew a dirk, which he held in his left hand in case they should run in under his sword. I, on my part, clambered up into the berth with an armful of pistols and something of a heavy heart, and set open the window where I was to watch. It was a small part of the deck that I could overlook, but enough for our purpose. The sea had gone down, and the wind was steady and kept the sails quiet; so that there was a great stillness in the ship, in which I made sure I heard the sound of muttering voices. A little after, and there came a clash of steel upon the deck, by which I knew they were dealing out the cutlasses and one had been let fall; and after that, silence again.

I do not know if I was what you call afraid; but my heart beat like a bird's, both quick and little; and there was a dimness came before my eyes which I continually rubbed away, and which continually returned. As for hope, I had none; but only a darkness of despair and a sort of anger against all the world that made me long to sell my life as dear as I was able. I tried to pray, I remember, but that same hurry of my mind, like a man running, would not suffer me to think upon the words; and my chief wish was to have the thing begin and be done with it.

It came all of a sudden when it did, with a rush of feet and a roar, and then a shout from Alan, and a sound of blows and some one crying out as if hurt. I looked back over my shoulder, and saw Mr. Shuan in the doorway, crossing blades with Alan.

"That's him that killed the boy!" I cried.

"Look to your window!" said Alan; and as I turned back to my place, I saw him pass his sword through the mate's body.

It was none too soon for me to look to my own part; for my head was scarce back at the window, before five men, carrying a spare yard for a battering-ram, ran past me and took post to drive the door in. I had never fired with a pistol in my life, and not often with a gun; far less against a fellowcreature. But it was now or never; and just as they swang the yard, I cried out: "Take that!" and shot into their midst.

I must have hit one of them, for he sang out and gave back a step, and the rest stopped as if a little disconcerted. Before they had time to recover, I sent another ball over their heads; and at my third shot (which went as wide as the second) the whole party threw down the yard and ran for it.

Then I looked round again into the deckhouse. The whole place was full of the smoke of my own firing, just as my ears seemed to be burst with the noise of the shots. But there was Alan, standing as before; only now his sword was running blood to the hilt, and himself so swelled with triumph and fallen into so fine an attitude, that he looked to be invincible. Right before him on the floor was Mr. Shuan, on his hands and knees; the blood was pouring from his mouth, and he was sinking slowly lower, with a terrible, white face; and just as I looked, some of those from behind caught hold of him by the heels and dragged him bodily out of the roundhouse. I believe he died as they were doing it.

"There's one of your Whigs for ye!" cried Alan; and then turning to me, he asked if I had done much execution.

I told him I had winged one, and thought it was the captain.

"And I've settled two," says he. "No, there's not enough blood let; they'll be back again. To your watch, David. This was but a dram before meat."

I settled back to my place, re-charging the three pistols I had fired, and keeping watch with both eye and ear.

Our enemies were disputing not far off upon the deck, and that so loudly that I could hear a word or two above the washing of the seas.

"It was Shuan bauchled it," I heard one say.

And another answered him with a "Wheesht, man! He's paid the piper."

After that the voices fell again into the same muttering as before. Only now, one person spoke most of the time, as though laying down a plan, and first one and then another answered him briefly, like men taking orders. By this, I made sure they were coming on again, and told Alan.

"It's what we have to pray for," said he. "Unless we can give them a good distaste of us, and be done with it, there'll be nae sleep for either you or me. But this time, mind, they'll be in earnest."

By this, my pistols were ready, and there was nothing to do but listen and wait. While the brush lasted, I had not the time to think if I was frighted; but now, when all was still again, my mind ran upon nothing else. The thought of the sharp swords and the cold steel was strong in me; and presently, when I began to hear stealthy steps and a brushing of men's clothes against the roundhouse wall, and knew they were taking their places in the dark, I could have found it in my mind to cry out aloud.

All this was upon Alan's side; and I had begun to think my share of the fight was at an end, when I heard some one drop softly on the roof above me. Then there came a single call on the seapipe, and that was the signal. A knot of them made one rush of it, cutlass in hand, against the door; and at the same moment, the glass of the skylight was dashed in a thousand pieces, and a man leaped through and landed on the floor. Before he got his feet, I had clapped a pistol to his back, and might have shot him, too; only at the touch of him (and him alive) my whole flesh misgave me, and I could no more pull the trigger than I could have flown.

He had dropped his cutlass as he jumped, and when he felt the pistol, whipped straight round and laid hold of me, roaring out an oath; and at that either my courage came again, or I grew so much afraid as came to the same thing; for I gave a shriek and shot him in the midst of the body. He gave the most horrible, ugly groan and fell to the floor. The foot of a second fellow, whose legs were dangling through the skylight, struck me at the same time upon the head; and at that I snatched another pistol and shot this one through the thigh, so that he slipped through and tumbled in a lump on his companion's body. There was no talk of missing, any more than there was time to aim; I clapped the muzzle to the very place and fired. I might have stood and stared at them for long, but I heard Alan shout as if for help, and that brought me to my senses. He had kept the door so long; but one of the seamen, while he was engaged with others, had run in under his guard and caught him about the body. Alan was dirking him with his left hand, but the fellow clung like a leech. Another had broken in and had his cutlass raised. The door was thronged with their faces. I thought we were lost, and catching up my cutlass, fell on them in flank.

But I had not time to be of help. The wrestler dropped at last; and Alan, leaping back to get his distance, ran upon the others like a bull, roaring as he went. They broke before him like water, turning, and running, and falling one against another in their haste. The sword in his hands flashed like quicksilver into the huddle of our fleeing enemies; and at every flash there came the scream of a man hurt. I was still thinking we were lost, when lo! they were all gone, and Alan was driving them along the deck as a sheepdog chases sheep.

Yet he was no sooner out than he was back again, being as cautious as he was brave; and meanwhile the seamen continued running and crying out as if he was still behind them; and we heard them tumble one upon another into the forecastle, and clapto the hatch upon the top.

The roundhouse was like a shambles; three were dead inside, another lay in his death agony across the threshold; and there were Alan and I victorious and unhurt.

He came up to me with open arms. "Come to my arms!" he cried, and embraced and kissed me hard upon both cheeks.

"David," said he, "I love you like a brother. And O, man," he cried in a kind of ecstasy, "am I no a bonny fighter?"

Thereupon he turned to the four enemies, passed his sword clean through each of them, and tumbled them out of doors one after the other. As he did so, he kept humming and singing and whistling to himself, like a man trying to recall an air; only what he was trying was to make one. All the while, the flush was in his face, and his eyes were as bright as a five-year-old child's with a new toy. And presently he sat down upon the table, sword in hand; the air that he was making all the time began to run a little clearer, and then clearer still; and then out he burst with a great voice into a Gaelic song.

I have translated it here, not in verse (of which I have no skill) but at least in the king's English. He sang it often afterwards, and the thing became popular; so that I have heard it, and had it explained to me, many's the time.

*This is the song of the sword of Alan;*
*The smith made it,*
*The fire set it;*
*Now it shines in the hand of Alan Breck.*

*Their eyes were many and bright,*
*Swift were they to behold,*
*Many the hands they guided:*
*The sword was alone.*

*The dun deer troop over the hill,*
*They are many, the hill is one;*
*The dun deer vanish,*
*The hill remains.*

*Come to me from the hills of heather,*
*Come from the isles of the sea.*
*O far-beholding eagles,*
*Here is your meat.*

Now this song which he made (both words and music) in the hour of our victory, is something less than just to me, who stood beside him in the tussle. Mr. Shuan and five more were either killed outright or thoroughly disabled; but of these, two fell by my hand, the two that came by the skylight. Four more were hurt, and of that number, one (and he not the least important) got his hurt from me. So that, altogether, I did my fair share both of the killing and the wounding, and might have claimed a place in Alan's verses. But poets have to think upon their rhymes; and in good prose talk, Alan always did me more than justice.

In the meanwhile, I was innocent of any wrong being done me. For not only I knew no word of the Gaelic; but what with the long suspense of the waiting, and the scurry and strain of our two spirts of fighting, and more than all, the horror I had of some of my own share in it, the thing was no sooner over than I was glad to stagger to a seat. There was that tightness on my chest that I could hardly breathe; the thought of the two men I had shot sat upon me like a nightmare; and all upon a sudden, and before I had a guess of what was coming, I began to sob and cry like any child.

Alan clapped my shoulder, and said I was a brave lad and wanted nothing but a sleep. "I'll take the first watch," said he. "Ye've done well by me, David, first and last; and I wouldn't lose you for all Appin—no, nor for Breadalbane."

So I made up my bed on the floor; and he took the first spell, pistol in hand and sword on knee, three hours by the captain's watch upon the wall. Then he roused me up, and I took my turn of three hours; before the end of which it was broad day, and a very quiet morning, with a smooth, rolling sea that tossed the ship and made the blood run to and fro on the round-house floor, and a heavy rain that drummed upon the roof. All my watch there was nothing stirring; and by the banging of the helm, I knew they had even no one at the tiller. Indeed (as I learned afterwards) there were so many of them hurt or dead, and the rest in so ill a temper, that Mr. Riach and the captain had to take turn and turn like Alan and me, or the brig might have gone ashore and nobody the wiser. It was a mercy the night had fallen so still, for the wind had gone down as soon as the rain began. Even as it was, I judged by the wailing of a great number of gulls that went crying and fishing round the ship, that she must have drifted pretty near the coast of one of the islands of the Hebrides; and at last, looking out of the door of the round-house, I saw the great stone hills of Skye on the right hand, and, a little more astern, the strange isle of Rum.

# Owen Chase's Narrative

## *Owen Chase*

I HAVE NOT BEEN ABLE TO RECUR TO THE SCENES WHICH ARE now to become the subject of description, although a considerable time has elapsed, without feeling a mingled emotion of horror and astonishment at the almost incredible destiny that has preserved me and my surviving companions from a terrible death. Frequently, in my reflections on the subject, even after this lapse of time, I find myself shedding tears of gratitude for our deliverance, and blessing God, by whose divine aid and protection we were conducted through a series of unparalleled suffering and distress, and restored to the bosoms of our families and friends. There is no knowing what a stretch of pain and misery the human mind is capable of contemplating, when it is wrought upon by the anxieties of preservation; nor what pangs and weaknesses the body is able to endure, until they are visited upon it; and when at last deliverance comes, when the dream of hope is realized, unspeakable gratitude takes possession of the soul, and tears of joy choke the utterance. We require to be taught in the school of some signal suffering, privation, and despair, the great lessons of constant dependence upon an almighty forbearance and mercy. In the midst of the wide ocean, at night, when the sight of the heavens was shut out, and the dark tempest came upon us, then it was that we felt ourselves ready to exclaim, "Heaven have mercy upon us, for nought but that can save us now." But I proceed to the recital. On the 20th of November (cruising in latitude 0° 40' S., longitude 119° 0' W.), a shoal of whales was discovered off the leebow.

The weather at this time was extremely fine and clear, and it was about 8 o'clock in the morning that the man at the mast-head gave the usual cry of, "There she blows." The ship was immediately put away, and we ran down in the direction for them. When we had got within half a mile of the place where they were observed, all our boats were lowered down, manned, and we started in pursuit of them. The ship, in the meantime, was brought to the wind, and the maintop-sail hove back, to wait for us. I had the harpoon in the second boat; the captain preceded me in the first. When I arrived at the spot where we calculated they were, nothing was at first to be seen. We lay on our oars in anxious expectation of discovering them come up somewhere near us. Presently one rose, and spouted a short distance ahead of my boat; I made all speed towards it, came up with, and struck it; feeling the harpoon in him, he threw himself, in agony, over towards the boat (which at that time was up alongside of him), and, giving a severe blow with his tail, struck the boat near the edge of the water, amidships, and stove a hole in her.

I immediately took up the boat hatchet, and cut the line, to disengage the boat from the whale, which by this time was running off with great velocity. I succeeded in getting clear of him, with the loss of the harpoon and line; and finding the water to pour fast in the boat, I hastily stuffed three or four of our jackets in the hole, ordered one man to keep constantly bailing, and the rest to pull immediately for the ship; we succeeded in keeping the boat free, and shortly gained the ship. The captain and the second mate, in the other two boats, kept up the pursuit, and soon struck another whale. They being at this time a considerable distance to leeward, I went forward, braced around the mainyard, and put the ship off in a direction for them; the boat which had been stove was immediately hoisted in, and after examining the hole, I found that I could, by nailing a piece of canvas over it, get her ready to join in a fresh pursuit, sooner than by lowering down the other remaining boat which belonged to the ship.

I accordingly turned her over upon the quarter, and was in the act of nailing on the canvas, when I observed a very large spermaceti whale, as well as I could just about eighty-five feet in length; he broke water about twenty rods off our weather-bow, and was lying quietly, with his head in a direction for the ship. He spouted two or three times, and then disappeared. In less than two or three seconds he came up again, about the length of the ship off, and made directly for us, at the rate of about three knots. The ship was then going with about the same velocity. His appearance and attitude gave us at first no alarm; but while I stood watching his movements, and observing him but a ship's length off, coming down for us with great celerity, I involuntarily ordered the boy at the helm to put it hard up; intending to sheer off and avoid him. The words were scarcely out of my mouth, before he came down upon us with full speed, and struck the ship with his head, just forward of the forechains; he gave us such an appalling and tremendous jar, as nearly threw us all on our faces. The ship brought up as suddenly and violently as if she had struck a rock, and trembled for a few seconds like a leaf.

We looked at each other with perfect amazement, deprived almost of the power of speech. Many minutes elapsed before we were able to realize the dreadful accident; during which time he passed under the ship, grazing her keel as he went along, came up alongside of her to leeward, and lay on the top of the water (apparently stunned with the violence of the blow) for the space of a minute; he then suddenly started off, in a direction to leeward. After a few moments' reflection, and recovering, in some measure, from the sudden consternation that had seized us, I of course concluded that he had stove a hole in the ship, and that it would be necessary to set the pumps going. Accordingly they were rigged, but had not been in operation more than one minute before I perceived the head of the ship to be gradually settling down in the water; I then ordered the signal to be set for the other boats, which, scarcely had I dispatched, before

I again discovered the whale, apparently in convulsions, on the top of the water, about one hundred rods to leeward. He was enveloped in the foam of the sea, that his continual and violent thrashing about in the water had created around him, and I could distinctly see him smite his jaws together, as if distracted with rage and fury. He remained a short time in this situation, and then started off with great velocity, across the bows of the ship, to windward. By this time the ship had settled down a considerable distance in the water, and I gave her up for lost.

I, however, ordered the pumps to be kept constantly going, and endeavoured to collect my thoughts for the occasion. I turned to the boats, two of which we then had with the ship, and with an intention of clearing them away, and getting all things ready to embark in them, if there should be no other resource left; and while my attention was thus engaged for a moment, I was aroused with the cry of a man at the hatchway, "Here he is—he is making for us again." I turned around, and saw him about one hundred rods directly ahead of us, coming down apparently with twice his ordinary speed, and to me at that moment, it appeared with tenfold fury and vengeance in his aspect. The surf flew in all directions about him, and his course towards us was marked by a white foam of a rod in width, which he made with the continual violent thrashing of his tail; his head was about half out of the water, and in that way he came upon, and again struck the ship. I was in hopes when I descried him making for us, that by a dexterous movement of putting the ship away immediately, I should be able to cross the line of his approach, before he could get up to us, and thus avoid what I knew, if he should strike us again, would prove our inevitable destruction.

I bawled out to the helmsman, "Hard up!" but she had not fallen off more than a point, before we took the second shock. I should judge the speed of the ship to have been at this time about three knots, and that of the whale about six. He struck her to windward, directly under the cathead, and completely stove in her bows. He passed under the ship again, went off to leeward, and we saw no more of him. Our situation at this junction can be more readily imagined than described. The shock to our feelings was such, as I am sure none can have an adequate conception of that were not there: the misfortune befell us at a moment when we least dreamt of any accident, and from the pleasing anticipations we had formed, of realizing the certain profits of our labour, we were dejected by a sudden, most mysterious, and overwhelming calamity. Not a moment, however, was to be lost in endeavouring to provide for the extremity to which it was now certain we were reduced. We were more than a thousand miles from the nearest land, and with nothing but a light open boat, as the resource of safety for myself and companions. I ordered the men to cease pumping, and every one to provide for himself; seizing a hatchet at the same time, I cut away the lashings of the spare boat, which lay bottom up across two spars directly over the quarter deck, and cried out to those near me to take her as she came down. They did so accordingly, and bore her on their shoulders as far as the waist of the ship. The steward had in the meantime gone down into the cabin twice, and saved two quadrants, two practical navigators, and the captain's trunk and mine; all of which were hastily thrown into the boat, as she lay on the deck, with the two compasses which I snatched from the binnacle. He attempted to descend again; but the water by this time had rushed in, and he returned without being able to effect his purpose. By the time we had got the boat to the waist, the ship had filled with water, and was going down on her beam-ends: we shoved our boat as quickly as possible from the plankshear into the water, all hands jumping in her at the same time, and launched off clear of the ship. We were scarcely two boat lengths distant from her, when she fell over to windward, and settled down in the water.

Amazement and despair now wholly took possession of us. We contemplated the frightful situation the ship lay in, and thought with horror upon the sudden and dreadful calamity that had overtaken us. We looked upon each other, as if to gather some consolatory sensation from an interchange of sentiments, but every countenance was marked with the paleness of despair. Not a word was spoken for several minutes by any of us; all appeared to be bound in a spell of stupid consternation; and from the time we were first attached by the whale, to the period of the fall of the ship, and of our leaving her in the boat, more than ten minutes could not certainly have elapsed! God only knows in what way, or by what means, we were enabled to accomplish in that short time what we did; the cutting away and transporting the boat from where she was deposited would of itself, in ordinary circumstances, have consumed as much time as that, if the whole ship's crew had been employed in it. My companions had not saved a single article but what they had on their backs; but to me it was a source of infinite satisfaction, if any such could be gathered from the horrors of our gloomy situation, that we had been fortunate enough to have preserved our compasses, navigators, and quadrants. After the first shock of my feelings was over, I enthusiastically contemplated them as the probable instruments of our salvation; without them all would have been dark and hopeless. Gracious God! What a picture of distress and suffering now presented itself to my imagination. The crew of the ship were saved, consisting of twenty human souls. All that remained to conduct these twenty beings through the stormy terrors of the ocean, perhaps many thousand miles, were three open light boats.

The prospect of obtaining any provisions or water from the ship, to subsist upon during the time, was at least now doubtful. How many long and watchful nights, thought I, are to be passed? How many tedious days of partial starvation are to be endured, before the least relief or mitigation of our sufferings can be reasonably anticipated. We lay at this time in our boat, about two ship lengths off from the wreck, in perfect silence, calmly contemplating her situation, and absorbed in our own melancholy reflections, when the other boats were discovered rowing up to us. They had but shortly before been discovered by the boatsteerer in the captain's boat, and with a horror-struck countenance and voice, he suddenly exclaimed, "Oh, my God! Where is the ship?"

Their operations upon this were instantly suspended, and a general cry of horror and despair burst from the lips of every man, as their looks were directed for her, in vain, over every part of the ocean. They immediately made all haste towards us. The captain's boat was the first that reached us. He stopped about a boat's length off, but had no power to utter a single syllable: he was so completely overpowered with the spectacle before him that he sat down in his boat, pale and speechless. I could scarcely recognize his countenance, he appeared to be so much altered, awed, and overcome with the oppression of his feelings, and the dreadful reality that lay before him. He was in a short time however enabled to address the inquiry to me. "My God, Mr. Chase, what is the matter?" I answered, "We have been stove by a whale." I then briefly told him the story. After a few moments' reflection he observed that we must cut away her masts, and endeavour to get something out of her to eat. Our thoughts were now all accordingly bent on endeavours to save from the wreck whatever we might possibly want, and for this purpose we rowed up and got on to her. Search was made for every means of gaining access to her hold; and for this purpose the lanyards were cut loose, and with our hatchets we commenced to cut away the masts, that she might right up again, and enable us to scuttle her decks. In doing which we were occupied about three-quarters of an hour, owing to our having no axes, nor indeed any other instruments, but the small hatchets belonging to the boats. After her masts were gone she came up about twothirds of the way upon an even keel. While we were employed about the masts the captain took his quadrant, shoved off from the ship, and got an observation. We found ourselves in latitude 0° 40' S., longitude 119° W. We now commenced to cut a hole through the planks, directly above two large casks of bread, which most fortunately were between decks, in the waist of the ship, and which being in the upper side, when she upset, we had strong hopes was not wet. It turned out according to our wishes, and from these casks we obtained six hundred pounds of hard bread. Other parts of the deck were then scuttled, and we got without difficulty as much fresh water as we dared to take in the boats, so that each was supplied with about sixty-five gallons; we got also from one of the lockers a musket, a small canister of powder, a couple of files, two rasps, about two pounds of boat nails, and a few turtles.

In the afternoon the wind came on to blow a strong breeze; and having obtained every thing that occurred to us could then be got out, we began to make arrangements for our safety during the night. A boat's line was made fast to the ship, and to the other end of it one of the boats was moored, at about fifty fathoms to leeward; another boat was then attached to the first one, about eight fathoms astern; and the third board, the like distance astern of her. Night came on just as we had finished our operations; and such a night as it was to us! so full of feverish and distracting inquietude, that we were deprived entirely of rest. The wreck was constantly before my eyes. I could not, by any effort, chase away the horrors of the preceding day from my mind: they haunted me the live-long night. My companions—some of them were like sick women; they had no idea of the extent of their deplorable situation. One or two slept unconcernedly, while others wasted the night in unavailing murmurs. I now had full leisure to examine, with some degree of coolness, the dreadful circumstances of our disaster. The scenes of yesterday passed in such quick succession in my mind that it was not until after many hours of severe reflection that I was about to discard the idea of the catastrophe as a dream. Alas! It was one from which there was no awaking; it was too certainly true, that but yesterday we had existed as it were, and in one short moment had been cut off from all the hopes and prospects of the living! I have no language to paint out the horrors of our situation. To shed tears was indeed altogether unavailing, and withal unmanly; yet I was not able to deny myself the relief they served to afford me. After several hours of idle sorrow and repining I began to reflect upon the accident, and endeavoured to realize by what unaccountable destiny or design (which I could not at first determine) this sudden and most deadly attach had been made upon us: by an animal, too, never before suspected of premeditated violence, and proverbial for its insensibility and inoffensiveness.

Every fact seemed to warrant me in concluding that it was anything but chance which directed his operations; he made two several attacks upon the ship, at a short interval between them, both of which, according to their direction, were calculated to do us the most injury, by being made ahead, and thereby combining the speed of the two objects for the shock; to effect which, the exact manoeuvres which he made were necessary. His aspect was most horrible, and such as indicated resentment and fury. He came directly from the shoal which we had just before entered, and in which we had struck three of his companions, as if fired with revenge for their sufferings. But to do this it may be observed, that the mode of fighting which they always adopt is either with repeated strokes of their tails, or snapping of their jaws together; and that a case, precisely similar to this one, has never been heard of amongst the oldest and most experienced whalers. To this I would answer, that the structure and strength of the whale's head is admirably designed for this mode of attach; the most prominent part of which is almost as hard and as tough as iron; indeed, I can compare it to nothing else but the inside of a horse's hoof, upon which a lance or harpoon would not make the slightest impression. The eyes and ears are removed nearly onethird the length of the whole fish, from the front part of the head, and are not in the least degree endangered in this mode of attack. At all events, the whole circumstances taken together, all happening before my own eyes, and producing, at the time, impressions in my mind of decided, calculating mischief on the part of the whale (many of which impressions I cannot now recall) induce me to be satisfied that I am correct in my opinion. It is certainly, in all its bearings, a hitherto unheard of circumstance, and constitutes, perhaps, the most extraordinary one in the annals of the fishery.

# The White Whale

## *Herman Melville*

### First Day

THAT NIGHT, IN THE MIDWATCH, WHEN THE OLD MAN—AS his wont at intervals—stepped forth from the scuttle in which he leaned, and went to his pivothole, he suddenly thrust out his face fiercely, snuffing up the sea air as a sagacious ship's dog will, in drawing nigh to some barbarous isle. He declared that a whale must be near. Soon that peculiar odor, sometimes to a great distance given forth by the living Sperm Whale, was palpable to all the watch; nor was any mariner surprised when, after inspecting the compass, and then the dog-vane, and then ascertaining the precise bearing of the odor as nearly as possible, Ahab rapidly ordered the ship's course to be slightly altered, and the sail to be shortened.

The acute policy dictating these movements was sufficiently vindicated at daybreak by the sight of a long sleek on the sea directly and lengthwise ahead, smooth as oil, and resembling in the pleated watery wrinkles bordering it, the polished metalliclike marks of some swift tiderip, at the mouth of a deep, rapid stream.

"Man the mastheads! Call all hands!"

Thundering with the butts of three clubbed handspikes on the forecastle deck, Daggoo roused the sleepers with such judgment claps that they seemed to exhale from the scuttle, so instantaneously did they appear with their clothes in their hands.

"What d'ye see?" cried Ahab, flattening his face to the sky.

"Nothing, nothing, sir!" was the sound hailing down in reply.

"T'gallantsails! stunsails alow and aloft, and on both sides!"

All sail being set, he now cast loose the lifeline, reserved for swaying him to the mainroyal masthead; and in a few moments they were hoisting him thither, when, while but twothirds of the way aloft, and while peering ahead through the horizontal vacancy between the maintopsail and topgallantsail, he raised a gull-like cry in the air, "There she blows!—there she blows! A hump like a snowhill! It is Moby Dick!"

Fired by the cry which seemed simultaneously taken up by the three lookouts, the men on deck rushed to the rigging to behold the famous whale they had so long been pursuing. Ahab had now gained his final perch, some feet above the other lookouts, Tashtego standing just beneath him on the cap of the topgallant-mast, so that the Indian's head was almost on a level with Ahab's heel. From this height the whale was now seen some mile or so ahead, at every roll of the sea revealing his high sparking hump, and regularly jetting his silent spout into the air. To the credulous mariners it seemed the same silent spout they had so long ago beheld in the moonlit Atlantic and Indian Oceans.

"And did none of ye see it before?" cried Ahab, hailing the perched men all around him.

"I saw him almost that same instant, sir, that Captain Ahab did, and I cried out," said Tashtego.

"Not the same instant; not the same—no, the doubloon is mine, Fate reserved the doubloon for me. I only; none of ye could have raised the White Whale first. There she blows! There she blows!—there she blows! There again!—there again!" he cried, in long-drawn, lingering, methodic tones, attuned to the gradual prolongings of the whale's visible jets. "He's going to found! In stunsails! Down top-gallant-sails! stand by three boats. Mr. Starbuck, remember, stay on board, and keep the ship. Helm there! Luff, luff a point! So; steady, man, steady! There go flukes! No, no; only black water! All ready the boats there? Stand by, stand by! Lower me, Mr. Starbuck; lower, lower,—quick, quicker!" and he slid through the air to the deck.

"He is heading straight to leeward, sir," cried Stubb; "right away from us; cannot have seen the ship yet."

"Be dumb, man! Stand by the braces! Hard down the helm!—brace up! Shiver her!—shiver her! So; well that! Boats, boats!"

Soon all the boats but Starbuck's were dropped; all the boatsails set—all the paddles plying; with rippling swiftness, shooting to leeward; and Ahab heading the onset. A pale, deathglimmer lit up Fedallah's sunken eyes; a hideous motion gnawed his mouth.

Like noiseless nautilus shells, their light prows sped through the sea; but only slowly they neared the foe. As they neared him, the ocean grew still more smooth; seemed drawing a carpet over its waves; seemed a noon-meadow, so serenely it spread. At length the breathless hunter came so nigh his seemingly unsuspecting prey, that his entire dazzling hump was distinctly visible, sliding along the sea as if an isolated thing, and continually set in a revolving ring of finest, fleecy, greenish foam. He saw the vast involved wrinkles of the slightly projecting head beyond. Before it, far out on the soft Turkishrugged waters, went the glistening white shadow from his broad, milky forehead, a musical ripping playfully accompanying the shade; and behind, the blue waters interchangeably flowed over into the moving valley of his steady wake; and on either hand bright bubbles arose and danced by his side. But these were broken again by the light toes of hundreds of gay fowl softly feathering the sea, alternate with their fitful flight; and like to some flagstaff rising from the painted hull of an argosy, the tall but shattered pole of a recent lance projected from the White Whale's back; and at intervals one of the cloud of softtoed fowls hovering, and to and fro skimming like a canopy over the fish, silently perched and rocked on this pole, the long tail feathers streaming like pennons.

A gentle joyousness—a mighty mildness of repose in swiftness, invested the gliding whale. Not the white bull Jupiter swimming away with ravished Europa clinging to his graceful horns; his lovely, leering eyes sideways intent upon the maid; with smooth bewitching fleetness, rippling straight for the nuptial bower in Crete; not Jove did surpass the glorified White Whale as he so divinely swam.

On each soft side—coincident with the parted swell, that but once laving him, then flowed so wide away—on each bright side, the whale shed off enticings. No wonder there had been some among the hunters who namelessly transported and allured by all this serenity, had ventured to assail it; but had fatally found that quietude but the vesture of tornadoes. Yet calm, enticing calm, oh, whale! thou glidest on, to all who for the first time eye thee, no matter how many in that same way thou may'st have bejuggled and destroyed before.

And thus, through the serene tranquilities of the tropical sea, among waves whose handclappings were suspended by exceeding rapture, Moby Dick moved on, still withholding from sight the full terrors of his submerged trunk, entirely hiding the wretched hideousness of his jaw. But soon the fore part of him slowly rose from the water; for an instant his whole marbleized body formed a high arch, like Virginia's Natural Bride, and warningly waving his bannered flukes in the air; the giant god revealed himself, sounded, and went out of sight. Hoveringly halting, and dipping on the wing, the white seafowls longingly lingered over the agitated pool that he left.

With oars apeak, and paddles down, the sheets of their sails adrift, the three boats now stilly floated, awaiting Moby Dick's reappearance.

"An hour," said Ahab, standing rooted in his boat's stern, and he gazed beyond the whale's place, towards the dim blue spaces and wide wooing vacancies to leeward. It was only an instant; for again his eyes seemed whirling round in his head as he swept the watery circle. The breeze now freshened; the sea began to swell.

"The birds!—the birds!" cried Tashtego.

In long Indian file, as when herons take wing, the white birds were now all flying towards Ahab's boat; and when within a few yards began fluttering over the water there, wheeling round and round, with joyous, expectant cries. Their vision was keener than man's; Ahab could discover no sign in the sea. But suddenly as he peered down and down into its depths, he profoundly saw a white living spot no bigger than a white weasel, with wonderful celerity uprising, and magnifying as it rose, till it turned, and then there were plainly revealed two long crooked rows of white, glistening teeth, floating up from the undiscoverable bottom. It was Moby Dick's open mouth and scrolled jaw; his vast, shadowed bulk still half blending with the blue of the sea. The glittering mouth yawned beneath the boat like an open-doored marble tomb; and giving one sidelong sweep with his steering oar, Ahab whirled the craft aside from this tremendous apparition. Then, calling upon Fedallah to change places with him, he went forward to the bows, and seizing Perth's harpoon, commanded his crew to grasp their oars and stand by to stern.

Now, by reason of this timely spinning round the boat upon its axis, its bow, by anticipation, was made to face the whale's head while yet under water. But as if perceiving this stratagem.

Moby Dick, with that malicious intelligence ascribed to him, sidelingly transplanted himself, as it were, in an instant, shooting his plaited head lengthwise beneath the boat.

Through and through; through every plank and each rib, it thrilled for an instant, the whale obliquely lying on his back, in the manner of a biting shark, slowly and feelingly taking its bows full within his mouth, so that the long, narrow, scrolled lower jaw curled high up into the open air, and one of the teeth caught in a rowlock. The bluish pearlwhite of the inside of the jaw was within six inches of Ahab's head, and reached higher than that. In this attitude the White Whale now shook the slight cedar as a mildly cruel cat her mouse. With unastonished eyes Fedallah gazed and crossed his arms; but the tiger-yellow crew were tumbling over each other's heads to gain the uttermost stern.

And now, while both elastic gunwales were springing in and out, as the whale dallied with the doomed craft in this devilish way; and from his body being submerged beneath the boat, he could not be darted at from the bows, for the bows were almost inside of him, as it were, and while the other boats involuntarily paused, as before a quick crisis impossible to withstand, then it was that monomaniac Ahab, furious with this tantalizing vicinity of his foe, which placed him all alive and helpless in the very jaws he hated; frenzied with all this, he seized the long bone with his naked hands, and wildly strove to wrench it from its gripe. As now he thus vainly strove, the jaw slipped from him; the frail gunwales bent in, collapsed, and snapped, as both jaws, like an enormous shears, sliding further aft, bit the craft completely in twain, and locked themselves fast again in the sea, midway between the two floating wrecks. These floated aside, the broken ends drooping, the crew at the sternwreck clinging to the gunwales, and striving to hold fast to the oars to lash them across.

At that preluding moment, ere the boat was yet snapped, Ahab, the first to perceive the whale's intent, by the crafty upraising of his head, a movement that loosed his hold for the time; at that moment his hand had made one final effort to push the boat out of the bite. But only slipping further into the whale's mouth, and tilting over sideways as it slipped, the boat had shaken off his hold on the jaw; spilled him out of it, as he leaned to the push; and so he fell flat-faced upon the sea.

Ripplingly withdrawing from his prey, Moby Dick now lay at a little distance, vertically thrusting his oblong white head up and down in the billows; and at the same time slowly revolving his whole spindled body; so that when his vast wrinkled forehead rose—some twenty or more feet out of the water—the now rising swells, with all their confluent waves, dazzling broke against it; vindictively tossing their shivered spray still higher into the air. So, in a gale, the but half baffled channel billows only recoil from the base of the Eddystone, triumphantly to overleap its summit with their scud.

But soon resuming his horizontal attitude, Moby Dick swam swiftly round and round the wrecked crew; sideways churning the water in his vengeful wake, as if lashing himself up to still another and more deadly assault. The sight of the splintered boat seemed to madden him, as the blood of grapes and mulberries cast before Antiochus's elephants in the book of Maccabees. Meanwhile Ahab half smothered in the foam of the whale's insolent tail, and too much of a cripple to swim,—though he could still keep afloat, even in the heart of such a whirlpool as that; helpless Ahab's head was seen, like a tossed bubble which the least chance shock might burst. From the boat's fragmentary stern, Fedallah incuriously and mildly eyed him; the clinging crew, at the other drifting end, could not succor him; more than enough was it for them to look to themselves. For so revolvingly appalling was the White Whale's aspect, and so planetarily swift the evercontracting circles he made, that he seemed horizontally swooping upon them. And though the other boats, unharmed, still hovered hard by, still they dared not pull into the eddy to strike, lest that should be the signal for the instant destruction of the jeopardized castaways, Ahab and all; nor in that case could they themselves hope to escape. With straining eyes then, they remained on the outer edge of the direful zone, whose center had now become the old man's head.

Meantime, from the beginning all this had been descried from the ship's mastheads; and squaring her yards, she had borne down upon the scene; and was now so nigh, that Ahab in the water hailed her;—"Sail on the"—but that moment a breaking sea dashed on him from Moby Dick, and whelmed him for the time. But struggling out of it again, and chancing to rise on a towering crest, he shouted,—"Sail on the whale!—Drive him off!"

The *Pequod's* prows were pointed; and breaking up the charmed circle, she effectually parted the White Whale from his victim. As he sullenly swam off, the boats flew to the rescue.

Dragged into Stubb's boat with bloodshot, blinded eyes, the white brine caking in his wrinkles; the long tension of Ahab's bodily strength did crack, and helplessly he yielded to his body's doom: for a time, lying all crushed in the bottom of Stubb's boat, like one trodden under foot of herds of elephants. Far inland, nameless wails came from him, as desolate sounds from out ravines.

But this intensity of his physical prostration did but so much the more abbreviate it. In an instant's compass, great hearts sometimes condense to one deep pang, the sum-total of those shallow pains kindly diffused through feebler men's whole lives. And so, such hearts, though summary in each one suffering; still, if the gods decree it, in their lifetime aggregate a whole age of woe, wholly made up of instantaneous intensities; for even in their pointless centers, those noble natures contain the entire circumferences of inferior souls.

"The harpoon," said Ahab, halfway rising, and draggingly leaning on one bended arm—"is it safe?"

"Aye, sir, for it was not darted; this is it," said Stubb, showing it.

"Lay it before me;—any missing men?"

"One, two, three, four, five;—there were five oars, sir, and here are five men."

"That's good.—Help me, man; I wish to stand. So, so, I see him! there! there! going to leeward still; what a leaping spout!—Hands off from me! The eternal sap runs up in Ahab's bones again! Set the sail; out oars; the helm!"

It is often the case that when a boat is stove, its crew, being picked up by another boat, help to work that second boat; and the chase is thus continued with what is called doublebanked oars. It was thus now. But the added power of the boat did not equal the added power of the whale, but he seemed to have treblebanked his every fin; swimming with a velocity which plainly showed, that if now, under these circumstances, pushed on, the chase would prove an indefinitely prolonged, if not a hopeless one; nor could any crew endure for so long a period, such an unintermitted, intense straining at the oar; a thing barely tolerable only in some one brief vicissitude. The ship itself, then, as it sometimes happens, offered the most promising intermediate means of overtaking the chase. Accordingly the boats now made for her, and were soon swayed up to their cranes—the two parts of the wrecked boat having been previously secured by her—and then hoisting everything to her side, and stacking her canvas high up, and sideways outstretching it with stunsails, like the doublejointed wings of an albatross; the *Pequod* bore down in the leeward wake of Moby Dick. At the wellknown, methodic intervals, the whale's glittering spout was regularly announced from the manned mastheads; and when he would be reported as just gone down, Ahab would take the time, and then pacing the deck, binnaclewatch in hand, so soon as the last second of the allotted hours expired, his voice was heard.—"Whose is the doubloon now? D'ye see him?" and if the reply was, "No, sir!" straightway he commanded them to lift him to his perch. In this way the day wore on; Ahab, now aloft and motionless; anon, unrestingly pacing the planks.

As he was thus walking, uttering no sound, except to hail the men aloft, or to bid them hoist a sail still higher, or to spread one to a still greater breadth—thus to and fro pacing, beneath his slouched hat, at every turn he passed his own wrecked boat, which had been dropped upon the quarterdeck, and lay there reversed; broken bow to shattered stern. At last he paused before it; and as in an already overclouded sky fresh troops of clouds will sometimes sail across, so over the old man's face there now stole some such added gloom as this.

Stubb saw him pause; and perhaps intending, not vainly, though to evince his own unabated fortitude, and thus keep up a valiant place in his captain's mind, he advanced, and eyeing the wreck exclaimed—"the thistle the ass refused; it pricked his mouth too keenly, sir; ha! ha!"

"What soulless thing is this that laughs before a wreck? Man, man! did I not know thee brave as fearless fire (and as mechanical) I could swear thou wert poltroon. Groan nor laugh should be heard before a wreck."

"Aye, sir," said Starbuck, drawing near, "'tis a solemn sight; an omen, and an ill one."

"Omen? omen?—the dictionary! If the gods think to speak outright to man, they will honorably speak outright; not shake their heads, and give an old wife's darkling hint.— Begone! Ye two are the opposite poles of one thing; Starbuck is Stubb revered, and Stubb is Starbuck; and ye two are all mankind; and Ahab stands alone among the millions of the peopled earth, nor gods nor men his neighbors! Cold, cold—I shiver!—How now? Aloft there! D'ye see him? Sing out for every spout, though he spout ten times a second!"

The day was nearly done; only the hem of his golden robe was rustling. Soon, it was almost dark, but the lookout men still remained unset.

"Can't see the spout now, sir; too dark"—cried a voice from the air.

"How heading when last seen?"

"As before, sir,—straight to leeward."

"Good! he will travel slower now 'tis night. Down royals and topgallant stunsails, Mr. Starbuck. We must not run over him before morning; he's making a passage now, and may heaveto a while. Helm there! keep her full before the wind!—Aloft! come down!—Mr. Stubb, send a fresh hand to the foremast head and see it manned till morning."—Then advancing towards the doubloon in the mainmast—"Men, this gold is mine, for I earned it; but I shall let it abide here till the White Whale is dead; and then, whosoever of ye first raises him, upon the day he shall be killed, this gold is that man's; and if on that day I shall again raise him, then ten times its sum shall be divided among all of ye! Away now!—the deck is thine, sir."

And so saying, he placed himself halfway within the scuttle, and slouching his hat, stood there till dawn, except when at intervals rousing himself to see how the night wore on.

## Second Day

At daybreak, the three mastheads were punctually manned afresh.

"D'ye see him?" cried Ahab after allowing a little space for the light to spread.

"See nothing, sir."

"Turn up all hands and make sail! he travels faster than I thought for;—the top-gallant-sails!—aye, they should have been kept on her all night. But no matter—'tis but resting for the rush."

Here be it said, that this pertinacious pursuit of one particular whale, continued through day into night, and through night into day, is a thing by no means unprecedented in the South Sea fisher. For such is the wonderful skill, prescience of experience, and invincible confidence acquired by some great natural geniuses among the Nantucket commanders, that from the simple observation of a whale when last described, they will, under certain given circumstances, pretty accurately foretell both the direction in which he will continue to swim for a time, while out of sight, as well as his probable rate of progression during that period. And, in these cases, somewhat as a pilot, when about losing sight of a coast, whose general trending he well knows, and which he desires shortly to return to again, but at some further point; like as this pilot stands by his compass, and takes the precise bearing of the cape at present visible, in order the more certainly to hit aright the remote, unseen headland, eventually to be visited: so does the fisherman, at his compass, with the whale; for after being chased, and diligently marked, through several hours of daylight, then, when night obscures the fish, the creature's future wake through darkness is almost as established to the sagacious mind of the hunter, as the pilot's coast is to him. So that to this hunter's wondrous skill, the proverbial evanescence of a thing writ in water, a wake, is to all desired purposes well-nigh as reliable as the steadfast land. And as the mighty iron Leviathan of the modern railway is so familiarly known in its every pace, that, with watches in their hands, men time his rate as doctors that of a baby's pulse; and lightly say of it, "the up train or the down train will reach such or such a spot, at such or such an hour," even so, almost, there are occasions when these Nantucketers time that other Leviathan of the deep, according to the observed humor of his speed; and say to themselves, "So many hours hence this whale will have gone two hundred miles, will have about reached this or that degree of latitude or longitude." But to render this acuteness at all successful in the end, the wind and the sea must be the whaleman's allies; for of what present avail to the becalmed or windbound mariner is the skill that assures him he is exactly ninety-three leagues and a quarter from his port? Inferable from these statements are many collateral subtle matters touching the chase of whales.

The ship tore on; leaving such a furrow in the sea as when a cannonball, missent, becomes a ploughshare and turns up the level field.

"By salt and hemp!" cried Stubb, "but this swift motion of the deck creeps up one's legs and tingles at the heart. This ship and I are two brave fellows!—Ha! ha! Some one take me up, and launch me, spine-wise, on the sea,—for by live-oaks! My spine's a keel. Ha, ha! we go the gait that leaves no dust behind!"

"There she blows—she blows!—she blows!—right ahead!" was now the masthead cry.

"Aye, aye!" cried Stubb; "I knew it—ye can't escape—blow on and split your spout, O whale! the mad fiend himself is after ye! Blow your trump—blister your lungs!—Ahab will dam off your blood, as a miller shuts his water-gate upon the stream!"

And Stubb did but speak out for well-nigh all that crew. The frenzies of the chase had by this time worked them bub-blingly up, like old wine worked anew. Whatever pale fears and forebodings some of them might have felt before; these were not only now kept out of sight through the growing awe of Ahab, but they were broken up, and on all sides routed, as timid prairie hares that scatter before the bounding bison. The hand of Fate had snatched all their souls; and by the stirring perils of the previous day; the rack of the past night's sus-pense; the fixed, unfearing, blind, reckless way in which their wild craft went plunging towards its flying mark; by all these things, their hearts were bowled along. The wind that made great bellies of their sails, and rushed the vessel on by arms invisible as irresistible; this seemed the symbol of that unseen agency which so enslaved them to the race.

They were one man, not thirty. For as the one ship that held them all; though it was put together of all contrasting things—oak, and maple, and pine wood; iron, and pitch, and hemp—yet all these ran into each other in the one concrete hull, which shot on its way, both balanced and directed by the long central keel; even so, all the individualities of the crew. This man's valor, that man's fear; guilt and guiltiness, all varieties were welded into oneness, and were all directed to that fatal goal which Ahab their one lord and keel did point to.

The rigging lived. The mastheads, like the tops of tall palms, were outspreadingly tufted with arms and legs. Clinging to a spar with one hand, some reached forth the other with impatient wavings; others, shading their eyes from the vivid sunlight, sat far out on the rocking yards; all the spars in full bearing of mortals, ready and ripe for their fate. Ah! how they still strove through that infinite blueness to seek out the thing that might destroy them!

"Why sing ye not out for him, if ye see him?" cried Ahab, when, after the lapse of some minutes since the first cry, no more had been heard. "Sway me up, men; ye have been deceived; not Moby Dick casts one odd jet that way, and then disappears."

It was even so; in their headlong eagerness, the men had mistaken some other thing for the whale-spout, as the event itself soon proved; for hardly had Ahab reached his perch; hardly was the rope belayed to its pin on deck, when he struck the keynote to an orchestra, that made the air vibrate as with the combined discharges of rifles. The triumphant halloo of thirty buckskin lungs was heard, as—much nearer to the ship than the place of the imaginary jet, less than a mile ahead—Moby Dick bodily burst into view! For not by any calm and indolent spoutings; not by the peaceable gush of that mystic fountain in his head, did the White Whale now reveal his vicinity; but by the far more wondrous phenomenon of breaching. Rising with his utmost velocity from the further depths, the Sperm Whale thus booms his entire bulk into the pure element of air, and piling up a mountain of dazzling foam, shows his place to the distance of seven miles and more. In those moments, the torn, enraged waves he shakes off seem his mane; in some cases this breaching is his act of defiance.

"There she breaches! there she breaches!" was the cry, as in his immeasurable bravadoes the White Whale tossed himself salmonlike to Heaven. So suddenly seen in the blue plain of the sea, and relieved against the still bluer margin of the sky, the spray that he raised, for the moment, intolerably glittered and glared like a glacier; and stood there gradually fading and fading away from its first sparkling intensity, to the dim mistiness of an advancing shower in a vale.

"Aye, breach your last to the sun, Moby Dick!" cried Ahab, "thy hour and thy harpoon are at hand!—Down! down all of ye, but one man at the fore. The boats!—stand by!"

Unmindful of the tedious rope-ladders of the shrouds, the men, like shooting starts, slid to the deck by the isolated backstays and halyards; while Ahab, less dartingly, but still rapidly, was dropped from his perch.

"Lower away," he cried, so soon as he had reached his boat—a spare one, rigged the afternoon previous. "Mr. Starbuck, the ship is thine—keep away from the boats but keep near them. Lower, all!"

As if to strike a quick terror into them, by this time being the first assailant himself, Moby Dick had turned, and was now coming for the three crews. Ahab's boat was central; and cheering his men, he told them he would take the whale head-and-head,—that is pull straight up to his forehead,—a not uncommon thing; for when within a certain limit, such a course excludes the coming onset from the whale's sidelong vision. But ere that close limit was gained, and while yet all three boats were plain as the ship's three masts to his eye; the White Whale churning himself into furious speed, almost in an instant as it were, rushing among the boats with open jaws, and a lashing tail, offered appalling battle on every side; and heedless of the irons darted at him from every boat, seemed only intent on annihilating each separate plank of which those boats were made. But skilfully maneuvered, incessantly wheeling like trained chargers in the field; the boats for a while eluded him, though, at times, but by a plank's breadth; while all the time, Ahab's unearthly slogan tore every other cry but his to shreds.

But at last in his untraceable evolutions, the White Whale so crossed and re-crossed, and in a thousand ways entangled the slack of the three lines now fast to him, that they foreshortened, and, of themselves, warped the devoted boats towards the planted irons in him; though now for a moment the whale drew aside a little, as if to rally for a more tremendous charge. Seizing that opportunity, Ahab first paid out more line: and then was rapidly hauling and jerking in upon it again—hoping that way to disencumber it of some snarls—when lo!—a sight more savage than the embattled teeth of sharks!

Caught and twisted—corkscrewed in the mazes of the line—loose harpoons and lances, with all their bristling barbs and points, came flashing and dripping up to the chocks in the bows of Ahab's boat. Only one thing could be done. Seizing the boat-knife, he critically reached within—through—and then, without—the rays of steel; dragged in the line beyond, passed it, inboard, to the bowsman, and then, twice sundering the rope near the chocks—dropped the intercepted fagot of steel into the sea; and was all fast again. That instant, the White Whale made a sudden rush among the remaining tangles of the other lines; by so doing, irresistibly dragged the more involved boats of Stubb and Flask towards his flukes; dashed them together like two rolling husks on a surf-beaten beach, and then, diving down into the sea, disappeared in a boiling maelstrom, in which, for a space, the odorous cedar chips of the wrecks danced round and round, like the grated nutmeg in a swiftly stirred bowl of punch.

While the two crews were yet circling in the waters, reaching out after the revolving linetubs, oars, and other floating furniture, while aslope little Flask bobbed up and down like an empty vial, twitching his legs upwards to escape the dreaded jaws of sharks; and Stubb was lustily singing out for someone to ladle him up; and while the old man's line—now parting—admitted of his pulling into the creamy pool to rescue whom he could;—in that wild simultaneousness of a thousand concreted perils,—Ahab's yet unstricken boat seemed drawn up toward Heaven by invisible wires,—as arrow-like, shooting perpendicularly from the sea, the White Whale dashed his broad forehead against its bottom, and sent it, turning over and over, into the air; till it fell again—gunwale downwards—and Ahab and his men struggled out from under it, like seals from a seaside cave.

The first uprising momentum of the whale—modifying its direction as he struck the surface—involuntarily launched him along it, to a little distance from the center of the destruction he had made; and with his back to it, he now lay for a moment slowly feeling with his flukes from side to side; and whenever a stray oar, bit of plank, the least chip or crumb of the boats touched his skin, his tail swiftly drew back and came sideways, smiting the sea. But soon, as if satisfied that his work for that time was done, he pushed his plaited forehead through the ocean, and trailing after him the intertangled lines, continued his leeward way at a traveler's method pace.

As before, the attentive ship having described the whole fight, again came bearing down to the rescue, and dropping a boat, picked up the floating mariners, tubs, oars, and whatever else could be caught at, and safely landed them on her decks. Some sprained shoulders, wrists, and ankles; livid contusions; wrenched harpoons and lances: inextricable intricacies of rope; shattered oars and planks; all these were there; but no fatal or even serious ill seemed to have befallen anyone. As with Fedallah the day before, so Ahab was now found grimly clinging to his boat's broken half, which afforded a comparatively easy float; nor did it so exhaust him as the previous day's mishap.

But when he was helped to the deck, all eyes were fastened upon him; as instead of standing by himself he still half-hung upon the shoulder of Starbuck, who had thus far been the foremost to assist him. His ivory leg had been snapped off, leaving but one short sharp splinter.

"Aye, aye, Starbuck, 'tis sweet to lean sometimes, be the leaner who he will; and would old Ahab had leaned oftener than he has."

"The ferrule has not stood, sir," said the carpenter, now coming up; "I put good work into that leg."

"But no bones broken, sir, I hope," said Stubb with true concern.

"Aye! and all splintered to pieces, Stubb—d'ye see it.—But even with a broken bone, old Ahab is untouched; and I account no living bone of mine one jot more me, than this dead one that's lost. Nor White Whale, nor man, nor fiend, can so much as graze old Ahab in his own proper and inaccessible being. Can any lead touch younger floor, any mast scrape yonder roof?—Aloft there! which way?"

"Dead to leeward, sir."

"Up helm, then; pile on the sail again, shipkeepers! down the rest of the spare boats and rig them—Mr. Starbuck, away, and muster the boat's crews."

"Let me first help thee towards the bulwarks, sir."

"Oh, oh, oh! how this splinter gores me now! Accursed fate! that the unconquerable captain in the soul should have such a craven mate!"

"Sir?"

"My body, man, not thee. Give me something for a cane—there, that shivered lance will do. Muster the men. Surely I have not seen him yet. By heaven, it cannot be!—missing?—quick! call them all."

The old man's hinted thought was true. Upon mustering the company, the Parsee was not there.

"The Parsee!" cried Stubb—"he must have been caught in———"

"The black vomit wrench thee!—run all of ye above, alow, cabin, forecastle—find him—not gone—not gone!"

But quickly they returned to him with the tidings that the Parsee was nowhere to be found.

"Aye, sir," said Stubb—"caught among the tangles of your line—I thought I saw him dragging under."

"*My* line? *my* line? Gone?—gone? What means that little word?—What deathknell rings in it, that old Ahab shakes as if he were the belfry. The harpoon, too!—toss over the litter there,—d'ye see it?—the forged iron, men, the White Whale's—no, no, no,—blistered fool! this hand did dart it!—'tis in the fish—Aloft there! Keep him nailed—Quick!—all hands to the rigging of the boats—collect the oars—harpooneers!—the irons, the irons!—hoist the royals higher—a pull on the sheets!—helm there! steady, steady for your life! I'll ten times girdle the unmeasured globe; yea and dive straight through it, but I'll slay him yet!"

"Great God! but for one single instant show thyself," cried Starbuck; "never never wilt thou capture him, old man.—In Jesus' name no more of this, that's worse than devil's madness. Two days chased; twice stove to splinters; thy very leg once more snatched from under thee; thy evil shadow gone—all good angels mobbing thee with warnings:—what more wouldst thou have?—Shall we keep chasing this murderous fish till he swamps the last man? Shall we be dragged by him to the bottom of the sea? Shall we be towed by him to the infernal world? Oh, oh!—Impiety and blasphemy to hunt him more!"

"Starbuck, of late I've felt strangely moved to thee; ever since that hour we both saw—though know'st what, in one another's eyes. But in this matter of the whale, be the front of thy face to me as the palm of this hand—a lipless, unfeatured blank. Ahab is for ever Ahab, man. This whole act's immutably decreed. 'Twas rehearsed by thee and me a billion years before this ocean rolled. Fool! I am the Fates' lieutenant; I act under orders. Look thou, underling! that thou obeyest mine.—Stand round me, men. Ye see an old man cut down to the stump; leaning on a shivered lance; propped up on a lonely foot. 'Tis Ahab—his body's part; but Ahab's soul's a centipede, that moves upon a hundred legs. I feel strained, half stranded, as ropes that tow dismasted frigates in a gale; and I may look so. But ere I break, ye'll hear me crack; and till ye hear that, know that Ahab's hawser tows his purpose yet. Believe ye, men, in the things called omens? Then laugh aloud, and cry encore! For ere they drown, drowning things will twice rise to the surface; then rise again, to sink for evermore. So with Moby Dick—two days he's floated—tomorrow will be the third. Aye, man, he'll rise once more—but only to spout his last! D'ye feel brave men, brave?"

"As fearless fire," cried Stubb.

"And as mechanical," muttered Ahab. Then as the men went forward, he muttered on:—"The things called omens! And yesterday I talked the same to Starbuck there, concerning my broken boat. Oh! how valiantly I seek to drive out of others' hearts what's clinched so fast in mine!—The Parsee—the Parsee!—gone, gone? And he was to go before:—but still was to be seen again ere I could perish—How's that?—There's a riddle now might baffle all the lawyers backed by the ghosts of the whole line of judges:—like a hawk's beak it pecks my brain. *I'll, I'll* solve it, though!"

When dusk descended, the whale was still in sight to leeward.

So once more the sail was shortened, and everything passed nearly as on the previous night; only, the sound of hammers, and the hum of the grindstone was heard till nearly daylight, as the men toiled by lanterns in the complete and careful rigging of the spare boats and sharpened their fresh weapons for the morrow. Meantime, of the broken keel of Ahab's wrecked craft the carpenter made him another leg; while still as on the night before, slouched Ahab stood fixed within his scuttle; his hid heliotrope glance anticipatingly gone backward on its dial; set due eastward for the earliest sun.

## THIRD DAY

The morning of the third day dawned fair and fresh, and once more the solitary nightman at the foremasthead was relieved by crowds of the daylight lookouts, who dotted every mast and almost every spar.

"D'ye see him?" cried Ahab; but the whale was not yet in sight.

"In his infallible wake, though; but follow that wake, that's all. Helm there; steady as thou goest, and hast been going. What a lovely day again! were it a new-made world, and made for a summerhouse to the angels, and this morning the first of its throwing open to them, a fairer day could not dawn upon that world. Here's food for thought, had Ahab time to think, but Ahab never thinks; he only feels, feels, feels, *that's* tingling enough for mortal man! to think's audacity. God only has that right and privilege. Thinking is, or ought to be a coolness and a calmness; and our poor hearts throb, and our poor brains beat too much for that. And yet, I've sometimes thought my brain was very calm—frozen calm, this old skull cracks so, like a glass in which the contents turn to ice, and shiver it. And still this hair is growing now; this moment growing, and heat must breed it; but no, it's like that sort of common grass that will grow anywhere, between the earthly clefts of Greenland ice or in Vesuvius lava. How the wild winds blow it; they whip it about me as the torn shreds of split sails lash the tossed ship they cling to. A vile wind that has no doubt blown ere this through prison corridors and cells, and wards of hospitals, and ventilated them, and now comes blowing hither as innocent as fleeces. Out upon it!—it's tainted. Were I the wind, I'd blow no more on such a wicked, miserable world. I'd crawl somewhere to a cave, and slink there. And yet, 'tis a noble and heroic thing, the wind! Who ever conquered it? In every fight it has the last and bitterest blow. Run tilting at it, and you but run through it. Ha! a coward wind that strikes stark naked men, but will not stand to receive a single blow. Even Ahab is a braver thing—a nobler thing than *that*. Would now the wind but had a body; but all the things that most exasperate and outrage mortal man, all these things are bodiless, but only bodiless as objects, not as agents. There's a most special, a most cunning, oh a most malicious difference! And yet, I say again, and swear it now, that there's something all glorious and gracious in the wind.

These warm Trade Winds, at least, that in the clear heavens blow straight on, in strong and steadfast, vigorous mildness; and veer not from their mark, however the baser current of the sea may turn and tack, and the mightiest Mississippis of the land shift and swerve about, uncertain where to go at last. And by the eternal Poles; these same Trades that so directly blow my good ship on; these Trades, or something like them— something so unchangeable, and full as strong, blow my keeled soul along! To it! Aloft there! What d'ye see?"

"Nothing, sir."

"Nothing! and noon at hand! The doubloon goes a-begging! See the sun! Aye, aye it must be so. I've oversailed him. How, got the start? Aye, he's chasing me now; not I, *him*—that's bad; I might have known it, too. Fool! The lines—the harpoons he's towing. Aye, aye, I have run him by last night. About! about! Come down, all of ye, but the regular lookouts! Man the braces!"

Steering as she had done, the wind had been somewhat on the *Pequod*'s quarter, so that now being pointed in the reverse direction, the braced ship sailed hard upon the breeze as she rechurned the cream in her own white wake.

"Against the wind he now steers for the open jaw," murmured Starbuck to himself, as he coiled the new-hauled mainbrace upon the rail. "God keep us, but already my bones feel damp within me, and from the inside wet my flesh. I misdoubt me that I disobey my God in obeying him!"

"Stand by to sway me up!" cried Ahab, advancing to the hempen basket. "We should meet him soon."

"Aye, aye, sir," and straightway Starbuck did Ahab's bidding, and once more Ahab swung on high.

A whole hour now passed; gold-beaten out to ages. Time itself now held long breaths with keen suspense. But at last, some three points off the weatherbow, Ahab descried the spout again, and instantly from the three mastheads three shrieks went up as if the tongues of fire had voiced it.

"Forehead to forehead I meet thee, this third time, Moby Dick! On deck there!—brace sharper up; crowd her into the wind's eye. He's too far off to lower yet, Mr. Starbuck. The sails shake! Stand over the helmsman with a topmaul! So, so; he travels fast, and I must down. But let me have one more good round look aloft here at the sea; there's time for that. An old, old sight, and yet somehow so young; aye, and not changed a wink since I first saw it, a boy, from the sandhills of Nantucket! The same!—the same!—the same to Noah as to me. There's a soft shower to leeward. Such lovely leewardings! They must lead somewhere—to something else than common land, more palmy than the palms. Leeward! the White Whale goes that way; look to windward, then; the better if the bitter quarter. But goodbye, good-bye, old masthead! What's this?—green? aye, tiny mosses in these warped cracks. No such green weather stains on Ahab's head! There's the difference now between man's old age and matter's. But aye, old mast, we both grow old together; sound in our hulls, though, are we not, my ship? Aye, minus a leg, that's all. By heaven! this dead wood has the better of my live flesh every way, I can't compare with it; and

I've known some ships made of dead trees outlast the lives of man made of the most vital stuff of vital fathers. What's that he said? he should still go before me, my pilot; and yet to be seen again? But where? Shall I have eyes at the bottom of the sea, supposing I descend those endless stairs? and all night I've been sailing from him, wherever he did sink to. Aye, aye, like many more thou told'st direful truth as touching thyself, O Parsee; but, Ahab, there thy shot fell short. Goodbye, mast-head—keep a good eye upon the whale, the while I'm gone. We'll talk tomorrow, nay, tonight, when the White Whale lies down there, tied by head and tail." He gave the word; and still gazing round him, was steadily lowered through the cloven blue air to the deck.

In due time the boats were lowered; but as standing in his shallop's stern, Ahab just hovered upon the point of the descent, he waved to the mate,—who held one of the tackle-ropes on deck—and bade him pause.

"Starbuck!"

"Sir?"

"For the third time my soul's ship starts upon this voyage, Starbuck."

"Aye, sir, thou wilt have it so."

"Some ships sail from their ports, and ever afterwards are missing, Starbuck!"

"Truth, sir: saddest truth."

"Some men die at ebb tide; some at low water; some at the full of the flood;—and I feel now like a billow that's all one crested comb, Starbuck. I am old;—shake hands with me, man."

Their hands met; their eyes fastened; Starbuck's tears the glue.

"Oh, my captain, my captain!—noble heart—go not—go not!—see, it's a brave man that weeps; how great the agony of the persuasion then!"

"Lower away!"—cried Ahab, tossing the mate's arm from him. "Stand by the crew?"

In an instant the boat was pulling round close under the stern.

"The sharks! the sharks!" cried a voice from the low cabin window there; "O master, my master, come back!"

But Ahab heard nothing; for his own voice was highlifted then; and the boat leaped on.

Yet the voice spake true; for scarce had he pushed from the ship, when numbers of sharks, seemingly rising from out dark waters beneath the hull, maliciously snapped at the blades of the oars, every time they dipped in the water; and in this way accompanied the boat with their bites. It is a thing not uncommonly happening to the whaleboats in those swarming seas; the sharks at times apparently following them in the same prescient way that vultures hover over the banners of marching regiments in the east. But these were the first sharks that had been observed by the *Pequod* since the White Whale had been first described; and whether it was that Ahab's crew were all such tigeryellow barbarians, and therefore their flesh more musky to the senses of the sharks—a matter sometimes well known to affect them,—however it was, they seemed to follow that one boat without molesting the others.

"Heart of wrought steel!" murmured Starbuck, gazing over the side, and following with his eyes the receding boat—"canst thou yet ring boldly to that sight?—lowering thy keel among ravening sharks, and followed by them, openmouthed, to the chase; and this the critical third day?—For when three days flow together in one continuous intense pursuit; be sure the first is the morning, the second the noon, and the third the evening and the end of that thing—be that end what it may. Oh! my God! what is this that shoots through me, and leaves me so deadly calm, yet expectant,—fixed at the top of a shudder! Future things swim before me, as in empty outlines and skeletons; all the past is somehow grown dim. Mary, girl! thou fadest in pale glories behind me; boy! I seem to see but thy eyes grown wondrous blue. Strangest problems of life seem clearing; but clouds sweep between—Is my journey's end coming? My legs feel faint; like his who has footed it all day. Feel thy heart,—beats it yet?—Stir thyself, Starbuck!—stave it off—move, move! speak aloud!—Masthead there! See ye my boy's hand on the hill?—Crazed;—aloft there!—keep thy keenest eye upon the boats:—mark well the whale—Ho! again!—drive off that hawk! see! he pecks—he tears the vane"—pointing to the red flag flying at the maintruck—"Ha! he soars away with it!—Where's the old man now? sees't thou that sight, oh Ahab!—shudder, shudder!"

The boats had not gone very far, when by a signal from the mastheads—a downward pointed arm, Ahab knew that the whale had sounded; but intending to be near him at the next rising, he held on his way a little sideways from the vessel; the becharmed crew maintaining the profoundest silence, as the head-beat waves hammered and hammered against the opposing bow.

"Drive, drive in your nails, oh ye waves! To their uttermost heads drive them in! ye but strike a thing without a lid; and no coffin and no hearse can be mine:—and hemp only can kill me! Ha! ha!"

Suddenly the waters around them slowly swelled in broad circles; then quickly upheaved, as if sideways sliding from a submerged berg of ice, swiftly rising to the surface. A low rumbling sound was heard; a subterraneous hum; and then all held their breaths; as bedraggled with trailing ropes, and harpoons, and lances, a vast form shot lengthwise, but obliquely from the sea. Shrouded in a thin drooping veil of mist, it hovered for a moment in the rainbowed air; and then fell swamping back into the deep. Crushed thirty feet upwards, the waters flashed for an instant like heaps of fountains, then brokenly sank in a shower of flakes, leaving the circling surface creamed like new milk round the marble trunk of the whale.

"Give way!" cried Ahab to the oarsmen and the boats darted forward to the attack; but maddened by yesterday's fresh irons that corroded in him, Moby Dick seemed combinedly possessed by all the angels that fell from heaven. The wide tiers of welded tendons overspreading his broad white forehead, beneath the transparent skin, looked knitted together, as head on, he came churning his tail among the boats; and once more flailed them apart; spilling out the irons and lances from the two mates' boats, and dashing in one side of the upper part of their bows, but leaving Ahab's almost without a scar.

While Daggoo and Queequeg were stopping the strained planks; and as the whale swimming out from them, turned, and showed one entire flank as he shot by them again; at that moment a quick cry went up. Lashed round and round to the fish's back; pinioned in the turns upon turns in which during the past night, the whale had reeled the involutions of the lines around him, the half torn body of the Parsee was seen, his sable raiment frayed to shreds; his distended eyes turned full upon old Ahab.

The harpoon dropped from his hand.

"Befooled, befooled!"—drawing in a long lean breath—"aye, Parsee! I see thee again.—Aye, and thou goest before; and this, *this* then is the hearse that thou didst promise. But I hold thee to the last letter of thy word. Where is the second hearse? Away, mates, to the ship! Those boats are useless now; repair them if ye can in time, and return to me; if not Ahab is enough to die—

"Down men! the first thing that but offers to jump from this boat I stand in, that thing I harpoon. Ye are not other men, but my arms and my legs; and so obey me.—Where's the whale? gone down again?"

But he looked too nigh the boat; for as if bent upon escaping with the corpse he bore and as if the particular place of the last encounter had been but a stage in his leeward voyage, Moby Dick was now again steadily swimming forward; and had almost passed the ship,—which thus far had been sailing in the contrary direction to him, though for the present her headway had been stopped. He seemed swimming with his utmost velocity, and now only intent upon pursuing his own straight path in the sea.

"Oh! Ahab," cried Starbuck, "not too late is it, even now, the third day, to desist. See! Moby Dick seeks thee not. It is thou, thou, that madly seekest him!"

Setting sail to the rising wind, the lonely boat was swiftly impelled to leeward, by both oars and canvas. And at last when Ahab was sliding by the vessel, so near as plainly to distinguish Starbuck's face as he leaned over the rail, he hailed him to turn the vessel about, and follow him, not too swiftly, at a judicious interval. Glancing upwards, he saw Tashtego, Queequeg, and Daggoo, eagerly mounting to the three mastheads; while the oarsmen were rocking in the two staved boats which had just been hoisted to the side, and were busily at work in repairing them. One after the other, through the port-holes, as he sped, he also caught flying glimpses of Stubb and Flask, busying themselves on deck among bundles of new irons and lances. As he saw all this; as he heard the hammers in the broken boats; far other hammers seemed driving a nail into his heart. But he rallied. And now marking that the vane or flag was gone from the main masthead, he shouted to Tashtego, who had just gained that perch, to descend again for another flag, and a hammer and nails, and so nail it to the mast.

Whether fagged by the three days' running chase, and the resistance to his swimming in the knotted hamper he bore; or whether it was some latent deceitfulness and malice in him: whichever was true, the White Whale's way now began to abate, as it seemed, from the boat so rapidly nearing him once more; though indeed the whale's last start had not been so long a one as before. And still as Ahab glided over the waves the unpitying sharks accompanied him, and so pertinaciously stuck to the boat; and so continually bit at the plying oars, that the blades became jagged and crunched, and left small splinters in the sea, at almost every dip.

"Heed them not! those teeth but give new rowlocks to your oars. Pull on! 'tis the better rest, the sharks' jaw than the yielding water."

"But at every bite, sir, the thin blades grow smaller and smaller."

"They will last long enough! pull on!—But who can tell"— he muttered—"whether these sharks swim to feast of a whale or on Ahab?—But pull on! Aye, all alive, now—we near him. The helm! take the helm; let me pass,"—and so saying, two of the oarsmen helped him forward to the bows of the still flying boat.

At length as the craft was cast to one side, and ran ranging along with the White Whale's flank, he seemed strangely oblivious of its advance—as the whale sometimes will—and

Ahab was fairly within the smoky mountain mist, which thrown off from the whale's spout, curled round his great, Monadnock hump. He was even thus close to him; when, with body arched back, and both arms lengthwise highlifted to the poise, he darted his fierce iron, and his far fiercer curse into the hated whale. As both steel and curse sank to the socket, as if sucked into a morass, Moby Dick sideways writhed; spasmodically rolled his nigh flank against the bow, and, without staving a hole in it, so suddenly canted the boat over, that had it not been for the elevated part of the gunwale to which he then clung, Ahab would once more have been tossed into the sea. As it was, three of the oarsmen—who foreknew not the precise instant of the dart, and were therefore unprepared for its effects—these were flung out; but so fell, that in an instant two of them clutched the gunwale again, and rising to its level on a combing wave, hurled themselves bodily inboard again; the third man helplessly drooping astern, but still afloat and swimming.

Almost simultaneously, with a mighty volition of ungraduated, instantaneous swiftness, the White Whale darted through the weltering sea. But when Ahab cried out to the steersman to take new turns with the line, and hold it so; and commanded the crew to turn round on their seats, and tow the boat up to the mark; the moment the treacherous line felt that double strain and tug, it snapped in the empty air!

"What breaks in me? Some sinew cracks!—'tis whole again; oars! oars! Burst in upon him!"

Hearing the tremendous rush of the sea-crashing boat, the whale wheeled round to present his blank forehead at bay; but in that evolution, catching sight of the nearing black hull of the ship; seemingly seeing in it the source of all his persecutions; bethinking it—it may be—a larger and nobler foe; of a sudden, he bore down upon its advancing prow, smiting his jaws amid fiery showers of foam.

Ahab staggered; his hand smote his forehead. "I grow blind; hands! Stretch out before me that I may yet grope my way. Is't nigh?"

"The whale! The ship!" cried the cringing oarsman.

"Oars! Oars! Slope downwards to thy depths, O sea, that ere it be for ever too late, Ahab may slide this last, last time upon his mark! I see: the ship! The ship! Dash on, my men! Will ye not save my ship?"

But as the oarsmen violently forced their boat through the sledge-hammering seas, the before whalesmitten bowends of two planks burst through, and in an instant almost, the temporarily disabled boat lay nearly level with the waves; its half-wading, splashing crew, trying hard to stop and gap and bail out the pouring water.

Meantime, for that one beholding instant, Tashtego's masthead hammer remained suspended in his hand; and the red flag, half-wrapping him as with a plaid, then streamed itself straight out from him, as his own forwardflowing heart; while Starbuck and Stubb, standing upon the bowsprit beneath, caught sight of the down-coming monster just as soon as he.

"The whale, the whale! Up helm, up helm! Oh, all ye sweet powers of air, now hug me close! Let not Starbuck die, if die he must, in a woman's fainting fit. Up helm, I say—ye fools, the jaw! The jaw! Is this the end of all my bursting prayers? all my lifelong fidelities? Oh, Ahab, Ahab, lo, thy work. Steady! helmsman, steady. Nay, nay! Up helm again! He turns to meet us! Oh, his unappeasable brow drives on towards one, whose duty tells him he cannot depart. My God, stand by me now!"

"Stand not by me, but stand under me, whoever you are that will now help Stubb; for Stubb, too, sticks here. I grin at thee, thou grinning whale! Whoever helped Stubb, or kept Stubb awake, but Stubb's own unwinking eye? And now poor Stubb goes to bed upon a mattress that is all too soft; would it were stuffed with brushwood! I grin at thee, thou grinning whale! Look ye, sun, moon and stars! I call ye assassins of as good a fellow as ever spouted up his ghost. For all that, I would yet ring glasses with ye, would ye but hand the cup! Oh, oh, oh, oh! thou grinning whale, but there'll be plenty of gulping soon! Why fly ye not, O Ahab? For me, off shoes and jacket to it, let Stubb die in his drawers! A most moldy and oversalted death, though;—cherries! cherries! cherries! Oh, Flask, for one red cherry ere we die!"

"Cherries? I only wish that we were where they grow. Oh, Stubb, I hope my poor mother's drawn my partpay ere this; if not, few coppers will come to her now, for the voyage is up."

From the ship's bows, nearly all the seamen now hung inactive; hammers, bits of plank, lances, and harpoons, mechanically retained in their hands, just as they had darted from their various employments; all their enchanted eyes intent upon the whale, which from side to side strangely vibrating his predestinating head, sent a broad band of overspreading semicircular foam before him as he rushed. Retribution, swift vengeance, eternal malice were in his whole aspect, and spite of all that mortal man could do, the solid white buttress of his forehead smote the ship's starboard bow, till men and timbers reeled. Some fell flat upon their faces. Like dislodged trucks, the heads of the harpooneers aloft shook on their bulllike necks. Through the breach, they heard the waters pour, as mountain torrents down a flume.

"The ship! The hearse!—the second hearse!" cried Ahab from the boat; "its wood could only be American!"

Diving beneath the settling ship, the whale ran quivering along its keel, but turning under water, swiftly shot to the surface again, far off the other bow, but within a few yards of Ahab's boat, where, for a time, he lay quiescent.

"I turn my body from the sun. What ho, Tashtego! let me hear thy hammer. Oh! ye three unsurrendered spires of mine; thou uncracked keel; and only god-bullied hull; thou firm deck, and haughty helm, and Polepointed prow,—deathglorious ship! Must ye then perish, and without me? Am I cut off from the last fond pride of meanest shipwrecked captains? Oh, lonely death on lonely life! Oh, now I feel my topmost greatness lies in my topmost grief. Ho, ho! from all your furthest bounds, pour ye now in, ye bold billows of my whole foregone life, and top this one piled comber of my death! Towards thee I roll, thou all-destroying but unconquering whale; to the last I grapple with thee; from hell's heart I stab at thee; for hate's sake I spit my last breath at thee. Sink all coffins and all hearses to one common pool! and since neither can be mine let me then tow to pieces, while still chasing thee, though tied to thee, thou damned whale! *Thus*, I give up the spear!" The harpoon was darted; the stricken whale flew forward; with igniting velocity the line ran through the groove; ran foul. Ahab stopped to clear it; he did clear it; but the flying turn caught him round the neck, and voicelessly as Turkish mutes bowstring their victim, he was shot out of the boat, ere the crew knew he was gone. Next instant, the heavy eyesplice in the rope's final end flew out of the starkempty tub, knocked down an oarsman, and smiting the sea, disappeared in its depths.

For an instant, the tranced boat's crew stood still; then turned. "The ship? Great God, where is the ship?" Soon they through dim bewildering mediums saw her sidelong facing phantom, as in the gaseous Fata Morgana; only the uppermost masts out of water; while fixed by infatuation, or fidelity, or fate, to their once lofty perches, the pagan harpooneers still maintained their sinking lookouts on the sea. And now, concentric circles seized the lone boat itself, and all its crew, and each floating oar, and every lancepole, and spinning, animate and inanimate, all round and round in one vortex, carried the smallest chip of the *Pequod* out of sight.

But as the last whelmings intermixingly poured themselves over the sunken head of the Indian at the mainmast, leaving a few inches of the erect spar yet visible, together with long streaming yards of the flag, which calmly undulated, with ironical coincidings, over the destroying billows they almost touched;—at that instant, a red arm and a hammer hovered backwardly uplifted in the open air, in the act of nailing the flag faster and yet faster to the subsiding spar. A sky-hawk that tauntingly had followed the maintruck downwards from its natural home among the start, pecking at the flag, and incommoding Tashtego there, this bird now chanced to intercept its broad fluttering wing between the hammer and the wood; and simultaneously feeling that ethereal thrill, the submerged savage beneath, in his deathgasp, kept his hammer frozen there; and so the bird of heaven, with unearthly shrieks, and his imperial beak thrust upwards, and his whole captive form folded in the flag of Ahab, went down with his ship, which, like Satan, would not sink to hell till she had dragged a living part of heaven along with her, and helmeted herself with it.

Now small fowls flew screaming over the yet yawning gulf; a sullen white surf beat against its steep sides; then all collapsed, and the great shroud of the sea rolled on as it rolled five thousand years ago.

# Escape from the Ice

## *Ernest Shackleton*

On April 7 at daylight the longdesired peak of Clarence Island came into view; bearing nearly north from our camp. At first it had the appearance of a huge berg, but with the growing light we could see plainly the black lines of scree and the high, precipitous cliffs of the island, which were miraged up to some extent. The dark rocks in the white snow were a pleasant sight.

So long had our eyes looked on icebergs that apparently grew or dwindled according to the angles at which the shadows were cast by the sun; so often had we discovered rocky islands and brought in sight the peaks of Joinville Land, only to find them, after some change of wind or temperature, floating away as nebulous cloud or ordinary berg; that not until Worsley, Wild, and Hurley had unanimously confirmed my observation was I satisfied that I was really looking at Clarence Island. The land was still more than sixty miles away, but it had to our eyes something of the appearance of home, since we expected to find there our first solid footing after all the long months of drifting on the unstable ice. We had adjusted ourselves to the life on the floe, but our hopes had been fixed all the time on some possible landingplace. As one hope failed to materialize, our anticipations fed themselves on another. Our drifting home had no rudder to guide it, no sail to give it speed. We were dependent upon the caprice of wind and current; we went whither those irresponsible forces listed. The longing to feel solid earth under our feet filled our hearts. In the full daylight Clarence Island ceased to look like land and had the appearance of a berg of more than eight or ten miles away, so deceptive are distances in the clear air of the Antarctic. The sharp white peaks of Elephant Island showed to the west of north a little later in the day. "I have stopped issuing sugar now, and our meals consist of seal meat and blubber only, with 7 ozs. of dried milk per day for the party," I wrote. "Each man receives a pinch of salt, and the milk is boiled up to make hot drinks for all hands. The diet suits us, since we cannot get much exercise on the floe and the blubber supplies heat. Fried slices of blubber seem to our taste to resemble crisp bacon. It certainly is no hardship to eat it, though persons living under civilized conditions probably would shudder at it. The hardship would come if we were unable to get it."

I think that the palate of the human animal can adjust itself to anything. Some creatures will die before accepting a strange diet if deprived of their natural food. The Yaks of the Himalayan uplands must feed from the growing grass, scanty and dry though it may be, and would starve even if allowed the best oats and corn.

"We still have the dark water-sky of the last week with us to the southwest and west, round to the north-east. We are leaving all the bergs to the west and there are few within our range of vision now. The swell is more marked today, and I feel sure we are at the verge of the floe-ice. One strong gale, followed by a calm would scatter the pack, I think, and then we could push through. I have been thinking much of our prospects. The appearance of Clarence Island after our long drift seems, somehow, to convey an ultimatum. The island is the last outpost of the south and our final chance of a landingplace. Beyond it lies the broad Atlantic. Our little boats may be compelled any day now to sail unsheltered over the open sea with a thousand leagues of ocean separating them from the land to the north and east. It seems vital that we shall land on Clarence Island or its neighbour, Elephant Island.

"The latter island has attraction for us, although as far as I know nobody has ever landed there. Its name suggests the presence of the plump and succulent seaelephant. We have an increasing desire in any case to get firm ground under our feet. The floe has been a good friend to us, but it is reaching the end of its journey, and it is liable at any time now to break up and fling us into the unplumbed sea."

A little later, after reviewing the whole situation in the light of our circumstances, I made up my mind that we should try to reach Deception Island. The relative positions of Clarence, Elephant, and Deception Islands can be seen on the chart. The two islands first named lay comparatively near to us and were separated by some eighty miles of water from Prince George Island, which was about 160 miles away from our camp on the berg. From this island a chain of similar islands extends westward, terminating in Deception Island. The channels separating these desolate patches of rock and ice are from ten to fifteen miles wide. But we knew from the Admiralty sailing directions that there were stores for the use of shipwrecked mariners on Deception Island, and it was possible that the summer whalers had not yet deserted its harbour.

Also we had learned from our scanty records that a small church had been erected there for the benefit of the transient whalers. The existence of this building would mean to us a supply of timber, from which, if dire necessity urged us, we could construct a reasonably seaworthy boat. We had discussed this point during our drift on the floe. Two of our boats were fairly strong, but the third, the *James Caird*, was light, although a little longer than the others. All of them were small for the navigation of these notoriously stormy seas, and they would be heavily loaded, so a voyage in open water would be a serious undertaking. I fear that the carpenter's fingers were already itching to convert pews into topsides and decks. In any case, the worst that could befall us when we had reached Deception Island would be a wait until the whalers returned about the middle of November.

Another bit of information gathered from the records of the west side of the Weddell Sea related to Prince George Island. The Admiralty "Sailing Directions," referring to the South Shetlands, mentioned a cave on this island. None of us had seen that cave or could say if it was large or small, wet or dry; but as we drifted on our floe and later, when navigating the treacherous leads and making our uneasy night camps, that cave seemed to my fancy to be a palace which in contrast would dim the splendours of Versailles.

The swell increased that night, and the movement of the ice became more pronounced. Occasionally a neighbouring floe would hammer against the ice on which we were camped, and the lesson of these blows was plain to read. We must get solid ground under our feet quickly. When the vibration ceased after a heavy surge, my thoughts flew round to the problem ahead. If the party had not numbered more than six men a solution would not have been so hard to find; but obviously the transportation of the whole party to a place of safety, with the limited means at our disposal, was going to be a matter of extreme difficulty. There were twentyeight men on our floating cake of ice, which was steadily dwindling under the influence of wind, weather, charging floes, and heavy swell. I confess that I felt the burden of responsibility sit heavily on my shoulders; but, on the other hand, I was stimulated and cheered by the attitude of the men. Loneliness is the penalty of leadership, but the man who has to make the decisions is assisted greatly if he feels that there is no uncertainty in the minds of those who follow him, and that his orders will be carried out confidently and in expectation of success.

The sun was shining in the blue sky on the following morning (April 8). Clarence Island showed clearly on the horizon, and Elephant Island could also be distinguished. The single snow-clad peak of Clarence Island stood up as a beacon of safety, though the most optimistic imagination could not make an easy path of the ice and ocean that separated us from that giant, white and austere.

"The pack was much looser this morning, and the long rolling swell from the north-east is more pronounced than it was yesterday. The floes rise and fall with the surge of the sea. We evidently are drifting with the surface current, for all the heavier masses of floe, bergs, and hummocks are being left behind. There has been some discussion in the camp as to the advisability of making one of the bergs our home for the time being and drifting with it to the west. The idea is not sound. I cannot be sure that the berg would drift in the right direction. If it did move west and carried us into the open water, what would be our fate when we tried to launch the boats—down the steep sides of the berg in the sea-swell after the surrounding floes had left us? One must reckon, too, the chance of the berg splitting or even overturning during our stay. It is not possible to gauge the condition of a big mass of ice by surface appearance. The ice may have a fault, and when the wind, current, and swell set up strains and tensions, the line of weakness may reveal itself suddenly and disastrously. No, I do not like the idea of drifting on a berg. We must stay on our floe till conditions improve and then make another attempt to advance towards the land."

At 6.30 p.m. a particularly heavy shock went through our floe. The watchman and other members of the party made an immediate inspection and found a crack right under the *James Baird* and between the other two boats and the main camp. Within five minutes the boats were over the crack and close to the tents. The trouble was not caused by a blow from another floe. We could see that the piece of ice we occupied had slewed and now presented its long axis towards the oncoming swell. The floe, therefore, was pitching in the manner of a ship, and it had cracked across when the swell lifted the centre, leaving the two ends comparatively unsupported. We were now on a triangular raft of ice, the three sides measuring, roughly, 90, 100, and 120 yds. Night came down dull and overcast, and before midnight the wind had freshened from the west. We could see that the pack was opening under the influence of wind, wave, and current; and I felt that the time for launching the boats was near at hand. Indeed, it was obvious that even if the conditions were unfavourable for a start during the coming day, we could not safely stay on the floe many hours longer. The movement of the ice in the swell was increasing, and the floe might split right under our camp. We had made preparations for quick action if anything of the kind occurred. Our case would be desperate if the ice broke into small pieces not large enough to support our party and not loose enough to permit the use of the boats.

The following day was Sunday (April 9), but it proved no day of rest for us. Many of the important events of our Expedition occurred on Sundays, and this particular day was to see our forced departure from the floe on which we had lived for nearly six months, and the start of our journeyings in the boats.

"This has been an eventful day. The morning was fine, though somewhat overcast by stratus and cumulus clouds; moderate southsouthwesterly and south-easterly breezes. We hoped that with this wind the ice would drift nearer to Clarence Island. At 7 a.m. lanes of water and leads could be seen on the horizon to the west. The ice separating us from the lanes was loose, but did not appear to be workable for the boats. The long swell from the north-west was coming in more freely than on the previous day and was driving the floes together in the utmost confusion. The loose brash between the masses of ice was being churned to mudlike consistency, and no boat could have lived in the channels that opened and closed around us. Our own floe was suffering in the general disturbance, and after breakfast I ordered the tents to be struck and everything prepared for an immediate start when the boats could be launched."

I had decided to take the *James Caird* myself, with Wild and eleven men. This was the largest of our boats, and in addition to her human complement she carried the major portion of the stores. Worsley had charge of the *Dudley Docker* with nine men, and Hudson and Crean were the senior men on the *Stancomb Wills*.

Soon after breakfast the ice closed again. We were standing by, with our preparations as complete as they could be made, when at 11 a.m. our floe suddenly split right across under the boats. We rushed our gear on to the larger of the two pieces and watched with strained attention for the next development.

The crack had cut through the site of my tent. I stood on the edge of the new fracture, and, looking across the widening channel of water, could see the spot where for many months my head and shoulders had rested when I was in my sleeping bag. The depression formed by my body and legs was on our side of the crack. The ice had sunk under my weight during the months of waiting in the tent, and I had many times put snow under the bag to fill the hollow. The lines of stratification showed clearly the different layers of snow. How fragile and precarious had been our restingplace! Yet usage had dulled our sense of danger. The floe had become our home, and during the early months of the drift we had almost ceased to realize that it was but a sheet of ice floating on unfathomed seas. Now our home was being shattered under our feet, and we had a sense of loss and incompleteness hard to describe.

The fragments of our floe came together again a little later, and we had our lunch of seal meat, all hands eating their fill. I thought that a good meal would be the best possible preparation for the journey that now seemed imminent, and as we would not be able to take all our meat with us when we finally moved, we could regard every pound eaten as a pound rescued. The call to action came at 1 p.m. The pack opened well and the channels became navigable. The conditions were not all one could have desired, but it was best not to wait any longer. The *Dudley Docker* and the *Stancomb Wills* were launched quickly. Stores were thrown in, and the two boats were pulled clear of the immediate floes towards a pool of open water three miles broad, in which floated a lone and mighty berg. The *James Caird* was the last boat to leave, heavily loaded with stores and odds and ends of camp equipment. Many things regarded by us as essentials at that time were to be discarded a little later as the pressure of the primitive became more severe. Man can sustain life with very scanty means. The trappings of civilization are soon cast aside in the face of stern realities, and given the barest opportunity of winning food and shelter, man can live and even find his laughter ringing true.

The three boats were a mile away from our floe home at 2 p.m. We had made our way through the channels and had entered the big pool when we saw a rush of foamclad water and tossing ice approaching us, like the tidal bore of a river. The pack was being impelled to the east by a tide-rip, and two huge masses of ice were driving down upon us on converging courses. The *James Caird* was leading.

Starboarding the helm and bending strongly to the oars, we managed to get clear. The two other boats followed us, though from their position astern at first they had not realized the immediate danger. The *Stancomb Wills* was the last boat and she was very nearly caught; but by great exertion she was kept just ahead of the driving ice. It was an unusual and startling experience. The effect of tidal action on ice is not often as marked as it was that day. The advancing ice, accompanied by a large wave, appeared to be travelling at about three knots; and if we had not succeeded in pulling clear we would certainly have been swamped.

We pulled hard for an hour to windward of the berg that lay in the open water. The swell was crashing on its perpendicular sides and throwing spray to a height of sixty feet. Evidently there was an ice-foot at the east end, for the swell broke before it reached the bergface and flung its white spray on to the blue icewall. We might have paused to have admired the spectacle under other conditions; but night was coming on apace, and we needed a campingplace. As we steered northwest, still amid the icefloes, the *Dudley Docker* got jammed between two masses while attempting to make a short cut. The old adage about a short cut being the longest way round is often as true in the Antarctic as it is in the peaceful countryside. The *James Caird* got a line aboard the *Dudley Docker*, and after some hauling the boat was brought clear of the ice again. We hastened forward in the twilight in search of a flat, old floe, and presently found a fairly large piece rocking in the swell. It was not an ideal campingplace by any means, but darkness had overtaken us. We hauled the boats up, and by 8 p.m. had the tents pitched and the blubberstove burning cheerily. Soon all hands were well fed and happy in their tents, and snatches of song came to me as I wrote up my log. Some intangible feeling of uneasiness made me leave my tent about 11 p.m. that night and glance around the quiet camp. The stars between the snow-flurries showed that the floe had swung round and was end on to the swell, a position exposing it to sudden strains. I started to walk across the floe in order to warn the watchman to look carefully for cracks, and as I was passing the men's tent the floe lifted on the crest of a swell and cracked right under my feet. The men were in one of the domeshaped tents, and it began to stretch apart as the ice opened. A muffled sound, suggestive of suffocation, came from beneath the stretching tent. I rushed forward, helped some emerging men from under the canvas, and called out,

"Are you all right?"

"There are two in the water," somebody answered. The crack had widened to about four feet, and as I threw myself down at the edge, I saw a whitish object floating in the water. It was a sleepingbag with a man inside. I was able to grasp it, and with a heave lifted man and bag on to the floe. A few seconds later the iceedges came together again with tremendous force. Fortunately, there had been but one man in the water, or the incident might have been a tragedy. The rescued bag contained Holness, who was wet down to the waist but otherwise unscathed. The crack was now opening again. The *James Caird* and my tent were on one side of the opening and the remaining two boats and the rest of the camp on the other side. With two or three men to help me I struck my tent; then all hands manned the painter and rushed the *James Caird* across the opening crack. We held to the rope while, one by one, the men left on our side of the floe jumped the channel or scrambled over by means of the boat. Finally I was left alone. The night had swallowed all the others and the rapid movement of the ice forced me to let go the painter. For a moment I felt that my piece of rocking floe was the loneliest place in the world. Peering into the darkness, I could just see the dark figures on the other floe. I hailed Wild, ordering him to launch the *Stancomb Wills*, but I need not have troubled. His quick brain had anticipated the order and already the boat was being manned and hauled to the iceedge. Two or three minutes later she reached me, and I was ferried across to the Camp.

We were now on a piece of flat ice about 200 ft. long and 100 ft. wide. There was no more sleep for any of us that night. The killers were blowing in the lanes around, and we waited for daylight and watched for signs of another crack in the ice. The hours passed with laggard feet as we stood huddled together or walked to and fro in the effort to keep some warmth in our bodies. We lit the blubber-stove at 3 a.m., and with pipes going and a cup of hot milk for each man, we were able to discover some bright spots in our outlook. At any rate, we were on the move at last, and if dangers and difficulties lay ahead we could meet and overcome them. No longer were we drifting helplessly at the mercy of wind and current.

The first glimmerings of dawn came at 6 a.m., and I waited anxiously for the full daylight. The swell was growing, and at times our ice was surrounded closely by similar pieces. At 6.30 a.m. we had hot hoosh, and then stood by waiting for the pack to open. Our chance came at 8, when we launched the boats, loaded them, and started to make our way through the lanes in a northerly direction; the *James Caird* was in the lead, with the *Stancomb Wills* next and the *Dudley Docker* bringing up the rear. In order to make the boats more seaworthy we had left some of our shovels, picks, and dried vegetables on the floe, and for a long time we could see the abandoned stores forming a dark spot on the ice. The boats were still heavily loaded. We got out of the lanes, and entered a stretch of open water at 11 a.m. A strong easterly breeze was blowing, but the fringe of pack lying outside protected us from the full force of the swell, just as the coralreef of a tropical island checks the rollers of the Pacific. Our way was across the open sea, and soon after noon we swung round the north end of the pack and laid a course to the westward, the *James Caird* still in the lead. Immediately our deeply laden boats began to make heavy weather. They shipped sprays, which, freezing as they fell, covered men and gear with ice, and soon it was clear that we could not safely proceed. I put the *James Caird* round and ran for the shelter of the pack again, the other boats following. Back inside the outer line of ice the sea was not breaking. This was at 3 p.m., and all hands were tired and cold. A big floeberg resting peacefully ahead caught my eye, and half an hour later we had hauled up the boats and pitched camp for the night. It was a fine, big, blue berg with an attractively solid appearance, and from our camp we could get a good view of the surrounding sea and ice. The highest point was about 15 ft. above sealevel. After a hot meal all hands, except the watchman, turned in. Every one was in need of rest after the troubles of the previous night and the unaccustomed strain of the last thirty-six hours at the oars. The berg appeared well able to withstand the battering of the sea, and too deep and massive to be seriously affected by the swell; but it was not as safe as it looked. About midnight the watchman called me and showed me that the heavy north-westerly swell was undermining the ice. A great piece had broken off within eight feet of my tent. We made what inspection was possible in the darkness, and found that on the westward side of the berg the thick snow covering was yielding rapidly to the attacks of the sea. An ice-foot had formed just under the surface of the water. I decided that there was no immediate danger and did not call the men. The north-westerly wind strengthened during the night. The morning of April 11 was overcast and misty. There was a haze on the horizon, and daylight showed that the pack had closed round our berg, making it impossible in the heavy swell to launch the boats. We could see no sign of the water. Numerous whales and killers were blowing between the floes, and Cape pigeons, petrels, and fulmars were circling round our berg. The scene from our camp as the daylight brightened was magnificent beyond description, though I must admit that we viewed it with anxiety. Heaving hills of pack and floe were sweeping towards us in long undulations, later to be broken here and there by the dark lines that indicated open water. As each swell lifted around our rapidly dissolving berg it drove floe-ice on to the icefoot, shearing off more of the top snowcovering and reducing the size of our camp. When the floes retreated to attack again the water swirled over the icefoot, which was rapidly increasing in width. The launching of the boats under such conditions would be difficult. Time after time, so often that a track was formed, Worsley, Wild, and I, climbed to the highest point of the berg and stared out to the horizon in search of a break in the pack. After long hours had dragged past, far away on the lift of the swell then appeared a dark break in the tossing field of ice. Aeons seemed to pass, so slowly it approached. I noticed enviously the calm, peaceful attitudes of two seals which lolled lazily on a rocking floe. They were at home and had no reason for worry or cause for fear. If they thought at all, I suppose they counted it an ideal day for a joyous journey on the tumbling ice. To us it was a day that seemed likely to lead to no more days. I do not think I had ever before felt the anxiety that belongs to leadership quite so keenly. When I looked down at the camp to rest my eyes from the strain of watching the wide white expanse broken by that one black ribbon of open water, I could see that my companions were waiting with more than ordinary interest to learn what I thought about it all. After one particularly heavy collision somebody shouted sharply, "She has cracked in the middle." I jumped off the lookout station and ran to the place the men were examining. There was a crack, but investigation showed it to be a mere surface-break in the snow with no indication of a split in the berg itself. The carpenter mentioned calmly that earlier in the day he had actually gone adrift on a fragment of ice. He was standing near the edge of our camping-ground when the ice under his feet parted from the parent mass. A quick jump over the widening gap saved him.

The hours dragged on. One of the anxieties in my mind was the possibility that we would be driven by the current through the eightymile gap between Clarence Island and Prince George Island into the open Atlantic; but slowly the open water came nearer, and at noon it had almost reached us. A long lane, narrow but navigable, stretched out to the southwest horizon. Our chance came a little later. We rushed our boats over the edge of the reeling berg and swung them clear of the ice-foot as it rose beneath them. The *James Caird* was nearly capsized by a blow from below as the berg rolled away, but she got into deep water. We flung stores and gear aboard and within a few minutes were away. The *James Caird* and *Dudley Docker* had good sails and with a favourable breeze could make progress along the lane, with the rolling fields of ice on either side. The swell was heavy and spray was breaking over the icefloes. An attempt to set a little rag of sail on the *Stancomb Wills* resulted in serious delay. The area of sail was too small to be of much assistance, and while the men were engaged in this work the boat drifted down towards the ice-floe, where her position was likely to be perilous. Seeing her plight, I sent the *Dudley Docker* back for her and tied the *James Caird* up to a piece of ice. The *Dudley Docker* had to tow the *Stancomb Wills*, and the delay cost us two hours of valuable daylight. When I had the three boats together again we continued down the lane, and soon saw a wider stretch of water to the west; it appeared to offer us release from the grip of the pack. At the head of an icetongue that nearly closed the gap through which we might enter the open space was a wave-worn berg shaped like some curious antediluvian monster, an icy Cerberus guarding the way. It had head and eyes and rolled so heavily that it almost overturned. Its sides dipped deep in the sea, and as it rose again the water seemed to be streaming from its eyes, as though it were weeping at our escape from the clutch of the floes. This may seem fanciful to the reader, but the impression was real to us at the time. People living under civilized conditions, surrounded by Nature's varied forms of life and by all the familiar work of their own hands, may scarcely realize how quickly the mind, influenced by the eyes, responds to the unusual and weaves about it curious imaginings like the firelight fancies of our childhood days. We had lived long amid the ice, and we halfunconsciously strove to see resemblances to human faces and living forms in the fantastic contours and massively uncouth shapes of berg and floe.

At dusk we made fast to a heavy floe, each boat having its painter fastened to a separate hummock in order to avoid collisions in the swell. We landed the blubber-stove, boiled some water in order to provide hot milk, and served cold rations. I also landed the dome tents and stripped the coverings from the hoops. Our experience of the previous day in the open sea had shown us that the tents must be packed tightly. The spray had dashed over the bows and turned to ice on the cloth, which had soon grown dangerously heavy. Other articles of our scanty equipment had to go that night. We were carrying only the things that had seemed essential, but we stripped now to the barest limit of safety. We had hoped for a quiet night, but presently we were forced to cast off, since pieces of loose ice began to work round the floe. Driftice is always attracted to the lee side of a heavy floe, where it bumps and presses under the influence of the current. I had determined not to risk a repetition of the last night's experience and so had not pulled the boats up. We spent the hours of darkness keeping an offing from the main line of pack under the lee of the smaller pieces. Constant rain and snow squalls blotted out the stars and soaked us through, and at times it was only by shouting to each other that we managed to keep the boats together. There was no sleep for anybody owing to the severe cold, and we dared not pull fast enough to keep ourselves warm since we were unable to see more than a few yards ahead. Occasionally the ghostly shadows of silver, snow, and fulmar petrels flashed close to us, and all around we could hear the killers blowing, their short, sharp hisses sounding like sudden escapes of steam. The killers were a source of anxiety, for a boat could easily have been capsized by one of them coming up to blow. They would throw aside in a nonchalant fashion pieces of ice much bigger than our boats when they rose to the surface, and we had an uneasy feeling that the white bottoms of the boats would look like ice from below. Shipwrecked mariners drifting in the Antarctic seas would be things not dreamed of in the killers' philosophy, and might appear on closer examination to be tasty substitutes for seal and penguin. We certainly regarded the killers with misgivings.

Early in the morning of April 12 the weather improved and the wind dropped. Dawn came with a clear sky, cold and fearless. I looked around at the faces of my companions in the *James Caird* and saw pinched and drawn features. The strain was beginning to tell. Wild sat at the rudder with the same calm, confident expression that he would have worn under happier conditions; his steelblue eyes looked out to the day ahead. All the people, though evidently suffering, were doing their best to be cheerful, and the prospect of a hot breakfast was inspiriting. I told all the boats that immediately we could find a suitable floe the cooker would be started and hot milk and Bovril would soon fix everybody up. Away we rowed to the westward through open pack, floes of all shapes and sizes on every side of us, and every man not engaged in pulling looking eagerly for a suitable campingplace. I could gauge the desire for food of the different members by the eagerness they displayed in pointing out to me the floes they considered exactly suited to our purpose. The temperature was about 10 degrees Fahr., and the Burberry suits of the rowers crackled as the men bent to the oars. I noticed little fragments of ice and frost falling from arms and bodies. At eight o'clock a decent floe appeared ahead and we pulled up to it. The galley was landed, and soon the welcome steam rose from the cooking food as the blubber-stove flared and smoked. Never did a cook work under more anxious scrutiny. Worsley, Crean, and I stayed in our respective boats to keep them steady and prevent collisions with the floe, since the swell was still running strong, but the other men were able to stretch their cramped limbs and run to and fro "in the kitchen," as somebody put it. The sun was now rising gloriously. The Burberry suits were drying and the ice was melting off our beards. The steaming food gave us new vigour, and within threequarters of an hour were off again to the west with all sails set. We had given an additional sail to the *Stancomb Wills* and she was able to keep up pretty well. We could see that we were on the true pack-edge, with the blue, rolling sea just outside the fringe of ice to the north. White-capped waves vied with the glittering floes in the setting of blue water, and countless seals basked and rolled on every piece of ice big enough to form a raft.

We had been making westward with oars and sails since April 9, and fair easterly winds had prevailed. Hopes were running high as to the noon observation for position. The optimists thought that we had done sixty miles towards our goal, and the most cautious guess gave us at least thirty miles. The bright sunshine and the brilliant scene around us may have influenced our anticipations. As noon approached I saw Worsley, as navigating officer, balancing himself on the gunwale of the *Dudley Docker* with his arm around the mast, ready to snap the sun. He got his observation and we waited eagerly while he worked out the sight. Then the *Dudley Docker* ranged up alongside the *James Caird* and I jumped into Worsley's boat in order to see the result. It was a grievous disappointment. Instead of making a good run to the westward we had made a big drift to the south-east. We were actually thirty miles to the east of the position we had occupied when we left the floe on the 9th. It has been noted by sealers operating in this area that there are often heavy sets to the east in the Belgica Straits, and no doubt it was one of these sets that we had experienced. The originating cause would be a north-westerly gale off Cape Horn, producing the swell that had already caused us so much trouble. After a whispered consultation with Worsley and Wild, I announced that we had not made as much progress as we expected, but I did not inform the hands of our retrograde movement.

The question of our course now demanded further consideration. Deception Island seemed to be beyond our reach. The wind was foul for Elephant Island, and as the sea was clear to the southwest, I discussed with Worsley and Wild the advisability of proceeding to Hope Bay on the mainland of the Antarctic Continent, now only eighty miles distant. Elephant Island was the nearest land, but it lay outside the main body of pack, and even if the wind had been fair we would have hesitated at that particular time to face the high sea that was running in the open. We laid a course roughly for Hope Bay, and the boats moved on again. I gave Worsley a line for a berg ahead and told him, if possible, to make fast before darkness set in. This was about three o'clock in the afternoon. We had set sail, and as the *Stancomb Wills* could not keep up with the other two boats I took her in tow, not being anxious to repeat the experience of the day we left the reeling berg. The *Dudley Docker* went ahead, but came beating down towards us at dusk. Worsley had been close to the berg, and he reported that it was unapproachable. It was rolling in the swell and displaying an ugly ice-foot. The news was bad. In the failing light we turned towards a line of pack, and found it so tossed and churned by the sea that no fragment remained big enough to give us an anchorage and shelter. Two miles away we could see a larger piece of ice, and to it we managed, after some trouble, to secure the boats. I brought my boat bow on to the floe, whilst Howe, with the painter in his hand, stood ready to jump. Standing up to watch our chance, while the oars were held ready to back the moment Howe had made his leap, I could see that there would be no possibility of getting the galley ashore that night. Howe just managed to get a footing on the edge of the floe, and then made the painter fast to a hummock. The other two boats were fastened alongside the *James Caird*. They could not lie astern of us in a line, since cakes of ice came drifting round the floe and gathering under its lee. As it was we spent the next two hours poling off the drifting ice that surged towards us. The blubberstove could not be used, so we started the Primus lamps. There was a rough, choppy sea, and the *Dudley Docker* could not get her Primus under way, something being adrift. The men in that boat had to wait until the cook on the *James Caird* had boiled up the first pot of milk.

The boats were bumping so heavily that I had to slack away the painter of the *Stancomb Wills* and put her astern. Much ice was coming round the floe and had to be poled off. Then the *Dudley Docker*, being the heavier boat, began to damage the *James Caird*, and I slacked the *Dudley Docker* away. The *James Caird* remained moored to the ice, with the

*Dudley Docker* and the *Stancomb Wills* in line behind her. The darkness had become complete, and we strained our eye to see the fragments of ice that threatened us. Presently we thought we saw a great berg bearing down upon us, its form outlined against the sky, but this startling spectacle resolved itself into a lowlying cloud in front of the rising moon. The moon appeared in a clear sky. The wind shifted to the southeast as the light improved and drove the boats broadside on towards the jagged edge of the floe. We had to cut the painter of the *James Caird* and pole her off, thus losing much valuable rope. There was no time to cast off. Then we pushed away from the floe, and all night long we lay in the open, freezing sea, the *Dudley Docker* now ahead, the *James Caird* astern of her, and the *Stancomb Wills* third in the line. The boats were attached to one another by their painters. Most of the time the *Dudley Docker* kept the *James Caird* and the *Stancomb Wills* up to the swell, and the men who were rowing were in better pass than those in the other boats, waiting inactive for the dawn. The temperature was down to 4 degrees below zero, and a film of ice formed on the surface of the sea. When we were not on watch we lay in each other's arms for warmth. Our frozen suits thawed where our bodies met, and as the slightest movement exposed these comparatively warm spots to the biting air, we clung motionless, whispering each to his companion our hopes and thoughts. Occasionally from an almost clear sky came snow-showers, falling silently on the sea and laying a thin shroud of white over our bodies and our boats.

The dawn of April 13 came clear and bright, with occasional passing clouds. Most of the men were now looking seriously worn and strained. Their lips were cracked and their eyes and eyelids showed red in their saltencrusted faces. The beards even of the younger men might have been those of patriarchs, for the frost and the salt spray had made them white. I called the *Dudley Docker* alongside and found the condition of the people there was no better than in the *James Caird*. Obviously we must make land quickly, and I decided to run for Elephant Island. The wind had shifted fair for that rocky isle, then about one hundred miles away, and the pack that separated us from Hope Bay had closed up during the night from the south. At 6 p.m. we made a distribution of stores among the three boats, in view of the possibility of their being separated. The preparation of a hot breakfast was out of the question. The breeze was strong and the sea was running high in the loose pack around us. We had a cold meal, and I gave orders that all hands might eat as much as they pleased, this concession being due partly to a realization that we would have to jettison some of our stores when we reached open sea in order to lighten the boats. I hoped, moreover, that a full meal of cold rations would compensate to some extent for the lack of warm food and shelter. Unfortunately, some of the men were unable to take advantage of the extra food owing to sea-sickness. Poor fellows, it was bad enough to be huddled in the deeply laden, spray-swept boats, frostbitten and half-frozen, without having the pangs of sea-sickness added to the list of their woes. But some smiles were caused even then by the plight of one man, who had a habit of accumulating bits of food against the day of starvation that he seemed always to think was at hand, and who was condemned now to watch impotently while hungry comrades with undisturbed stomachs made biscuits, rations, and sugar disappear with extraordinary rapidity.

We ran before the wind through the loose pack, a man in the bow of each boat trying to pole off with a broken oar the lumps of ice that could not be avoided. I regarded speed as essential. Sometimes collisions were not averted. The *James Caird* was in the lead, where she bore the brunt of the encounter with lurking fragments, and she was holed above the water-line by a sharp spur of ice, but this mishap did not stay us. Later the wind became stronger and we had to reef sails, so as not to strike the ice too heavily. The *Dudley Docker* came next to the *James Caird* and the *Stancomb Wills* followed. I had given orders that the boats should keep 30 or 40 yds. apart, so as to reduce the danger of a collision if one boat was checked by the ice. The pack was thinning, and we came to occasional open areas where thin ice had formed during the night. When we encountered this new ice we had to shake the reef out of the sails in order to force a way through. Outside of the pack the wind must have been of hurricane force. Thousands of small dead fish were to be seen, killed probably by a cold current and the heavy weather. They floated in the water and lay on the ice, where they had been cast by the waves. The petrels and skua-gulls were swooping down and picking them up like sardines off toast.

We made our way through the lanes till at noon we were suddenly spewed out of the pack into the open ocean. Dark blue and sapphire green ran the seas. Our sails were soon up; and with a fair wind we moved over the waves like three Viking ships on the quest of a lost Atlantis. With the sheet well out and the sun shining bright above, we enjoyed for a few hours a sense of the freedom and magic of the sea, compensating us for pain and trouble in the days that had passed. At last we were free from the ice, in water that our boats could navigate. Thoughts of home, stifled by the deadening weight of anxious days and nights, came to birth once more, and the difficulties that had still to be overcome dwindled in fancy almost to nothing.

During the afternoon we had to take a second reef in the sails, for the wind freshened and the deeply laden boats were shipping much water and steering badly in the rising sea. I had laid the course for Elephant Island and we were making good progress. The *Dudley Docker* ran down to me at dusk and Worsley suggested that we should stand on all night; but already the *Stancomb Wills* was barely discernible among the rollers in the gathering dusk, and I decided that it would be safer to heave to and wait for the daylight. It would never have done for the boats to have become separated from one another during the night. The party must be kept together, and, moreover, I thought it possible that we might overrun our goal in the darkness and not be able to return. So we made a sea-anchor of oars and hove to, the *Dudley Docker* in the lead, since she had the longest painter. The *James Caird* swung astern of the *Dudley Docker* and the *Stancomb Wills* again had the third place. We ate a cold meal and did what little we could to make things comfortable for the hours of darkness. Rest was not for us. During the greater part of the night the sprays broke over the boats and froze in masses of ice, especially at the stern and bows. This ice had to be broken away in order to prevent the boats' growing too heavy. The temperature was below zero and the wind penetrated our clothes and chilled us almost unbearably. I doubted if all the men would survive that night. One of our troubles was lack of water. We had emerged so suddenly from the pack into the open sea that we had not had time to take aboard ice for melting in the cookers, and without ice we could not have hot food. The *Dudley Docker* had one lump of ice weighing about ten pounds, and this was shared out among all hands. We sucked small pieces and got a little relief from thirst engendered by the salt spray, but at the same time we reduced our bodily heat. The condition of most of the men was pitiable. All of us had swollen mouths and we could hardly touch the food. I longed intensely for the dawn. I called out to the other boats at intervals during the night, asking how things were with them. The men always managed to reply cheerfully. One of the people on the *Stancomb Wills* shouted, "We are doing all right, but I would like some dry mits." The jest brought a smile to cracked lips. He might as well have asked for the moon. The only dry things aboard the boats were swollen mouths and burning tongues. Thirst is one of the troubles that confront the traveller in polar regions. Ice may be plentiful on every hand, but it does not become drinkable until it is melted, and the amount that may be dissolved in the mouth is limited. We had been thirsty during the days of heavy pulling in the pack, and our condition was aggravated quickly by the salt spray. Our sleepingbags would have given us some warmth, but they were not within our reach. They were packed under the tents in the bows, where a mail-like coating of ice enclosed them, and we were so cramped that we could not pull them out.

At last daylight came, and with the dawn the weather cleared and the wind fell to a gentle southwesterly breeze. A magnificent sunrise heralded in what we hoped would be our last day in the boats. Rose-pink in the growing light, the lofty peak of Clarence Island told of the coming glory of the sun. The sky grew blue above us and the crests of the waves sparkled cheerfully. As soon as it was light enough we chipped and scraped the ice off the bows and sterns. The rudders had been unshipped during the night in order to avoid the painters catching them. We cast off our iceanchor and pulled the oars aboard. They had grown during the night to the thickness of telegraphpoles while rising and falling in the freezing seas, and had to be chipped clear before they could be brought inboard.

We were dreadfully thirsty now. We found that we could get momentary relief by chewing pieces of raw seal meat and swallowing the blood, but thirst came back with redoubled force owing to the saltiness of the flesh. I gave orders, therefore, that meat was to be served out only at stated intervals during the day or when thirst seemed to threaten the reason of any particular individual. In the full daylight Elephant Island showed cold and severe to the north north-west. The island was on the bearings that Worsley had laid down, and I congratulated him on the accuracy of his navigation under difficult circumstances, with two days dead reckoning while following a devious course through the pack-ice and after drifting during two nights at the mercy of wind and waves. The *Stancomb Wills* came up and McIlroy reported that Blackborrow's feet were very badly frost-bitten. This was unfortunate, but nothing could be done. Most of the people were frost-bitten to some extent, and it was interesting to notice that the "oldtimers," Wild, Crean, Hurley, and I, were all right. Apparently we were acclimatized to ordinary Antarctic temperature, though we learned later that we were not immune.

All day, with a gentle breeze on our port bow, we sailed and pulled through a clear sea. We would have given all the tea in China for a lump of ice to melt into water, but no ice was within our reach. Three bergs were in sight and we pulled towards them, hoping that a trail of brash would be floating on the sea to leeward; but they were hard and blue, devoid of any sign of cleavage, and the swell that surged around them as they rose and fell made it impossible for us to approach closely. The wind was gradually hauling ahead, and as the day wore on the rays of the sun beat fiercely down from a cloudless sky on painracked men. Progress was slow, but gradually Elephant Island came nearer. Always while I attended to the other boats, signalling and ordering, Wild sat at the tiller of the *James Caird*. He seemed unmoved by fatigue and unshaken by privation. About four o'clock in the afternoon a stiff breeze came up ahead and, blowing against the current, soon produced a choppy sea. During the next hour of hard pulling we seemed to make no progress at all. The *James Caird* and the *Dudley Docker* had been towing the *Stancomb Wills* in turn, but my boat now took the *Stancomb Wills* in tow permanently, as the *James Caird* could carry more sail than the *Dudley Docker* in the freshening wind.

We were making up for the southeast side of Elephant Island, the wind being between northwest and west. The boats, held as close to the wind as possible, moved slowly, and when darkness set in our goal was still some miles away. A heavy sea was running. We soon lost sight of the *Stancomb Wills*, astern of the *James Caird* at the length of the painter, but occasionally the white gleam of broken water revealed her presence. When the darkness was complete I sat in the stern with my hand on the painter, so that I might know if the other boat broke away, and I kept that position during the night. The rope grew heavy with the ice as the unseen seas surged past us and our little craft tossed to the motion of the waters. Just at dusk I had told the men on the *Stancomb Wills* that if their boat broke away during the night and they were unable to pull against the wind, they could run for the east side of Clarence Island and await our coming there. Even though we could not land on Elephant Island, it would not do to have the third boat adrift.

It was a stern night. The men, except the watch, crouched and huddled in the bottom of the boat, getting what little warmth they could from the soaking sleepingbags and each other's bodies. Harder and harder blew the wind and fiercer and fiercer grew the sea. The boat plunged heavily through the squalls and came up to the wind, the sail shaking in the stiffest gusts. Every now and then, as the night wore on, the moon would shine down through a rift in the driving clouds, and in the momentary light I could see the ghostly faces of men, sitting up to trim the boat as she heeled over to the wind. When the moon was hidden its presence was revealed still by the light reflected on the streaming glaciers of the island. The temperature had fallen very low, and it seemed that the general discomfort of our situation could scarcely have been increased; but the land looming ahead was a beacon of safety, and I think we were all buoyed up by the hope that the coming day would see the end of our immediate troubles. At least we would get firm land under our feet. While the painter of the *Stancomb Wills* tightened and drooped under my hand, my thoughts were busy with plans for the future.

Towards midnight the wind shifted to the south-west, and this change enabled us to bear up closer to the island. A little later the *Dudley Docker* ran down to the *James Caird*, and Worsley shouted a suggestion that he should go ahead and search for a landing-place. His boat had the heels of the *James Caird*, with the *Stancomb Wills* in tow. I told him he could try, but he must not lose sight of the *James Caird*. Just as he left me a heavy snowsquall came down, and in the darkness the boats parted. I saw the *Dudley Docker* no more. This separation caused me some anxiety during the remaining hours of the night. A crosssea was running and I could not feel sure that all was well with the missing boat. The waves could not be seen in the darkness, though the direction and force of the wind could be felt, and under such conditions, in an open boat, disaster might overtake the most experienced navigator. I flashed our compasslamp on the sail in the hope that the signal would be visible on board the *Dudley Docker*, but could see no reply. We strained our eyes to windward in the darkness in the hope of catching a return signal and repeated our flashes at intervals.

My anxiety, as a matter of fact, was groundless. I will quote Worsley's own account of what happened to the *Dudley Docker*:

"About midnight we lost sight of the *James Caird* with the *Stancomb Wills* in tow, but not long after saw the light of the *James Caird's* compasslamp, which Sir Ernest was flashing on their sail as a guide to us. We answered by lighting our candle under the tent and letting the light shine through. At the same time we got the direction of the wind and how we were hauling from my little pocketcompass, the boat's compass being smashed. With this candle our poor fellows lit their pipes, their only solace, as our raging thirst prevented us from eating anything. By this time we had got into a bad tiderip, which, combined with the heavy, lumpy sea, made it almost impossible to keep the *Dudley Docker* from swamping. As it was we shipped several bad seas over the stern as well as abeam and over the bows, although we were 'on a wind.' Lees, who owned himself to be a rotten oarsman, made good here by strenuous bailing, in which he was well seconded by Cheetham. Greenstreet, a splendid fellow, relieved me at the tiller and helped generally. He and Macklin were my right and left bowers as stroke-oars throughout. McLeod and Cheetham were two good sailors and oars, the former a typical old deepsea salt and growler, the latter a pirate to his fingertips. In the height of the gale that night Cheetham was buying matches from me for bottles of champagne, one bottle per match (too cheap; I should have charged him two bottles). The champagne is to be paid when he opens his pub in Hull and I am able to call that way. . . . We had now had one hundred and eight hours of toil, tumbling, freezing, and soaking, with little or no sleep. I think Sir Ernest, Wild, Greenstreet, and I could say that we had no sleep at all. Although it was sixteen months since we had been in a rough sea, only four men were actually sea-sick, but several others were off colour.

"The temperature was 20 degrees below freezingpoint; fortunately, we were spared the bitterly low temperature of the previous night. Greenstreet's right foot got badly frostbitten, but Lees restored it by holding it in his sweater against his stomach. Other men had minor frostbites, due principally to the fact that their clothes were soaked through with salt water. . . . We were close to the land as the morning approached, but could see nothing of it through the snow and spindrift. My eyes began to fail me. Constant peering to windward, watching for seas to strike us, appeared to have given me a cold in the eyes. I could not see or judge distance properly, and found myself falling asleep momentarily at the tiller. At 3 a.m. Greenstreet relieved me there. I was so cramped from long hours, cold, and wet, in the constrained position one was forced to assume on top of the gear and stores at the tiller, that the other men had to pull me amidships and straighten me out like a jackknife, first rubbing my thighs, groin, and stomach.

"At daylight we found ourselves close alongside the land, but the weather was so thick that we could not see where to make for a landing. Having taken the tiller again after an hour's rest under the shelter (save the mark!) of the dripping tent, I ran the *Dudley Docker* off before the gale, following the coast around to the north. This course for the first hour was fairly risky, the heavy sea before which we were running threatening to swamp the boat, but by 8 a.m. we had obtained a slight lee from the land. Then I was able to keep her very close in, along a glacier front, with the object of picking up lumps of freshwater ice as we sailed through them. Our thirst was intense. We soon had some ice aboard, and for the next hour and a half we sucked and chewed fragments of ice with greedy relish.

"All this time we were coasting along beneath towering rocky cliffs and sheer glacierfaces, which offered not the slightest possibility of landing anywhere. At 9:30 a.m. we spied a narrow, rocky beach at the base of some very high crags and cliffs, and made for it. To our joy, we sighted the *James Caird* and the *Stancomb Wills* sailing into the same haven just ahead of us. We were so delighted that we gave three cheers, which were not heard aboard the other boats owing to the roar of the surf. However, we soon joined them and were able to exchange experiences on the beach."

Our experiences on the *James Caird* had been similar, although we had not been able to keep up to windward as well as the *Dudley Docker* had done. This was fortunate as events proved, for the *James Caird* and *Stancomb Wills* went to leeward of the big bight the *Dudley Docker* entered and from which she had to turn out with the sea astern. We thus avoided the risk of having the *Stancomb Wills* swamped in the following sea. The weather was very thick in the morning. Indeed at 7 a.m. we were right under the cliffs, which plunged sheer into the sea, before we saw them. We followed the coast towards the north, and ever the precipitous cliffs and glacierfaces presented themselves to our searching eyes. The sea broke heavily against these walls and a landing would have been impossible under any conditions. We picked up pieces of ice and sucked them eagerly. At 9 a.m. at the northwest end of the island we saw a narrow beach at the foot of the cliffs. Outside lay a fringe of rocks heavily beaten by the surf but with a narrow channel showing as a break in the foaming water. I decided that we must face the hazards of this unattractive landing-place. Two days and nights without drink or hot food had played havoc with most of the men, and we could not assume that any safer haven lay within our reach. The *Stancomb Wills* was the lighter and handier boat—and I called her alongside with the intention of taking her through the gap first and ascertaining the possibilities of a landing before the *James Caird* made the venture. I was just climbing into the *Stancomb Wills* when I saw the *Dudley Docker* coming up astern under sail. The sight took a great load off my mind.

Rowing carefully and avoiding the blind rollers which showed where sunken rocks lay, we brought the *Stancomb Wills* towards the opening in the reef. Then, with a few strong strokes we shot through on the top of a swell and ran the boat on to a stony beach. The next swell lifted her a little farther. This was the first landing ever made on Elephant Island, and a thought came to me that the honour should belong to the youngest member of the Expedition, so I told Blackborrow to jump over. He seemed to be in a state almost of coma, and in order to avoid delay I helped him, perhaps a little roughly, over the side of the boat. He promptly sat down in the surf and did not move. Then I suddenly realized what I had forgotten, that both his feet were frost-bitten badly. Some of us jumped over and pulled him into a dry place. It was a rather rough experience for Blackborrow, but, anyhow, he is now able to say that he was the first man to sit on Elephant Island. Possibly at the time he would have been willing to forgo any distinction of the kind. We landed the cook with his blubber-stove, a supply of fuel and some packets of dried milk, and also several of the men. Then the rest of us pulled out again to pilot the other boats through the channel. The *James Caird* was too heavy to be beached directly, so after landing most of the men from the *Dudley Docker* and the *Stancomb Wills* I superintended the transhipment of the *James Caird*'s gear outside the reef. Then we all made the passage, and within a few minutes the three boats were aground. A curious spectacle met my eyes when I landed the second time. Some of the men were reeling about the beach as if they had found an unlimited supply of alcoholic liquor on the desolate shore. They were laughing uproariously, picking up stones and letting handfuls of pebbles trickle between their fingers like misers gloating over hoarded gold. The smiles and laughter, which caused cracked lips to bleed afresh, and the gleeful exclamations at the sight of two live seals on the beach made me think for a moment of that glittering hour of childhood when the door is open at last and the Christmas-tree in all its wonder bursts upon the vision. I remember that Wild, who always rose superior to fortune, bad and good, came ashore as I was looking at the men and stood beside me as easy and unconcerned as if he had stepped out of his car for a stroll in the park.

Soon half a dozen of us had the stores ashore. Our strength was nearly exhausted and it was heavy work carrying our goods over the rough pebbles and rocks to the foot of the cliff, but we dared not leave anything within reach of the tide. We had to wade kneedeep in the icy water in order to lift the gear from the boats. When the work was done we pulled the three boats a little higher on the beach and turned gratefully to enjoy the hot drink the cook had prepared. Those of us who were comparatively fit had to wait until the weaker members of the party had been supplied; but every man had his pannikin of hot milk in the end, and never did anything taste better. Seal steak and blubber followed, for the seals that had been careless enough to await our arrival on the beach had already given up their lives. There was no rest for the cook. The blubber-stove flared and spluttered fiercely as he cooked, not one meal, but many meals, which merged into a daylong bout of eating. We drank water and ate seal meat until every man had reached the limit of his capacity.

The tents were pitched with oars for supports, and by 3 p.m. our camp was in order. The original framework of the tents had been cast adrift on one of the floes in order to save weight. Most of the men turned in early for a safe and glorious sleep, to be broken only by the call to take a turn on watch. The chief duty of the watchman was to keep the blubber-stove alight, and each man on duty appeared to find it necessary to cook himself a meal during his watch, and a supper before he turned in again.

Wild, Worsley, and Hurley accompanied me on an inspection of our beach before getting into the tents. I almost wished then that I had postponed the examination until after sleep, but the sense of caution that the uncertainties of polar travel implant in one's mind had made me uneasy. The outlook we found to be anything but cheering. Obvious signs showed that at spring tides the little beach would be covered by the water right up to the foot of the cliffs. In a strong northeasterly gale, such as we might expect to experience at any time, the waves would pound over the scant barrier of the reef and break against the sheer sides of the rocky wall behind us. Well-marked terraces showed the effect of other gales, and right at the back of the beach was a small bit of wreckage not more than three feet long, rounded by the constant chafing it had endured. Obviously we must find some better restingplace. I decided not to share with the men the knowledge of the uncertainties of our situation until they had enjoyed the full sweetness of rest untroubled by the thought that at any minute they might be called to face peril again. The threat of the sea had been our portion during many, many days, and a respite meant much to weary bodies and jaded minds.

The cliffs at the back of the beach were inaccessible except at two points where there were steep snowslopes. We were not worried now about food, for, apart from our own rations, there were seals on the beach and we could see others in the water outside the reef. Every now and then one of the animals would rise in the shallows and crawl up on the beach, which evidently was a recognized place of resort for its kind. A small rocky island which protected us to some extent from the northwesterly wind carried a ringedpenguin rookery. These birds were of migratory habit and might be expected to leave us before the winter set in fully, but in the meantime they were within our reach. These attractions, however, were overridden by the fact that the beach was open to the attack of wind and sea from the northeast and east. Easterly gales are more prevalent than western in that area of the Antarctic during the winter.

Before turning in that night I studied the whole position and weighed every chance of getting the boats and our stores into a place of safety out of reach of the water. We ourselves might have clambered a little way up the snow-slopes, but we could not have taken the boats with us. The interior of the island was quite inaccessible. We climbed up one of the slopes and found ourselves stopped soon by overhanging cliffs. The rocks behind the camp were much weathered, and we noticed the sharp, unworn boulders that had fallen from above. Clearly there was a danger from overhead if we camped at the back of the beach. We must move on. With that thought in mind I reached my tent and fell asleep on the rubbly ground, which gave a comforting sense of stability. The fairy princess who would not rest on her seven downy mattresses because a pea lay underneath the pile might not have understood the pleasure we all derived from the irregularities of the stones, which could not possibly break beneath us or drift away; the very searching lumps were sweet reminders of our safety.

Early next morning (April 15) all hands were astir. The sun soon shone brightly and we spread out our wet gear to dry, till the beach looked like a particularly disreputable gipsy camp. The boots and clothing had suffered considerably during our travels. I had decided to send Wild along the coast in the *Stancomb Wills* to look for a new campingground, and he and I discussed the details of the journey while eating our breakfast of hot seal steak and blubber. The camp I wished to find was one where the party could live for weeks or even months in safety, without danger from sea or wind in the heaviest winter gale. Wild was to proceed westwards along the coast and was to take with him four of the fittest men, Marston, Crean, Vincent, and McCarthy. If he did not return before dark we were to light a flare, which would serve him as a guide to the entrance of the channel. The *Stancomb Wills* pushed off at 11 a.m. and quickly passed out of sight around the island. Then Hurley and I walked along the beach towards the west, climbing through a gap between the cliff and a great detached pillar of basalt. The narrow strip of beach was cumbered with masses of rock that had fallen from the cliffs. We struggled along for two miles or more in the search for a place where we could get the boats ashore and make a permanent camp in the event of Wild's search proving fruitless, but after three hours' vain toil we had to turn back. We had found on the far side of the pillar of basalt a crevice in the rocks beyond the reach of all but the heaviest gales. Rounded pebbles showed that the seas reached the spot on occasions. Here I decided to depot ten cases of Bovril sledging ration in case of our having to move away quickly. We could come back for the food at a later date if opportunity offered.

Returning to the camp, we found the men resting or attending to their gear. Clark had tried angling in the shallows off the rocks and had secured one or two small fish. The day passed quietly. Rusty needles were rubbed bright on the rocks and clothes were mended and darned. A feeling of tiredness— due, I suppose, to reaction after the strain of the preceding days—overtook us, but the rising tide, coming farther up the beach than it had done on the day before, forced us to labour at the boats, which we hauled slowly to a higher ledge. We found it necessary to move our makeshift camp nearer the cliff. I portioned out the available ground for the tents, the galley, and other purposes, as every foot was of value. When night arrived the *Stancomb Wills* was still away, so I had a blubberflare lit at the head of the channel.

About 8 p.m. we heard a hail in the distance. We could see nothing, but soon like a pale ghost out of the darkness came the boat, the faces of the men showing white in the glare of the fire. Wild ran her on the beach with the swell, and within a couple of minutes we had dragged her to a place of safety. I was waiting Wild's report with keen anxiety, and my relief was great when he told me that he had discovered a sandy spit seven miles to the west, about 200 yds. long, running out at right angles to the coast and terminating at the seaward end in a mass of rock. A long snowslope joined the spit at the shore end, and it seemed possible that a "dugout" could be made in the snow. The spit, in any case, would be a great improvement on our narrow beach. Wild added that the place he described was the only possible camping-ground he had seen. Beyond, to the west and southwest, lay a frowning line of cliffs and gla-ciers, sheer to the water's edge. He thought that in very heavy gales either from the south-west or east the spit would be sprayblown, but that the seas would not actually break over it. The boats could be run up on a shelving beach. After hearing this good news I was eager to get away from the beach camp. The wind when blowing was favourable for the run along the coast. The weather had been fine for two days and a change might come at any hour. I told all hands that we would make a start early on the following morning. A newly killed seal provided a luxurious supper of steak and blubber, and then we slept comfortably till the dawn.

The morning of April 17 came fine and clear. The sea was smooth, but in the offing we could see a line of pack, which seemed to be approaching. We had noticed already pack and bergs being driven by the current to the east and then sometimes coming back with a rush to the west. The current ran as fast as five miles an hour, and it was a set of this kind that had delayed Wild on his return from the spit. The rise and fall of the tide was only about five feet at this time, but the moon was making for full and the tides were increasing. The appearance of ice emphasized the importance of getting away promptly. It would be a serious matter to be prisoned on the beach by the pack. The boats were soon afloat in the shallows, and after a hurried breakfast all hands worked hard getting our gear and stores aboard. A mishap befell us when we were launching the boats. We were using oars as rollers, and three of these were broken, leaving us short for the journey that had still to be undertaken. The preparations took longer than I had expected; indeed, there seemed to be some reluctance on the part of several men to leave the barren safety of the little beach and venture once more on the ocean. But the move was imperative, and by 11 a.m. we were away, the *James Caird* leading. Just as we rounded the small island occupied by the ringed penguins the "willywaw" swooped down from the 2000-ft. cliffs behind us, a herald of the southerly gale that was to spring up within half an hour.

Soon we were straining at the oars with the gale on our bows. Never had we found a more severe task. The wind shifted from the south to the southwest, and the shortage of oars became a serious matter. The *James Caird*, being the heaviest boat, had to keep a full complement of rowers, while the *Dudley Docker* and the *Stancomb Wills* went short and took turns using the odd oar. A big swell was thundering against the cliffs and at times we were almost driven on to the rocks by swirling green waters. We had to keep close inshore in order to avoid being embroiled in the raging sea, which was lashed snow-white and quickened by the furious squalls into a living mass of sprays. After two hours of strenuous labour we were almost exhausted, but we were fortunate enough to find comparative shelter behind a point of rock. Overhead towered the sheer cliffs for hundreds of feet, the sea-birds that fluttered from the crannies of the rock dwarfed by the height. The boats rose and fell in the big swell, but the sea was not breaking in our little haven, and we rested there while we ate our cold ration. Some of the men had to stand by the oars in order to pole the boats off the cliff-face.

After half an hour's pause I gave the order to start again. The *Dudley Docker* was pulling with three oars, as the *Stancomb*

*Wills* had the odd one, and she fell away to leeward in a particularly heavy squall. I anxiously watched her battling up
against wind and sea. It would have been useless to take the
*James Caird* back to the assistance of the *Dudley Docker* since
we were hard pressed to make any progress ourselves in the
heavier boat. The only thing was to go ahead and hope for
the best. All hands were wet to the skin again and many men
were feeling the cold severely. We forged on slowly and passed
inside a great pillar of rock standing out to sea and towering to
a height of about 2400 ft. A line of reef stretched between the
shore and this pillar, and I thought as we approached that we
would have to face the raging sea outside; but a break in the
white surf revealed a gap in the reef and we laboured through,
with the wind driving clouds of spray on our port beam. The
*Stancomb Wills* followed safely. In the stinging spray I lost sight
of the *Dudley Docker* altogether. It was obvious she would have
to go outside the pillar as she was making so much leeway, but
I could not see what happened to her and I dared not pause.
It was a bad time. At last, about 5 p.m., the *James Caird* and
the *Stancomb Wills* reached comparatively calm water and we
saw Wild's beach just ahead of us. I looked back vainly for the
*Dudley Docker*.

Rocks studded the shallow water round the spit and the
sea surged amongst them. I ordered the *Stancomb Wills* to run
on to the beach at the place that looked smoothest, and in a
few moments the first boat was ashore, the men jumping out
and holding her against the receding wave. Immediately I saw

she was safe I ran the *James Caird* in. Some of us scrambled up the beach through the fringe of the surf and slipped the painter round a rock, so as to hold the boat against the back-wash. Then we began to get the stores and gear out, working like men possessed, for the boats could not be pulled up till they had been emptied. The blubberstove was quickly alight and the cook began to prepare a hot drink. We were labouring at the boats when I noticed Rickenson turn white and stag-ger in the surf. I pulled him out of reach of the water and sent him up to the stove, which had been placed in the shelter of some rocks. McIlroy went to him and found that his heart had been temporarily unequal to the strain placed upon it. He was in a bad way and needed prompt medical attention. There are some men who will do more than their share of work and who will attempt more than they are physically able to accomplish. Rickenson was one of these eager souls. He was suffering, like many other members of the Expedition, from bad salt-water boils. Our wrists, arms, and legs were attacked. Apparently this infliction was due to constant soaking with sea-water, the chafing of wet clothes, and exposure.

I was very anxious about the *Dudley Docker*, and my eyes as well as my thoughts were turned eastward as we car-ried the stores ashore; but within half an hour the missing boat appeared, labouring through the spume-white sea, and presently she reached the comparative calm of the bay. We watched her coming with that sense of relief that the mariner feels when he crosses the harbour-bar. The tide was going out rapidly, and Worsley lightened the *Dudley Docker* by placing some cases on an outer rock, where they were retrieved subsequently. Then he beached his boat, and with many hands at work we soon had our belongings ashore and our three craft above high-water mark. The spit was by no means an ideal campingground; it was rough, bleak, and inhospitable—just an acre or two of rock and shingle, with the sea foaming around it except where the snowslope, running up to a glacier, formed the landward boundary. But some of the larger rocks provided a measure of shelter from the wind, and as we clustered round the blubber-stove, with the acrid smoke blowing into our faces, we were quite a cheerful company. After all, another stage of the homeward journey had been accomplished and we could afford to forget for an hour the problems of the future. Life was not so bad. We ate our evening meal while the snow drifted down from the surface of the glacier, and our chilled bodies grew warm. Then we dried a little tobacco at the stove and enjoyed our pipes before we crawled into our tents. The snow had made it impossible for us to find the tideline and we were uncertain how far the sea was going to encroach upon our beach. I pitched my tent on the seaward side of the camp so that I might have early warning of danger, and, sure enough, about 2 a.m. a little wave forced its way under the tentcloth. This was a practical demonstration that we had not gone far enough back from the sea, but in the semi-darkness it was difficult to see where we could find safety. Perhaps it was fortunate that experience had inured us to the unpleasantness of sudden forced changes of camp. We took down the tents and repitched them close against the high rocks at the seaward end of the spit, where large boulders made an uncomfortable restingplace. Snow was falling heavily. Then all hands had to assist in pulling the boats farther up the beach, and at this task we suffered a serious misfortune. Two of our four bags of clothing had been placed under the bilge of the *James Caird*, and before we realized the danger a wave had lifted the boat and carried the two bags back into the surf. We had no chance of recovering them. This accident did not complete the tale of the night's misfortunes. The big eight-man tent was blown to pieces in the early morning. Some of the men who had occupied it took refuge in other tents, but several remained in their sleeping-bags under the fragments of cloth until it was time to turn out.

A southerly gale was blowing on the morning of April 18 and the drifting snow was covering everything. The outlook was cheerless indeed, but much work had to be done and we could not yield to the desire to remain in the sleepingbags. Some sea-elephants were lying about the beach above high-water mark, and we killed several of the younger ones for their meat and blubber. The big tent could not be replaced, and in order to provide shelter for the men we turned the *Dudley Docker* upside down and wedged up the weather side with boulders. We also lashed the painter and stern-rope round the heaviest rocks we could find, so as to guard against the danger of the boat being moved by the wind. The two bags of clothing

were bobbing about amid the brash and glacierice to the windward side of the spit, and it did not seem possible to reach
them. The gale continued all day, and the fine drift from the
surface of the glacier was added to the big flakes of snow falling from the sky. I made a careful examination of the spit with
the object of ascertaining its possibilities as a camping-ground.
Apparently, some of the beach lay above high-water mark
and the rocks that stood above the shingle gave a measure of
shelter. It would be possible to mount the snowslope towards
the glacier in fine weather, but I did not push my exploration
in that direction during the gale. At the seaward end of the
spit was the mass of rock already mentioned. A few thousand
ringed penguins, with some gentoos, were on these rocks, and
we had noted this fact with a great deal of satisfaction at the
time of our landing. The ringed penguin is by no means the
best of the penguins from the point of view of the hungry traveller, but it represents food. At 8 a.m. that morning I noticed
the ringed penguins mustering in orderly fashion close to the
water's edge, and thought that they were preparing for the daily
fishing excursion; but presently it became apparent that some
important move was on foot. They were going to migrate, and
with their departure much valuable food would pass beyond
our reach. Hurriedly we armed ourselves with pieces of sledge-
runner and other improvised clubs, and started towards the
rookery. We were too late. The leaders gave their squawk of
command and the columns took to the sea in unbroken ranks.
Following their leaders, the penguins dived through the surf

and reappeared in the heaving water beyond. A very few of the weaker birds took fright and made their way back to the beach, where they fell victims later to our needs; but the main army went northwards and we saw them no more. We feared that the gentoo penguins might follow the example of their ringed cousins, but they stayed with us; apparently they had not the migratory habit. They were comparatively few in number, but from time to time they would come in from the sea and walk up our beach. The gentoo is the most strongly marked of all the smaller varieties of penguins as far as colouring is concerned, and it far surpasses the adelie in weight of legs and breast, the points that particularly appealed to us.

The deserted rookery was sure to be above high-water mark at all times; and we mounted the rocky ledge in search of a place to pitch our tents. The penguins knew better than to rest where the sea could reach them even when the highest tide was supported by the strongest gale. The disadvantages of a camp on the rookery were obvious. The smell was strong, to put it mildly, and was not likely to grow less pronounced when the warmth of our bodies thawed the surface. But our choice of places was not wide, and that afternoon we dug out a site for two tents in the debris of the rookery, levelling it off with snow and rocks. My tent, No. 1, was pitched close under the cliff, and there during my stay on Elephant Island I lived. Crean's tent was close by, and the other three tents, which had fairly clean snow under them, were some yards away. The fifth tent was a ramshackle affair. The material of the torn eightman tent had been drawn over a rough framework of oars, and shelter of a kind provided for the men who occupied it.

The arrangement of our camp, the checking of our gear, the killing and skinning of seals and sea-elephants occupied us during the day, and we took to our sleeping-bags early. I and my companions in No. 1 tent were not destined to spend a pleasant night. The heat of our bodies soon melted the snow and refuse beneath us and the floor of the tent became an evil smelling yellow mud. The snow drifting from the cliff above us weighted the sides of the tent, and during the night a particularly stormy gust brought our little home down on top of us. We stayed underneath the snow-laden cloth till the morning, for it seemed a hopeless business to set about repitching the tent amid the storm that was raging in the darkness of the night.

The weather was still bad on the morning of April 19. Some of the men were showing signs of demoralization. They were disinclined to leave the tents when the hour came for turning out, and it was apparent they were thinking more of the discomforts of the moment than of the good fortune that had brought us to sound ground and comparative safety. The condition of the gloves and headgear shown me by some discouraged men illustrated the proverbial carelessness of the sailor. The articles had frozen stiff during the night, and the owners considered, it appeared, that this state of affairs provided them with a grievance, or at any rate gave them the right to grumble. They said they wanted dry clothes and that their health would

not admit of their doing any work. Only by rather drastic methods were they induced to turn to. Frozen gloves and helmets
undoubtedly are very uncomfortable, and the proper thing is
to keep these articles thawed by placing them inside one's shirt
during the night. The southerly gale, bringing with it much
snow, was so severe that as I went along the beach to kill a seal
I was blown down by a gust. The cookingpots from No. 2 tent
took a flying run into the sea at the same moment. A case of
provisions which had been placed on them to keep them safe
had been capsized by a squall. These pots, fortunately, were
not essential, since nearly all our cooking was done over the
blubber-stove. The galley was set up by the rocks close to my
tent, in a hole we had dug through the debris of the penguin
rookery. Cases of stores gave some shelter from the wind and
a spread sail kept some of the snow off the cook when he was
at work. He had not much idle time. The amount of seal and
sea-elephant steak and blubber consumed by our hungry party
was almost incredible. He did not lack assistance—the neigh-
bourhood of the blubber-stove had attractions for every member of the party; but he earned everybody's gratitude by his
unflagging energy in preparing meals that to us at least were
savoury and satisfying. Frankly, we needed all the comfort that
the hot food could give us. The icy fingers of the gale searched
every cranny of our beach and pushed relentlessly through our
worn garments and tattered tents. The snow, drifting from the
glacier and falling from the skies, swathed us and our gear and
set traps for our stumbling feet. The rising sea beat against

the rocks and shingle and tossed fragments of floeice within a few feet of our boats. Once during the morning the sun shone through the racing clouds and we had a glimpse of blue sky; but the promise of fair weather was not redeemed. The consoling feature of the situation was that our camp was safe. We could endure the discomforts, and I felt that all hands would be benefited by the opportunity for rest and recuperation.

# Sources

"The Sea, with a Ship—Afterwards an Island," from *The Tempest*, William Shakespeare, 1610–1611

"The Capture," from *The Attrocities of the Pirates*, Aaron Smith, 1824

"Dirty Weather," from *Typhoon*, Joseph Conrad, 1902

"An Introduction to Informality," from *The Riddle of the Sands*, Erskine Childers, 1903

"Yammerschooner," from *Sailing Alone Around the World*, Joshua Slocum, 1900

"Young Ironsides," from *Old Ironsides*, James Fenimore Cooper, 1853

"Rounding Cape Horn," from *White-Jacket*, Herman Melville, 1850

"Loss of a Man—Superstition," from *Two Years Before the Mast*, Richard Henry Dana, 1840

"Mal de Mer," from *Three Men in a Boat (To Say Nothing of the Dog)*, Jerome K. Jerome, 1889

"MS. Found in a Bottle," Edgar Alan Poe, 1831

"The Unfortunate Voyage" (The Unfortunate Voyage Made with the Jesus, the Minion, and Four Other Ships, to the Parts of Guinea and the West Indies, in the Years 1567 and 1568, by Master John Hawkins), from *The Principal Navigations, Voyages, and Discoveries of the English Nation*, Richard Hakluyt, 1589

"Seige of the RoundHouse," from *Kidnapped*, Robert Louis Stevenson, 1886

"Owen Chase's Narrative," from *Shipwreck of the Whaleship Essex*, Owen Chase, 1821

"The White Whale," from *Moby Dick*, Herman Melville, 1851

"Escape from the Ice," from *South*, Ernest Shackleton, 1919